SUSPICION

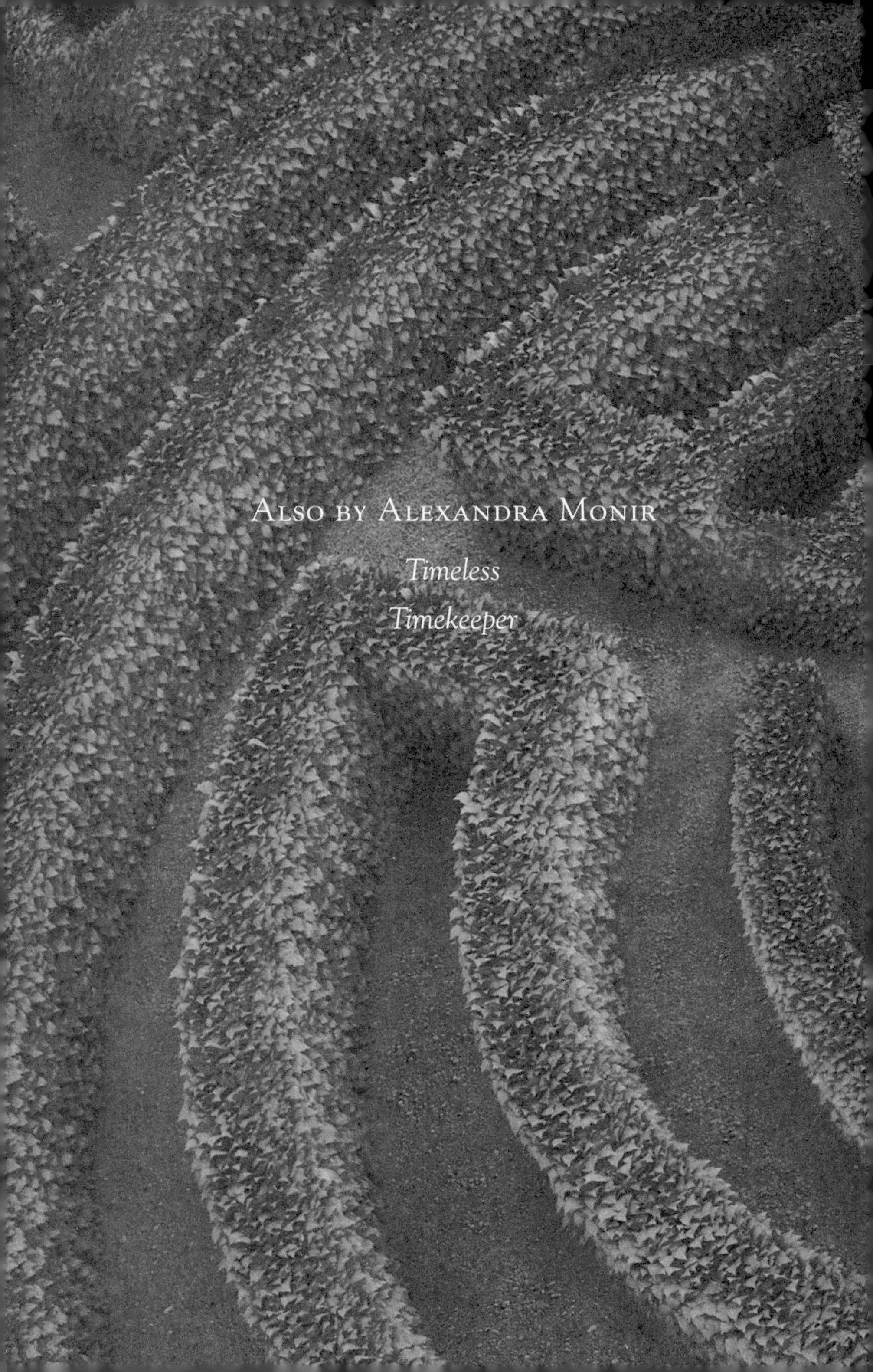

Also by Alexandra Monir

Timeless

Timekeeper

SUSPICION

ALEXANDRA MONIR

DELACORTE PRESS

Text copyright © 2014 by Alexandra Monir
Jacket photograph copyright © 2014 by Mopic/Shutterstock
Jacket photograph (girl) copyright © 2014 by Antenna/Getty Images

"Autumn Leaves"
English lyric by Johnny Mercer
French lyric by Jacques Prévert
Music by Joseph Kosma
© 1947, 1950 (Renewed) ENOCH ET CIE
Sole Selling Agent for U.S. and Canada: MORLEY MUSIC CO., by agreement with ENOCH ET CIE. All Rights Reserved.
Reprinted by Permission of Hal Leonard Corporation

randomhouse.com/teens

Educators and librarians, for a variety of teaching tools, visit us at
RHTeachersLibrarians.com

Library of Congress Cataloging-in-Publication Data
Monir, Alexandra.
Suspicion / Alexandra Monir. — First trade paperback edition.
pages cm
Summary: Seventeen-year-old Imogen Rockford turned away from her family and their English country manor after her parents' death, but assumes her duty as the new Duchess of Wickersham despite threats and strange occurrences.
ISBN 978-0-385-74389-1 (hc : alk. paper) — ISBN 978-0-385-37250-3 (ebook)
[1. Inheritance and succession—Fiction. 2. Aristocracy (Social class)—Fiction. 3. Duty—Fiction. 4. Supernatural—Fiction. 5. Orphans—Fiction. 6. England—Fiction.]
I. Title.
PZ7.M7495Sus 2014
[Fic]—dc23
2013040848

Printed in the United States of America
10 9 8 7 6 5 4 3 2 1

TO MY MOM, ZAZA,

the most loving mother in the entire world, and my best friend. Thank you for being at my side for every step of this journey!

AND IN MEMORY OF PAPA,

my beloved grandfather, now my angel. Thank you for bringing storytelling to my life and joy to my heart.

THE ROCKFORD FAMILY TREE

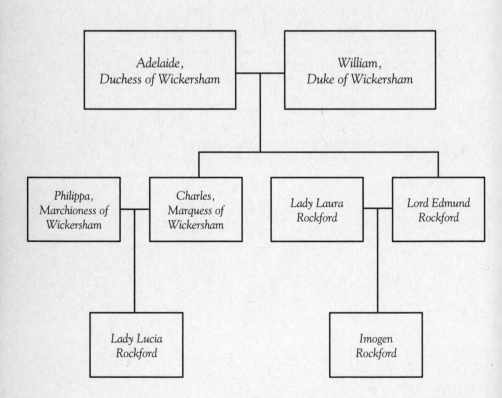

Adelaide,
Duchess of Wickersham

William,
Duke of Wickersham

Philippa,
Marchioness of
Wickersham

Charles,
Marquess of
Wickersham

Lady Laura
Rockford

Lord Edmund
Rockford

Lady Lucia
Rockford

Imogen
Rockford

SUSPICION

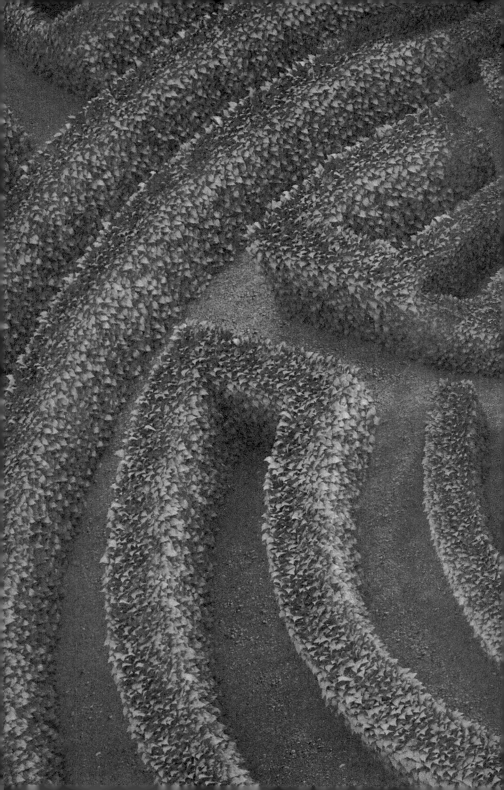

PART I

PROLOGUE

I should know this room. I've been inside countless times. But everything looks different now. The vibrant colors have all turned gray, the view out the windows is a foreign blur, and someone must have rearranged the furniture without telling me. Everything feels out of place, and as I move toward a favorite chair, I nearly sink into empty space.

I sense an arm hoisting me upright, steering me toward where the chair actually sits. Closing my eyes, I count to ten and promise myself that when I open them, the world will have returned to normal. But although the colors reappear and the furniture shifts back into position, I know there won't ever be such a thing as *normal* at Rockford Manor again.

I should have remembered what I learned firsthand years ago—that it only takes one night to transform a place; that a single event can crumble a stalwart structure and strip a home of a decade's worth of happy memories. But I never imagined it would happen twice. I let myself be taken in by Rockford once again, and even now, as I long to escape, I'm no match for the land. It pulls me under, seeping into my skin, until I don't know where I end and it begins. Maybe that's what it means to tie your identity to a place: it can betray you, shatter your illusions—and yet you can't stay away.

"Are you all right, Your Grace?"

I don't reply, the title failing to register at first. It's still new to me, and in my state of shock I find myself waiting for someone else, a real duchess, to answer. But then I remember, and glance up.

The butler, Oscar, stands before me, his face pale.

"I'm afraid the authorities require a statement from you. There's an officer waiting in the library."

My eyes drop to the floor.

"All you're expected to do is tell the truth," he says gently.

"The truth?" I echo. *Where do I start? And who would ever believe me?*

"Yes. From the beginning."

"That would mean going back seven years," I say under my breath.

Somehow I know that the events of tonight are connected to those from so many summers ago. But it will hurt to go back that far, to reminisce about when I was different—innocent, untouched by death or scandal.

Oscar's expression softens.

"Haven't you heard the old saying about the truth setting you free? Telling your story may lighten your burden."

I stare out the window at the trees strung with lights, still twinkling long after the party was abruptly halted. These same trees, which called Rockford Manor home centuries before me, are all witnesses to my story—they are wrapped up in it, just as I am.

"Your Grace, I'm afraid you don't have a choice," Oscar continues, pacing the drawing room. "A full statement from you is mandatory. However . . . I can see that you're in shock, and I might be able to make the officer understand that it would be best for him to return tomorrow."

I nod gratefully.

"Yes, please."

"But I suggest that when I come back you tell me the whole story, and together we can decide what to share with the authorities." Oscar's eyes warm as he looks at me. "You must know there isn't anything I wouldn't do to protect you. My whole life has been spent in service of your family. Tell me the truth—and let me be of service once again."

I remain silent, watching Oscar's retreating figure as he slips out of the room and into the corridor. I don't know what he could possibly do to help me . . . but in this moment, he's all I have.

Memories rise to the surface as I imagine what it would be like to finally tell my story. I feel my mind tumbling back through the days, months, years, until I am her again: ten-year-old Imogen Rockford, with the world at her feet.

Every dynasty has its stain. The reprobate, the scandalous, the fallen—each great house of the English aristocracy can lay claim to at least one of these characters. We know their stories inside and out; we've read them in books, witnessed them in our neighbors, and maybe even lived them in our own homes. But what happens when the family stain goes beyond what we understand or know to be possible? How do we categorize someone as "good" or "evil" based on that which we've never seen before, and never knew existed?

How do we judge them at all?

—"THE ROCKFORD DYNASTY: PERCEPTION VS. MISCONCEPTION," *THE ISIS* MAGAZINE

I

July 2007

I sit up straighter in the backseat, gripping Mum's hand with excitement as the car winds its way through the roads of Wickersham Village. When we reach the pair of black iron gates, gilded with the Rockford family crest, I know the moment I've been looking forward to has finally arrived: the first glimpse of my favorite view in England.

The gates part, and our car sweeps through the entrance. I lean out the window, gazing in awe at the rippling blue lake, the vast parkland stretching ahead for miles, and the curling tree branches pointing us toward a palace in the distance. Rockford Manor, the country house that's belonged to Dad's family since the eighteenth century, is more like a fairy-tale castle than a house, with its grand columns, domed towers, acres of gardens, and nearly two hundred rooms—most of which I still have yet to explore.

"We're home!" Dad says cheerfully, turning around in the passenger seat to smile at Mum and me.

"I wish it was home," I reply, bouncing in my seat as we draw closer to the house. "Lucia is so lucky she actually gets to live here."

"And *you're* lucky that you have such a nice home in New York to return to," Mum says pointedly, always on the lookout for any sign that our annual summer trips to Rockford are spoiling me.

"I know, I know."

And it's true. I love our Tribeca apartment, even more so since my friend Zoey Marino moved into the building. But each summer I find myself increasingly enchanted with Rockford Manor and the scenes of English country life: horseback riding through the park every morning with my cousin, playing cricket on the lawn, afternoon tea with buttery scones served in the Rose Garden, rainy days curled up in the vast library, wandering through long corridors filled with a museum's haul of artwork, and most of all . . . visits from the only boy I have ever cared to be friends with: Sebastian Stanhope.

I don't think I'll ever understand why Mum and Dad chose to move away when I was born, instead of staying in paradise at Rockford Manor. I've asked them about it dozens of times, but their answer is always that we moved to New York for Dad's job—which seems a bit strange, since England has lawyers too.

My thoughts slip away as we reach another gate beneath a towering stone arch, an indication that we're nearly there. The car's tires crunch against the gravel as we pull into the curving driveway, the perfectly mown lawns on either side of the road curving along with us. And suddenly we're in the Great Courtyard, bordered by the manor's stone-carved walls, columns, and towers. Yards away, on the steps leading into the mansion, I can see them forming two lines to greet us—the family in front, the staff in back.

"Mind your manners, Imogen," Mum says as the car slows to a stop in front of the house. I nod impatiently. The driver hurries to open the doors for us, and Mum and I follow Dad into the Great Courtyard. I draw in my breath as I take my first steps on Rockford soil, my heartbeat quickening at the sensations I only ever feel when I'm here. The wind whispers in my hair, the flowers brighten as I pass them, and my body feels different, awakened by adrenaline that I seem to be missing back home. It is stronger today than in past years, and I wonder if anyone will notice—or if my connection to the land is safely hidden in my imagination.

The leaves on the trees sway in a new direction, toward me, and I feel my palms nearly vibrating as I reach for them. But before I can greet the trees, Dad takes one of my hands and Mum clasps my other. I skip between them as we make our way toward the sea of people on the front steps.

My eyes meet Cousin Lucia's right away, but I know better than to greet her first. Instead, Mum, Dad, and I approach the gray-haired gentleman sitting in a wheelchair at the center of the group: my grandfather, the Duke of Wickersham. Dad bows solemnly and leans forward to kiss his father's cheek. Mum curtsies and I do the same, my face flushing as it always does whenever I have to curtsy in front of an audience.

I didn't know my family was different until the day I started elementary school. The other kids treated me normally enough, but everything changed when the final bell rang and the parents and nannies arrived to pick up their charges. For some reason, these unfamiliar grown-ups were eager to meet *me*, their eyes full of admiration as they spoke my name in hushed tones. And when Mum made her way into the classroom, the attention swiftly turned to her, with excited echoes of "Lady Rockford!" and clumsy curtsies. The whole scene was incredibly confusing, and Mum was forced to explain, as she led me away from the crowd, that my grandfather was the Duke of Wickersham—a title just below royalty. Anyone who watched coronations and royal weddings on TV, who followed the workings of the English aristocracy and read society magazines, knew just who we were.

As important as we might have seemed in America, I soon learned that there was another, superior branch of the family tree: Dad's older brother, Charles, the Marquess of Wickersham, who will inherit Rockford when Grandfather dies. So just as my uncle Charles and aunt Philippa take precedence over Mum and Dad, my cousin Lucia takes precedence over me. She's called *Lady* Lucia even though she's only twelve, while I'm just Imogen. But I don't mind. After all, they live at Rockford year-round, and we're only summertime visitors. It seems natural to me that they're more important.

I turn to them now, bowing my head to my aunt and uncle as I greet them, and after a giggly "Good afternoon, my lady!" to Cousin Lucia, I'm at last able to drop the formality. I throw my arms around her and she hugs me tightly, her smile letting me know how happy she is that I've arrived.

Lucia likes to say that I'm the little sister she's never had, and it's a role I'm glad to play. I've always been fascinated with my cousin, whose two-year age advantage over me makes her utterly glamorous and sophisticated in comparison. She has a look behind her brown eyes that hints at things she knows, things I haven't even begun to imagine—and every summer, I hold out hope that she might decide I'm old enough for her to confide her secrets in. Maybe this will be that summer.

Mum gives me a soft nudge, and the three of us move up a few steps to greet the household staff. I can't help but squeal in delight when I see Oscar the butler, my favorite person of them all.

"Oscar!"

"Miss Imogen." He smiles broadly and pulls me in for a bear hug. "You're getting so tall, I might not have recognized you."

"You always know just what to say, don't you, Oscar?" Mum grins, leaning over to kiss his cheek.

"It's good to see you, old boy." Dad embraces him warmly.

Oscar has been at Rockford Manor since Dad was a kid, so the two of them are especially close. No one on the staff could ever take Oscar's place—least of all the woman I see moving toward us now. The housekeeper, Mrs. Mulgrave.

I feel myself shrink under the shadow of her statuesque frame. Her eyes, the color of black coffee, stare down at me, and I have the uncomfortable feeling that she's sizing me up, judging and finding me wanting. Her thin black eyebrows arch as she looks the three of us over, and when she speaks, I don't meet her eyes—I focus instead on the little black mole on her chin.

"Welcome back, Lord and Lady Rockford," she says in her smooth voice. "Imogen."

"Thank you, Mrs. Mulgrave." Dad shakes her hand, and

then exchanges a quick glance with Mum that only I seem to catch.

"You remember my daughter, Maisie."

Mrs. Mulgrave gestures to the girl farther down the row of staff. She is a few inches taller than me, dressed in a black knee-length skirt and matching blouse, her hair pulled up into a bun.

"Of course." Mum moves down the line to greet her. "It's lovely to see you, Maisie."

I hang back awkwardly, unsettled as always by Maisie's presence. She stands in marked contrast to Lucia and me, despite the fact that she's around our age and resembles us enough to be mistaken for a third cousin. But her appearance and age are where the similarities end. While Lucia and I are Rockford heiresses, Maisie works at the manor as a junior maid. In my mind, this is the great flaw of my family's way of life. Someone like me can be born with so much, while another is forced to make do with so little. There is no rhyme or reason behind it . . . just luck.

As I glance at Maisie now, I find myself siding with her in an imaginary argument, thinking how unfair it is that she should have to live in the servants' quarters instead of enjoying a childhood like mine. But Dad says this is the norm for children of the staff in English homes—especially children like Maisie, with only one living parent—and he's promised me that she goes to school in Wickersham Village and is treated well at Rockford. Still . . . it doesn't seem right.

The cook, Mrs. Findlay, steps forward to greet us next, followed by her kitchen assistant, two footmen, two housemaids, and lastly, Max the gardener. After the long round of hellos, the footmen carry our luggage inside while the rest of the staff disperses. Lucia grabs my hand.

"Let's go to our boathouse."

I smile, thrilled that she considers the little haven next to the lake ours. As we turn to go, I sense a pair of eyes watching us. I look up and meet Maisie's gaze.

"Should we . . . invite her?" I nod toward Maisie.

Lucia gives me an incredulous look.

"Have you gone barmy? Of course not."

"You're right," I say quickly. "I don't know why I asked."

But as we run across the South Lawn toward the lake, despite my joy at being back at Rockford with Lucia, I feel a persistent sense of unease.

❧

The next afternoon finds us picnicking in the Shadow Garden, one of a dozen gardens nestled within the acres behind the main house. My favorite of them all, the Shadow Garden is the only patch of Rockford land that is closed to locals and tourists. A wrought-iron gate surrounds it, barring anyone without a key from entering.

I once asked Mum why the Shadow Garden wasn't open to the public, and she explained that it's so the family can have an outdoor retreat in the summer months, when Rockford Manor is crowded with day visitors. As much as I relish having the garden all to ourselves, I feel a pang of sadness at the thought of so few people getting to experience its beauty.

A petal-strewn gravel path divides the garden into two symmetrical sections, with lush meadows on either side, flanked by cherry blossom trees. The tree branches stretch out to meet each other, forming a canopy of evergreen leaves and pink blossoms overhead and creating the dancing shadows on the grass that give the garden its name. It's in this enchanting setting that the family gathers for afternoon tea, with a monogrammed blanket carpeting the grass and Mrs. Mulgrave and Maisie setting up a towering tea table laden with scones, finger sandwiches, and pastries.

As Dad chats animatedly with Grandfather, Uncle Charles, and Aunt Philippa, Mum pulls me onto her lap and begins rebraiding my unruly blond hair. I'm looking around for Lucia, wondering where she disappeared to, when I notice the twinkle in Mum's eyes and the knowing smile on her lips.

"The Stanhopes are here," she says in my ear.

I draw in a sharp breath, quickly hopping off Mum's lap before Sebastian can find me in such a babyish position. It's bad enough that I'm a mere ten years old when he's almost a teenager—I have to at least *act* grown-up.

The grass clings to my bare feet as I stand smiling, watching Sebastian Stanhope follow his younger brother, Theo, and their parents, the Earl and Countess Stanhope, through the gate and into the garden.

Sebastian's family lives at Stanhope Abbey in the nearby town of Great Milton, and they've been close friends of the Rockfords since before my parents were even born. "It's an inherited friendship," Dad once joked. "Two great families drawn together, for better or worse, by nothing more than proximity and influence." To me, the Stanhopes are far more than that. Especially Sebastian.

While the boys at my school in New York pay zero attention to me, Sebastian has been my friend for as long as I can remember. He held on to me so I wouldn't fall the first time I rode a bike, and every summer he's included me in his games and laughs. I feel a thrill whenever he pulls up a seat beside me, full of questions about my life in America and always calling me by the nickname he gave me, the name that only he is allowed to use: Ginny. Sebastian is different from any other boy I know; he's like a splash of color on a dull landscape. Maybe that's why he's the only boy I've ever *wanted* to know.

Just as I realize I'm staring a little too openly, Sebastian catches my eye and grins. I'm about to run over to him, when I see a lithe blond figure darting through the trees in his direction. Lucia.

Lucia beams at Sebastian as they greet each other, and she looks prettier than I've ever seen her. His smile softens, his expression turning suddenly shy. Their eyes rest on each other a moment too long, neither of them making a move to turn away—and I feel a slightly sickening twinge in my stomach. Has something changed since my last visit?

I can remember perfectly Lucia's words from last summer: "He'll be an earl when he grows up, and his parents are good friends with mine—but other than that, he's just a silly boy like all the rest."

This summer's Lucia seems to be singing an entirely different tune. She boldly takes Sebastian's hand, leading him to sit beside her on the outskirts of our picnic circle. My mouth falls open at the sight of them.

"Jolly good to see you, Imogen!"

I manage to tear my eyes away from Sebastian and Lucia to find his younger brother, Theo—the boy with the perpetually runny nose—standing before me. I give him a reluctant smile before greeting his parents the way I've been taught.

"Good afternoon, Lord and Lady Stanhope. How do you do?"

"Just fine, thank you, darling Imogen," Lady Stanhope coos. "And how are you? I say, you've grown up quite a bit since we saw you last."

"Really?" This perks me up slightly. "I sure hope so."

As the Stanhopes move on to greet the rest of the group, I sink back into the grass, and Theo plops down beside me. Mum hands us a plate of pastries to choose from, and I absently nibble on a blueberry scone while watching Lucia and Sebastian sit close together, the two of them flipping through one of his comic books. I know for a fact that Lucia doesn't even like comics, but today she appears engrossed in Sebastian's latest copy of Iron Man. What *happened* to the cousin I knew?

Before I can get caught staring again, Oscar interrupts Lucia and Sebastian's cozy moment and drags them over to me and Theo.

"How would the four of you like to plant the Shadow Garden's newest flowers?" he offers. "Max wants to show you how it's done."

"Let me guess," Lucia says, rolling her eyes. "Dad asked you to get us out of the way so he can drink and embarrass himself again. I'm right, aren't I, Oscar?" She laughs bitterly.

"Drink what?" I ask, confused by her strange outburst. But before anyone can answer me, Oscar shoots Lucia a stern look.

"We'll have no more of that smart mouth of yours, Lady Lucia. You know better than to speak about your father that way." He clears his throat. "Now, Max was kind enough to plan a fun activity for you children, and I hope you'll show him your appreciation by being polite."

With an emphatic sniff, Oscar leads the way to the flower beds on the other side of the garden. Apart from Lucia's parents and our grandfather, Oscar seems to be the only person allowed to give her a talking-to, and I'm always surprised when my willful cousin actually listens to him. But although she falls silent and follows Oscar along with the rest of us, her face settles into a frown. When a fly innocently whirs past, she catches it in her fist and squashes it in her hand, before carelessly tossing its corpse onto the grass. I shudder, looking away. I wonder if Sebastian noticed, if he even cared—or if I'm the only person in the world who could feel anything for a dead fly.

Max, the scruffy, middle-aged gardener, waits for us by a patch of empty flower beds. He hands us each a small bucket of water, a shovel, and bag of seeds as we form a line in front of the soil. I find myself standing beside Sebastian, and I feel my cheeks redden.

"Today we're planting the lovely bell-shaped flowers known as Canterbury bells," Max announces. "I'm afraid they take at least a year to bloom, but that means you have something exciting to return to next summer, Imogen!"

I try to look as enthusiastic as Max clearly expects me to be.

"Your first task is to pull out any weeds that you might find in the soil. Then you'll dig a small hole and pour a bit of water into the dirt. Sprinkle in your seeds, and then pat the dirt over them like so."

The four of us follow Max's instructions, and Lucia begins

to sing under her breath as she works, a melancholy song I've never heard before.

> *"I know dark clouds will gather round me,*
> *I know the road is rough and steep.*
> *But golden fields lie just beyond me,*
> *Where weary eyes no more will weep. . . ."*

Running my hands over the dirt, I suddenly feel an unfamiliar, electric charge buzzing through my fingertips. I jump back, hands trembling.

"Are you all right?" Sebastian asks, his green eyes glancing down at me with concern.

"Mm-hmm." I look away in embarrassment before returning to my task, gingerly spreading more dirt over the seeds. The buzzing shoots through my hands once again and my eyes squeeze shut in pain.

And then I hear Sebastian gasp. I open my eyes as Lucia shouts, "Where did her flower come from? Is this a trick?"

Bewildered, I glance in front of me—and stifle a scream.

A glorious Canterbury bell stands in full bloom, where moments ago there were only seeds. Its violet petals are damp from the water I just sprinkled over the dirt, and I gape at the impossible sight in disbelief.

"That patch was empty," Max says shakily, rubbing his temples as he stares at it. "I could have sworn there weren't any flowers there. How did you—you couldn't have—"

"You must have missed this one. It was there all along. I saw it when I first walked in," I lie, my voice coming out louder than I intended.

Sebastian gives me a sharp look, and my stomach drops. *He saw me do it.*

"I know every inch of the gardens. I would never miss a rogue flower like this one." Max gives me an uncomfortably perceptive look, as if he is probing for my secrets. "What did you do, Imogen?"

"I didn't do anything!" I snap. "What *could* I have done? Flowers don't appear out of thin air. It was there before."

But it wasn't. I know it wasn't.

Max finally seems to accept my explanation, and I release the breath I've been holding as he moves out of the way, instructing us to return to our planting. I turn to Sebastian, standing on my tiptoes to whisper in his ear.

"Whatever you saw—please don't tell."

"I don't know *what* I saw," he whispers back, his face pale. "One minute the flower bed was empty, the next . . ." He swallows hard. "That *thing* appeared. How did you do it?"

"I—I don't know. I've never done it before." Tears well in my eyes, and I turn away before he can see them. "Please, just promise me you won't tell anyone."

"Ginny," Sebastian says gently. "It's okay. I won't tell, I promise. But you have to promise to tell me if it ever happens again."

I nod, hoping with all my might that I'll never have to. I back away from the flower, which seems to taunt me with the knowledge that something is wrong, that I'm a freak, and I glance back up at Sebastian, wondering if I'll now see fear written across his face. But to my surprise, though he stares at me as if seeing me for the first time, he doesn't look afraid at all. How can that be? Still, I know I have to get out of this gardening exercise before I do anything else . . . unexpected. While Max and Theo seem to have moved on, Lucia keeps eyeing me curiously.

"I—I have to go tell my mum something," I say to no one in particular.

Without waiting for permission, I cross to the other side of the Shadow Garden, returning to the picnic. I find Grandfather napping in his wheelchair under the shade of the trees, while my parents, Aunt Philippa and Uncle Charles, and Lord and Lady Stanhope talk in a huddle, their voices hushed. At the sound of my footsteps, their conversation breaks off.

"Imogen." Mum's voice sounds unnatural, nervous. "Why aren't you with the other kids?"

I curl up beside her, hoping my mother's touch will calm my racing heart and make everything normal again.

"I decided I don't like gardening," I tell her. "I'm no good at it."

The rest of the picnic flashes by in a blur. I keep to myself, sitting quietly beside Mum and only half listening to the grownups' chatter, as my mind replays the image of the Canterbury bell blooming out of thin air. A small part of me itches to go back to the flower beds and see if it's still there, but my terror overrides my curiosity.

As the sun begins to set, Mrs. Mulgrave and Maisie reappear to clear the remains of our picnic. Mum and Aunt Philippa collect our belongings, while Uncle Charles gently wakes Grandfather, and Lord and Lady Stanhope gather Lucia,

Sebastian, and Theo. It's time to go inside, but where's Dad? It occurs to me now that I haven't seen him in over an hour.

"He went inside ahead of us," Mum says when I ask her. "The wind was giving him a chill."

I wrinkle my nose. Since when is Dad afraid of a little breeze?

The Stanhopes and Lucia are the first to head out of the garden, followed by Uncle Charles and Aunt Philippa, and Mum pushing Grandfather's wheelchair. I hang back, the last one out of the gate. I watch the others continue straight on the path toward the house, but I don't follow—because a quick glance at the Rockford Maze reveals something moving in its hedges.

I slowly turn to face the Maze, which towers high beside the Shadow Garden. Bordered on all sides by ten-foot-tall pine hedges, the Maze is rumored to be a marvel of a puzzle, filled with treacherous plants and surprises that make it suitable only for "mature children" and adults. I've never been inside, but Mum and Dad have promised that I can finally enter when I turn thirteen.

My breath catches in my throat as an arm snakes through the hedges. A familiar shock of brown hair emerges, and I exhale with relief.

"Dad! What were you doing in there? Mum said you'd gone inside."

He looks taken aback at the sound of my voice, but then he smiles.

"Imogen, darling. Can you keep a secret?"

"Of course I can!"

Dad seems different somehow—his face is redder than

usual, his eyes glassy—and I have the fleeting thought that perhaps he's eaten one too many tea sandwiches.

"There's something hidden in the Maze," he says quietly.

"Really?" My eyes widen. "Like buried treasure?"

"Something like that. But you'll have to be my good little girl and wait," he cautions. "We can't go get it, not for a while."

I frown, unaccustomed to waiting. Sensing my displeasure, Dad takes my hand.

"It's there for when you really need it. You'll know when that day comes." He looks at me intently. "If I'm not here to show you . . . just remember the hydrangeas. When you see them, that means you're close."

I squint up at my father, wondering if he's gone mad.

"What do you mean? Why *wouldn't* you be able to show me yourself?"

Dad's expression turns teasing.

"Because I'm your awfully important and busy father, that's why! Come on now, let's race back to the house."

I feel my trepidation start to fade, and I grin as he calls out, "On your mark . . . get set . . . go!"

Two summers ago, Lucia convinced our parents to let us have a slumber party in the Rockford boathouse—as close as we could get to sleeping under the stars while still being sheltered from the unpredictable English weather. After the night patrolman promised to keep watch outside the door, our parents gave in, and Lucia and I spent a jubilant evening sharing a treacle tart baked by Mrs. Findlay while watching our favorite movie, *Harry Potter and the Prisoner of Azkaban,* with the patter of rainfall outside adding to the ambience. The summer slumber party became our tradition, but tonight I'm surprised when Lucia reminds me about it. Watching her gaze at Sebastian and hold his hand earlier, it seemed to me that I was witnessing her growing up, leaving me and our childish rituals behind. But maybe I was wrong—because tonight finds us heading down the South Lawn toward the boathouse, Lucia carrying a covered pie dish from Mrs. Findlay while I aim the flashlight straight ahead.

Lucia unlocks the French doors and we enter a single airy room decorated entirely in whites and blues. White flowers peek out of blue vases; blue pillows adorn white couches; even the tile floor insists on an ivory-and-navy scheme. This is the most casual room at Rockford, the place where Lucia and I are free to play and snack indoors without worrying about breaking some priceless object or spilling soda on ancient linens. But instead of savoring our slumber party, like I normally would, I feel myself tense up every time Lucia speaks, afraid that she's going to tell me things I don't want to hear—about her and Sebastian, or worse, about what she saw me do with the Canterbury bell. Luckily she doesn't mention either, and I breathe a sigh of relief when she turns on *Prisoner of Azkaban.*

We curl up in sleeping bags on our respective couches in front of the TV, and I'm just drifting off to sleep at the end of the movie when I hear her speak softly.

"You're not upset about me and Sebastian . . . are you?"

My eyes snap open. *Me and Sebastian.* The phrase alone knots my stomach, but I force myself to lie.

"No." Still, I can't help asking, "Is he your boyfriend?"

I see her head bob up and down.

"I think so."

I turn to lie on my side, hugging my knees to my chest. I don't want to hear, but I'm desperate to know more.

"Have you . . . kissed him?"

"A peck. It was nicer than I expected," she giggles. "I'm so glad you don't mind, Imogen. I know you fancy Sebastian, but he and I are the right age for this sort of thing, you know? Maybe you and Theo will get together when you're older, and the four of us can double-date! Wouldn't that be brilliant?"

I open my mouth to speak, to tell her that I've always felt older than my years, that I belong with Sebastian just as much as she does. But I can't. So Lucia continues chattering on, oblivious to the tear trailing down my cheek. And I'm grateful for the darkness that hides my face.

I wake in the middle of the night to the earsplitting sound of sirens. The thick smell of smoke wafts its way into the boat-house, and I sit up frantically, turning to Lucia—but her sleeping bag is empty. *Where is she?*

I jump off the couch, heart in my throat. My shaking fingers make it impossible to switch on a lamp, so I use my hands to feel my way forward, stumbling over an ottoman in my path.

The door bursts open, revealing my cousin in a flash of light. Her pajama bottoms are caked in dirt, her face wet with tears or perspiration—I can't tell which.

"Imogen. Thank God you're okay," Lucia pants. "Something's happened."

"What's going on?" I whisper. "Where were you?"

But Lucia doesn't answer. She grabs my hand, silently pulling me toward the door. Once we're outside, I see a crowd of people—all watching the flames as they rise from the Shadow Garden and lick their way toward the Maze.

"There's something hidden in the Maze."

Remembering my father's words with a jolt, I drop Lucia's hand and race toward the smoke, ignoring her shouts.

"Imogen, stop!"

I cry out as Lord Stanhope blocks my path and sweeps me up into his arms, looking ridiculous in his velvet robe and bedroom slippers. I glance around wildly, struggling to register my surreal surroundings, which are so far removed from the idyllic picnic of just yesterday.

Fire trucks skid onto the lawn while Oscar and Mrs. Mulgrave race forward, shouting out instructions. Lady Stanhope wails hysterically on the back terrace, clutching Sebastian and Theo, surrounded by the rest of the disoriented staff in their pajamas. Maisie Mulgrave holds on to Grandfather's wheelchair, swaying in shock. The only people I can't seem to find are my aunt and uncle—and my parents.

The firemen leap out of the truck, blasting their way into the garden. Lord Stanhope covers my eyes with his hand.

"Don't look, Imogen."

But I have to. I pry his fingers away from my face, watching in silent horror as the firemen haul four stretchers out of the Shadow Garden—carrying bodies covered with sheets. A limp hand dangles out from under one of them, and I shake my head violently when I see the silver chain adorning the pale wrist. It is the bracelet I picked out for my mother on her last birthday.

Screams ring through my ears, anguished howls that I at first don't recognize as my own. My limbs kick and punch at Lord Stanhope until finally I break from his hold. I run blindly, tears blurring my vision, until somehow Lucia catches me. My cousin wraps her arms around me, holding on tight as my body convulses with sobs. I can hear her wailing for her mother, and the sound pierces my already shattered heart.

"We only have each other now," she whispers into my ear, tears trailing down her own cheeks.

I clutch her hand, my insides tightening and twisting with a grief too painful to bear. And suddenly, I feel a frighteningly familiar searing sensation in my hands. I pull away from Lucia, and a scream rises in my throat at the sight of the lines in my palms—sparking and blazing a fiery orange. Panicking, I close my hands into fists, but the sparks leap from my hands up into the air, forming a single large flame suspended between our two bodies. The flame casts an eerie glow over Lucia, from the wild look in her eyes to the spade-shaped birthmark on her wrist.

"What's happening?" Lucia cries, following my gaze. "How—how are you doing that?"

I back away from her, trembling. Without warning, my hands return to normal. The space between us is once again dark and empty.

I spin around, feeling everyone's eyes on me, watching me unravel—and all I can do is break into a run. I know they'll catch me, I know I'll have to face it all soon enough, but for now I sprint forward, directionless. As I'm running, I imagine that I'm shedding my old skin, the carefree little girl I used to be disintegrating into dust beneath my feet, until all that's left of me is an unrecognizable orphan—alone with terrifying new abilities.

II

TRIBECA, NEW YORK CITY
MAY 2014

I kneel before the fireplace, reaching my hand precariously close to the flame. I swipe a finger underneath the burning orange, and—nothing happens. I wince at the flash of heat and quickly withdraw, but it's still a victory: the flame failed to take on a life of its own at my touch. But then, I shouldn't be surprised. I haven't been able to grow anything out of thin air since I left Rockford Manor seven years ago. I guess that's one thing I can be grateful for. My frightening skill that day must have been a fluke.

"Imogen? Why in the world are you lighting a fire in the middle of May?"

The voice of my friend-turned-sister, Zoey Marino, echoes behind me. I turn around, my face flushed.

"Sorry, I was just . . ." I force a smile. "I got cold."

"O-kay, weirdo. You do know you can just turn on the

heater, right? Anyway, do you plan on getting dressed or are we going to be late again today?"

I roll my eyes at her.

"Chill out, Zoey. I'll be ready in ten minutes."

She flounces out of the living room, but I don't follow. The sound of the rain has me under a spell, and instead of going to my bedroom to change, I move toward the windows. The droplets form funny little patterns on the glass, and I trace them with my fingers.

The rain always reminds me of them, sending my thoughts spinning down the rabbit hole of what might have happened if there had been rain that night. Would my parents still be here, in this very apartment building, if rain had been there to thwart the fire?

"Sweetie, don't you think you'd better get a move on?"

I turn around to find Carole Marino—also known as my second mom—in the doorway. It's a good thing she wasn't the one to find me in front of the fireplace. She's always on the alert for signs that I might be succumbing to some kind of Orphan Madness.

"I know. I was just about to get ready."

Before she has a chance to question me any further, I hurry past her and turn the corner into my room. I quickly change into the Carnegie High uniform of a plain plaid skirt and white polo shirt, then twist my blond hair up into a messy bun and swipe on black mascara and my favorite cherry lip gloss. When I return to the living room, Carole hands me a wrapped bagel and a fruit smoothie.

"Here, take your breakfast to go," she says with a smile.

"Zoey's waiting for you downstairs. Oh, and don't forget you have Ms. Forman at three o'clock."

"Can't wait," I say dryly, before giving her a quick hug. "See you after school."

In the lobby of our apartment building, I find Zoey standing with her arms crossed, tapping her foot dramatically as she waits for me. Yeah, Zoey can definitely be annoying, but I have a soft spot for her. Our friendship is one of the few uncomplicated relationships in my life. I've known her since I was five years old and she was three, when my father became a partner in her dad's law firm, and there's an ease between us, a feeling of never having to explain myself or pretend around her.

"Don't worry, you're not going to miss your pre-homeroom gossip-fest," I say as I catch up to her.

"Ha, ha." She sticks out her tongue at me before leading the way out the door. As we weave through commuters on our walk to school, it occurs to me for the millionth time how different Zoey and I look. A stranger would never think we're sisters, or that I'm Keith and Carole's daughter. Zoey inherited Carole's dark hair and perpetually tanned olive skin, while her hazel eyes are the exact shade of Keith's. I'm the fair-skinned, blue-eyed oddity. But of course, Zoey and I aren't real sisters.

When the news came out that Mum and Dad had named their American neighbors and best friends as my guardians in their will, it sent shock waves through Wickersham. Newspapers wrote breathless stories about the duke's granddaughter "forced to live as an American commoner!" But somehow, Mum and Dad had known that the easiest thing for me in the face of an overwhelming tragedy would be to go home—to my street, my city, my school. They placed their faith in my love for "Aunt Carole and Uncle Keith" and my friendship with Zoey. But while their will dictated that the Marinos would be my legal guardians until I turned eighteen, it stipulated that I must retain my Rockford last name. The Marinos can never adopt me.

It shames me to admit it, but I wish my parents had cut that line from their will. Because of my different last name, I'm forced to explain the grim details of my past far more often than I'd like.

"You're pretty quiet this morning." Zoey's voice cuts through my thoughts. "What's wrong? Did Mom and Dad grill you about NYU again?"

Thanks for reminding me, Zoey.

"Not since the other night, but I'll bet you anything they're planning to have another big talk with me about it this weekend. Is it really so weird to take a gap year? Plenty of people do it. I don't know why it's such a foreign concept to Keith and Carole," I complain.

"Well, none of their friends' kids have taken a gap year, so that's probably why it seems weird. Besides, what will you do all day if you don't go to school?" Zoey asks.

"I don't know. I just don't understand how everyone else seems to magically know where they want to go to school and what they want to study and do with their lives. Since when did seventeen become the age when we're supposed to have it all figured out?"

"We do go to school with a lot of overachieving city kids," Zoey points out, rolling her eyes. "Maybe if we lived somewhere else, there wouldn't be so much, I don't know . . ."

"Expectation," I say, finishing her sentence as we wait to cross the street. "Well, thank goodness Carole and Keith have you to fulfill theirs."

"Stop it." Zoey gives me an affectionate shove. "They wouldn't want you any other way."

I don't fully believe that, but I smile at her anyway.

"Thanks, sis."

We turn onto Chambers Street, and the tall, redbrick building of Carnegie High comes into view, looming above the Tribeca Bridge.

"Home, sweet home," I deadpan.

As we climb the steps to the school's front courtyard, Zoey nudges me in the ribs.

"Look. Mark Wyatt is staring at you."

I feel an involuntary blush creep up my cheeks. Zoey and my best friend, Lauren Fox, are convinced that Mark has a thing for me, even though I keep telling them we're simply lab partners and friends. But lately, I've noticed him looking at me a certain way, and . . . I wonder if they might be right. I gaze across the courtyard at his lanky, soccer-player's build, his short brown hair and twinkling blue eyes. He's cute, sweet, and fun—I would be lucky to go out with him. So why does the idea make me more nervous than excited?

"I'll leave you two alone," Zoey says conspiratorially. Sure enough, once she's out of sight, Mark heads my way.

"Hey, Imogen," he greets me, his lips turning up in a charming smile. "What's up?"

"Nothing much. I'm just about to run to history before I miss the bell."

"I'm going in that direction too." Mark falls into step beside me, and I give him a sideways smile. He is *so* lying. I know he has math on the other side of the building.

I let myself move an inch closer to him as we walk together through the school doors. It feels good to be just a normal teenager. Not "Imogen, whose parents are dead" or "Imogen, with the uncertain future"—just a seventeen-year-old girl who is liked by a boy.

After our last class, Lauren walks me to Ms. Forman's office, linking her arm with mine as she fills me in on what she caught her older brother doing over the weekend.

"I only went into his room to tell him to turn down the music, because it was literally blaring through the walls. *Well.* I walked in to find two empty bottles of wine on the floor, a girl with her shirt off, and—this is the most embarrassing part—my brother was actually rapping to her. Like, drunkenly serenading her to that new Drake song."

I burst out laughing.

"If I didn't know Anthony so well, I'd almost call that sweet. But I do feel kinda sorry for him getting caught."

"See what happens when you live at home after high school?" Lauren wags a finger at me. "It's a constant state of getting busted. I keep telling Anthony he should just go live on campus, but of course he prefers our cushy apartment and Mom doing all his laundry and cooking to roughing it at the NYU dorms."

"I never said I'd live at home," I correct her. "I just don't know what I'm doing yet."

"Well, time to figure it out," Lauren says wryly as we stop in front of the school counselor's office. "Good luck, girl."

"Thanks. I'll text you later."

Lauren gives me a hug and continues down the hall, her black curls swinging behind her. With a sigh, I knock on Ms. Forman's door.

"Come in!"

She stands, giving me a warm smile as I enter her office. "Imogen, how *are* you today?"

I'd probably like Ms. Forman a lot more if she weren't so darn earnest. Being a school counselor rather than an actual therapist, she's thankfully a more relaxed version of the series of shrinks Carole and Keith sent me to after the fire—but I still wish she'd stop treating me like a delicate flower.

"I'm fine." I sink onto the brown suede couch while Ms. Forman pulls up a chair across from me. "I filled out those career assessment thingies you gave me."

Ms. Forman claps her hands together eagerly. "And?"

"And apparently I'm destined to be an architect. Which would make sense if it weren't for the fact that I nearly bombed geometry last year."

"Well . . ." Ms. Forman purses her lips. "Geometry is only one facet of architecture. NYU has plenty of courses that can cater to this interest of yours—"

Before she has a chance to whip out any more of her leaflets, I cut in.

"I'm not so sure it's an interest. I've never even thought about architecture before. Besides, isn't the plan for you to help convince the Marinos to let me take a gap year?"

"Imogen, really. I promised no such thing. I only said *if* I'm convinced it's the right move, I'll help you. But so far, I'm not." She leans forward. "It's not so much college that I'm focused on. There are plenty of great achievers who lack higher education, but they had talent and drive and direction. It's my job to help you find yours."

"Maybe I'd have a better sense of direction if I weren't in the wrong place."

The words tumble out of my mouth before I have a chance to think them through, before I even know what they mean.

Ms. Forman raises an eyebrow. "Why do you say that?"

I glance down at the faded carpeting. There's no way of getting out of this one.

"I don't know. It's like I told you before. Sometimes I feel like I'm not where I'm supposed to be, like I've . . . left something behind."

Ms. Forman gives me a perceptive look.

"You've been thinking about them more than usual lately . . . am I right?"

After a moment's pause, I nod.

"Maybe it's because their anniversary is coming up?" she suggests gently.

I flinch at the word. *Anniversary* conjures up images of celebration, not death. Catching my expression, Ms. Forman hurriedly adds, "I'm sorry, I just meant—"

"Yeah, I know," I interrupt. Nothing gets under my skin quite like watching people feel sorry for me, and I'm anxious to change the subject, but Ms. Forman won't let me off that easy.

"Have you talked to Carole and Keith about this?" she presses.

"No. Why would I?"

"Because they love you. They want to be there for you, to help you when you're going through these difficult times and feelings."

Feelings. Another one of Ms. Forman's favorite, overly used words.

"I know because they told me so themselves," she says softly. "They want so much for you to let them in."

"Haven't I let them in enough? What do you all expect, for me to start calling them Mom and Dad?" I snap, wishing I could take back the words as soon as they're out of my mouth. I jump to my feet, suddenly desperate to get away from Ms. Forman. "Can we just . . . call it a day? I'm not feeling so hot, and I don't think this is going to be all that productive a session."

Ms. Forman frowns.

"Imogen, we have another thirty minutes left."

"I know, but I'm just not up for talking right now." I give her a pleading look. "Can't we just finish this the next time we meet?"

Ms. Forman hesitates. "All right. I won't force you to stay." She eyes me carefully before scribbling something in her notepad. "Take care, Imogen."

And with that, I practically fly out of her office, able to breathe normally again now that I'm no longer being asked to rehash the past.

That night, as I'm setting the table for dinner, I hear the shrill ring of our landline.

"I'll get it," I call out, dashing into the empty kitchen and grabbing the phone. "Hello?"

"Good evening. May I please speak to Lady Imogen Rockford?"

My stomach lurches. The man's English accent reminds me of my father. And . . . why is this stranger calling me *Lady* Imogen? How does he even know that I'm a Rockford?

"This—this is Imogen," I finally answer, dizzily.

I hear a sharp intake of breath, but before the man on the other end of the line can respond, someone yanks the phone from my hands.

"Hey! That was for me—" I stop short at the look on Keith's face.

"For the last time, stop harassing my family," he says through gritted teeth. "My daughter has nothing to discuss with you."

I stare at him openmouthed as he throws the phone onto the kitchen counter.

"Um . . . *what* was that?"

Keith rubs his forehead wearily.

"Sorry, sweetie. I didn't mean to scare you. That was another lawyer from overseas. My firm beat his in an arbitration case and it's costing him a lot of money, so he's been trying to frighten me into paying him off, by bothering our family." He sighs heavily. "It's a long story."

"Jeez, that's terrible. I'm sorry." A thought suddenly occurs to me. "But how did he know my last name? If he thinks I'm your daughter, wouldn't he assume that I'm a Marino? And why would he call me *Lady* Imogen?"

Keith hesitates.

"He makes it his business to know these things, and especially being in England, he—he probably read about you in the papers. But don't worry, kiddo, he's all talk. Besides, you know I won't let anything happen to you."

"I won't let anything happen to you."

I shiver as I remember another, far-off voice saying those same words to me—the precociously polished voice of my cousin Lucia, begging me to stay.

"Let's forget about him. What do you say?" Keith gives me a reassuring smile.

"Yeah. Sure." My mind is already miles away.

I finish setting the table on autopilot, and moments later I'm sitting down to dinner with my second family, in the chair that I've occupied for the last seven years. After we've all filled our plates with Carole's signature salad and pot roast, Zoey clears her throat loudly, which is usually a sign that she's about to ask for something.

"So. Um. I got invited to Grad Night." She says it casually, but her bright eyes betray her excitement.

"You did? Isn't that only for seniors?" Carole asks skeptically.

"Yeah, but they can invite whoever they want. And today after school, Jason Mendes invited *me*." Her last word is practically a squeak. "You know what an honor it is for a sophomore to go. So . . . I can go, right?"

"It's Imogen's night, so it's up to her," Keith says, turning to me. "How do you feel about your sister being there, sweetie?"

I don't answer right away. Grad Night is supposed to be just for seniors, one last night for us all to be together and let loose, and I haven't exactly envisioned chaperoning Zoey as part of the equation. But when I look at her hopeful face, I know I could never let her down.

"It's cool," I tell her.

"Omigosh, thank you!" Zoey leaps out of her chair to give me a hug. "You're the best sister in the world."

I can't help feeling a warm glow as she squeezes me happily and Keith and Carole smile at me from across the table. I may not be a Marino by blood, but I know I'm loved all the same. And that makes it a little easier to be okay with the decision I made a long time ago—to say goodbye to Grandfather and Lucia and turn my back on Rockford Manor.

III

I fall asleep to memories floating before my eyes, like 3-D images I can almost reach out and touch. I am ten years old again, and sweating through my thick black mourning clothes. I glare up at the sky. How can the sun be so disloyal, choosing today to shine brilliantly when my whole world has turned dark?

It is my last day at Rockford Manor, and though desperate to be alone, I'm trailed by Carole and Keith, who have arrived to escort me home to New York. They follow me now as I climb the grassy hill to Rockford Chapel and Cemetery, at the farthest reaches of the Rockford grounds.

I approach the newest gravestones, and it seems as though I'm outside my own body—a pitying spectator watching a stranger perform the harrowing task of visiting her parents' graves. That grim-faced little girl can't actually be me; it *can't* be my mum and dad who are gone. I still hold out hope that at any moment I'll find my parents waiting for me, beaming as they tell me that it's all been a terrible mistake, that there's no need to worry, they're here and we're always going to be together—

Carole's choked sob shatters this fantasy. I watch as she kneels at Mum's gravestone, pressing her forehead against the marble. I long to do the same, to wrap my arms around my parents' graves and pretend they're hugging me back, to kiss their headstones and imagine that they can somehow feel me. But I can't—I'm afraid of my touch, of what it might do. So I can only stare, rereading the words on the two linked graves.

LORD EDMUND ALBERT ROCKFORD   LADY LAURA ROCKFORD
NOVEMBER 12, 1967–   FEBRUARY 8, 1970–
JULY 26, 2007   JULY 26, 2007

FATHER & MOTHER TO THEIR BELOVED IMOGEN
"WITH THE KEY TO THE PROMISED LAND, WE SHALL MEET AGAIN."

"What does that mean?" I ask Carole when she steps back beside me. "'The key to the Promised Land'?"

"I don't know." She glances up at Keith. "They must have specified that epitaph in their will."

The three of us turn around at the sound of footsteps crunching on the fallen leaves. My chest tightens when I see who's there: Lucia and Sebastian, hand in hand.

"Imogen. I knew I'd find you here," she says, catching her breath. "I—we've—come to tell you something. You can't go." She draws herself up to her full height. "I'm now the Marchioness of Wickersham, and I—I command you to stay."

I open my mouth to speak, but nothing comes out.

"I know you're scared," she says in a softer voice. "But I promise, I won't let anything happen to you."

Keith steps forward before I can answer, wrapping a protective arm around my shoulder.

"Lady Lucia, I can't tell you how sorry I am for your loss. There are no words. But I'm afraid Imogen does need to come home with us tonight. I know you two will miss each other, but you can still visit—"

"It's not fair!" Lucia cries, balling her hands into fists. "Our grandfather lives here, *I* live here. How can you just take her away and leave me alone, with no parents and now no cousin? It's not *right,* is it, Imogen?"

"Where did you go the night of the fire?" I blurt out instead. "Where were you?"

Lucia recoils, as if I've hurt her. Sebastian gives me an imploring glance.

"Ginny . . ."

But I don't want to hear his voice; I don't want him to talk me out of the one emotion that gives me any relief. Anger.

"I—I only went to get some air, I got hot!" Lucia sputters. "Is that a crime?"

"Did you see how the fire got started? No one else seems to know." I fold my arms across my chest. "You were wandering around in the middle of the night, so you must know something."

"Are you actually questioning *me*?" Lucia demands. "Because that's a laugh, coming from you."

"What do you mean?"

"I saw what you can do," she hisses. "How do we know the fire wasn't your fault?"

Her words feel like a slap across my face. I stumble backward, shaking my head no, *no*. It can't be my fault . . . or can it? Carole jumps between us.

"That's enough, girls. You don't mean any of what you're saying. You're both hurting, and it's natural to lash out at each other, but you have to remember that this terrible accident was just that—an accident. It's nobody's fault."

After a long pause, I hear Sebastian's voice, tinged with sadness.

"So . . . you're really going, then, Ginny?"

I nod.

"I know it's hard to understand after everything that's happened, but the fact is, Imogen's life is in New York," Carole tries to explain. "That's why her parents chose us to be her guardians in their will. They wouldn't want her life uprooted any more than it has to be. England is your home, but it's never been Imogen's."

"You won't miss me anyway," I tell Sebastian, my voice breaking on the last word. "You have each other."

I turn on my heels, leaving Carole and Keith to reason with a still-arguing Lucia. I keep my head down as I descend the hill toward Rockford Manor, not noticing that I'm being followed until I feel a hand on my shoulder.

"It's not true, what you said."

I turn around at Sebastian's voice, feeling a strange swooping in my stomach as I face him.

"What isn't true?"

"That I won't miss you. Because I will. I'll miss you every summer and every holiday if you don't come back," he says, looking at me earnestly. "I'll miss you every time I see a bell-flower or anything else that reminds me of my friend Ginny Rockford."

Tears prick at the back of my eyelids as he speaks. He can't know how much his words mean to me; how they make everything simultaneously better and worse. But before I can answer, Sebastian bends down and brushes his lips against my cheek. I gasp, reaching up to touch my face in awe. Nothing should be able to make me feel happy after all I've just lost—but this kiss, platonic though it may be, gives me a moment of pure joy.

"Goodbye, Ginny," he says softly. "Till we meet again."

"Goodbye," I echo, still touching my cheek as he walks back to rejoin Lucia. When he's no longer within earshot, I whisper, "I'll never forget you."

I wake from my dream with the nauseating pit in my stomach that I've come to associate with this memory—the last time I ever spoke to Lucia and Sebastian. For a long time, any recollection of Lucia left me tormented. Her name and face were inextricably tangled up in my mind with the horrors of the fire, and for reasons I still don't understand, I blamed her—I blamed *us*. And the only way I could get through it all was by pretending that the previous years belonged to somebody else, that my real life began at age ten with the Marinos.

It's not the bravest way of handling things, I know. And I can't help thinking my parents would be hurt and disappointed in me for not honoring their memory the way I should. If I were stronger, I'd be able to talk about them freely and celebrate their lives, instead of hiding them in my heart. But when I try—when I remember the comfort of Mum's arms and the adoring smile that Dad gave to only me—then I'm forced to also remember the gruesome images of the fire. Lucia leading me to witness the tragedy, my mother's limp hand . . . And I *can't*—I can't think about them or miss them, because then the darkness beckons. So I've avoided any reminiscing with the Marinos about my family, and I haven't stayed even remotely up to date on the happenings in Wickersham. My parents are reduced to names and photographs, their deaths a somber speech that I numbly recite whenever a curious new friend asks about my last name. It's so much easier to pretend I never had another life . . . and yet the pangs of guilt are a constant.

One of the side effects of growing up is seeing things in a different light. And now, when I'm alone and brutally honest with myself, I face a different type of torment: regret for turning my back on my cousin, and for refusing every one of my grandfather's invitations to visit Rockford. But then, as it turns out, Lucia didn't really need me after all. It wasn't long before she'd stopped writing and calling me altogether.

When I turned fourteen and the Marinos let me get a Facebook account, I couldn't contain my curiosity. I looked Lucia up right away—but unlike practically everyone around our age, she didn't have an account. In fact, she wasn't on *any* of the social networking sites my friends and I visited on a daily basis. I did find Sebastian, though. The sight of his profile picture sent a tremor through me. He was so handsome at seventeen, his eyes so painfully familiar as he smiled for the camera alongside a mystery girl, that I slammed my laptop shut, vowing to never look for him again. After all, what good would it do? We were half a world away from each other. But I always held out a sprig of hope that he might look for me—that he would find me on Facebook one day, and our friendship would start up again like no time had passed. Of course, it never happened. I guess I was right when I told Sebastian he wouldn't miss me.

The doorbell rings, jarring me out of my thoughts. With a sigh and a stretch, I roll out of bed. I reach the front door just as Carole sleepily pads out of the kitchen, clutching a mug of coffee. She does a double take when she sees me.

"Morning, sweetie. Are you okay? You don't need to be up for another hour."

"I'm fine, I just woke up early. Did you hear the doorbell? Who would be coming over now?"

"The doorman said he was sending up someone from a messenger service," Carole replies. "Who knew deliveries started at six a.m.?"

She opens the door. A scrawny twentysomething stands in the hallway, a thick envelope in his hands. He gives Carole a polite nod as he proffers the package.

"Good morning, ma'am. I have a delivery for a Lady Imogen Rockford."

"That's—that's me!" I exclaim. "Although I'm not a *lady*."

"She's a minor," Carole says hastily, grabbing the package.

"I'll sign for her." After scrawling her signature and mumbling a barely audible goodbye, Carole closes the door on him.

"Let me see it." I reach for the package, but to my astonishment, she holds it out of my grasp.

"Your father needs to see this first. It might be something to do with his—"

"I don't care if it's from the pissed-off lawyer! That package is mine, and I should be the one to open it," I snap.

I peer closer at the envelope clutched in Carole's fist. Unbeknownst to her, the return address peeks out through her fingers, and my heart nearly leaps into my throat as I make out the words.

MR. HARRY MORGAN, ESQ.
ROCKFORD MANOR
WICKERSHAM, OXFORDSHIRE, UK

"It's from my grandfather's house." My voice is barely above a whisper. "I haven't heard from him in . . . ages."

Carole looks from me to the envelope, her face paling.

"I'm sorry, but your father has to see this first. We can discuss it over dinner tonight."

"But—"

"No buts, Imogen. We'll talk about it tonight," she says firmly.

My shoulders slump in defeat, but then an idea strikes me. Without answering her, I turn on my heels and race back to my room.

I slide onto my desk chair, flip open my laptop, and Google "Harry Morgan Rockford Manor." The first link that pops up is the official tourist website for Rockford Manor. My hands hesitate over the mouse—but then I hold my breath and click on it.

Images and words rush toward me as the screen loads. My stomach clenches at the sight of the striking, monumental Elizabethan castle looming in the main photo, surrounded by picture-perfect parkland. Rockford Manor is achingly familiar, yet the passing of seven years gives it a distant quality, as though I'm looking at the set of a TV show, or another place that only feels real—but isn't.

I blink rapidly as ghosts descend upon the photo in my mind, strolling the grounds and looking out from the high balconies and arched windows. I can't look anymore. I quickly shift my eyes down toward the text.

> Welcome to Rockford Manor, home to the eleventh Duke of Wickersham. Known as the finest nonroyal palace in Britain, Rockford Manor is a National Trust Site. The Rockford family has called the manor home for more than three centuries. The palace and gardens are currently closed to the public but will reopen in June for the summer season.

I swallow hard, struggling to calm my racing heart, as I click the Contact Us tab. I scan the different titles and phone numbers until I find the name I'm looking for: *Mr. Harry Morgan, Estate Manager.*

Why in the world would the Rockford's estate manager

need to reach *me?* I wage a silent debate in my mind over whether or not to contact him, and once the little voice in my head urging me to do it has won, I question whether calling or emailing is the right move. Finally, I bite the bullet and reach for my cell. Calling Europe is probably going to cost me a fortune, but I'll deal with that later.

It strikes me that I have no clue what the country code is for England—the last time I ever called overseas was when Mum and Dad were still alive. I quickly Google "How to call England," and after dialing a myriad of numbers, I hear the drone of the international ringtone. At last, a prim woman's voice answers.

"Good afternoon, Harry Morgan's office."

"Hi." My voice comes out like a croak, and I clear my throat nervously. "Hi, um, can I speak to him, please?"

"Mr. Morgan is currently in America," she replies briskly. "May I take a message?"

"Where in America?" I ask, feeling suddenly light-headed.

The woman pauses. "May I ask who I'm speaking with?"

I take a deep breath.

"This is Imogen. Imogen Rockford."

I hear a sharp exhale on the other end of the line. When she speaks again, the woman's voice is entirely different. No longer sounding harried, she adopts a girlish tone brimming with excitement.

"Lady Imogen! I'm Liza, Harry Morgan's assistant. You can't imagine how long we've been trying to reach you. It's been quite a trial, so much so that hearing your voice now is just . . . well, I can't believe it!"

I hold the phone in front of me and stare at it, as if gazing deep into my iPhone will somehow make sense of her bizarre words.

"I'm just Imogen. No one calls me Lady," I say, baffled. "And I don't know what you mean about trying to reach me. I haven't gotten any calls or mail or anything, other than a package from Mr. Morgan just now."

"You didn't receive anything?" Liza echoes, her voice sounding bewildered. "But we've been writing and calling for weeks."

With a jolt, I realize this can mean only one of two things. Either this lady is off her rocker—or the Marinos have been withholding the correspondence from me.

"Where is Mr. Morgan?" I ask again. "I haven't opened his package yet. My guardians have it."

"He's in New York," she says softly. "He came to see you."

I nearly fall out of my desk chair.

"What? He's here?"

"Yes. He needs to speak with you. It's very important."

"Is it something bad?" I ask tentatively. What if the Marinos have a good reason for keeping this from me?

"Not exactly." As if sensing my hesitation over the phone, Liza continues, "You'll be glad to speak with him. You won't be sorry, I guarantee it."

"Okay . . ." I think quickly. "It's probably best that I meet him somewhere else, not at home."

I nervously rattle off the first place I think of, Lauren's address, and ask if Mr. Morgan can meet me there after school.

"I'll make sure he gets there at three-fifteen," Liza promises me. "I'm so glad I got to speak with you, Imogen. Have a wonderful day, and I—I hope we'll be seeing you at Rockford Manor soon."

"Oh, um, probably not, but thanks. Have a good day."

I click the phone off and fling myself onto my bed, suddenly overwhelmed by the magnitude of what I've just done. I can't imagine what's so important that an estate manager would travel halfway across the world to come talk to me about—and I'm both terrified and eager to find out what it is.

❧

"You said what?" Lauren exclaims through a mouthful of her turkey sandwich. We're sitting at our usual table in the school cafeteria and I've just finished giving her a quick, under-my-breath recap of the phone call. "What am I supposed to tell my mom when a strange old British guy shows up at our apartment?"

"I didn't know what else to say. I had to come up with something on the spot, and I wanted to meet him someplace where I wouldn't have to worry about anyone overhearing. And I obviously can't meet him at home when Carole and Keith are the ones trying to hide all this from me." I glance across the room at Zoey, who's chatting happily with her friends at a corner table, blissfully unaware of her parents' secrets—or my own. "Plus . . . I'd just feel a little better if you were there."

Lauren gives my arm a squeeze. "You're right, I'm sorry. Of course I'll be there for you. We just have to think of an alias for this Harry guy that won't make my mom suspicious."

"I guess we could say he's my uncle?" I suggest. "We

could pretend he's visiting me and that I brought him over to meet you."

Lauren wrinkles her nose.

"I don't know. I can totally see my mom mentioning that to the Marinos."

"Okay, then . . . what if he's my tutor and is helping us study for a test?"

"You know how often my mom talks to Carole," Lauren says, shaking her head. "Anything we come up with could get back to her, even if it's something as small as my mom commenting on how nice your fancy British tutor is."

I take a deep breath.

"Then I guess I'll have to be prepared to tell her the truth . . . later. First I've got to find out what Harry Morgan wants, without Carole and Keith getting in the way. So even if the tutor alias gives us just a couple of hours before my cover is blown, at least by then I'll have some answers. And if it comes down to it, I'll tell your parents I lied to you about who he is too, so you won't get in trouble."

Lauren stares at me. "I've never seen you like this."

"Like what?"

"You never talk about your family—the Rockfords," she says carefully. "I hardly know anything about them, or . . . or what your life was like before we met in middle school. But now some guy who works for them shows up and you're suddenly willing to risk being grounded till your eighteenth birthday, just to find out what he wants? That's not the Imogen I know."

I glance down at the cafeteria table, where someone has crudely etched their initials.

"I may not talk about it, but I think about them . . . often."
All those years ago, I shut my cousin and grandfather out, and
I haven't heard from them in so long that I figured they just let
me go. But now it turns out maybe they haven't. And I need
to know why."

Lauren reaches for my hand.

"I get it. And I'll be here to help you."

Literature, my last class of the day, drags on so long that every
time I look up at the clock expecting to see half an hour has
passed, it turns out I'm no closer to the final bell than before.
Normally this is my favorite subject, but today it's impossible
to focus. My teacher's voice is background noise, a droning
sound track to my thoughts, which swim with images from
the Rockford Manor website and imagined scenarios of what
Harry Morgan will say when we meet.

At last, the bell rings. I hurriedly toss my textbook and
binder into my bag, failing to notice that Mark Wyatt has
sidled up to my desk.

"Hey. Thank God that's over, right? Does anyone really
need to know that much about Tolstoy?" he says with a grin.

Oh, right. That's who our teacher was going on about.

"True." I smile back at him, and we fall into step together
as we leave the classroom.

"So are you doing anything right now?" he asks casually.
"Feel like a snack at Magnolia Bakery?"

"Oh . . ."

I stop short, caught off guard. Is he asking me on a date?

I mean, we've never hung out just the two of us before. And if the answer is yes, am I actually going to pass up a date in favor of an awkward meeting with a stranger? But . . . do I really like Mark, or am I just flattered by his attention? The truth is, I haven't had a real, honest-to-goodness crush since I was ten years old. The words I spoke when Sebastian and I said goodbye had been presciently true: *I'll never forget you.*

"Well?" He gives a self-conscious chuckle. "Tough decision?"

"No, of course not," I tell him, reddening. "I just promised I'd help Lauren cram for a test tomorrow and I was thinking maybe I could bail, but I . . . I can't. Rain check?"

"Yeah, no worries," he says as we reach the school exit. "See you tomorrow?"

I give him another smile, hoping my confusion isn't evident on my face.

"See you."

My stomach is jittery throughout the subway ride to Lauren's, and I know it has a lot more to do with the upcoming meeting than Mark's Magnolia Bakery offer. By the time I'm walking up to her family's SoHo loft, my throat is dry and my knuckles white.

I dash up the stairs to the second floor, and then let myself into her apartment—which isn't as rude as it sounds. Lauren and I have been going over to each other's apartments since we were thirteen, and as her mom once sweetly said, "I think we're past the point of knocking. You're one of us." Remembering that makes me feel guiltier about lying to her, but I swallow the feeling. There's no backing out now.

I find Lauren in the kitchen, rummaging for an after-school snack. She must have just beaten me here.

"Hey. So what should we serve our illustrious guest? Will Cheez-Its do the trick?"

"Sure. Thanks." I tap my foot apprehensively. "Did you tell your mom?"

"Yep, and I asked her to leave us alone in the living room so we can study. But she's still close enough to save us if he turns out to be a creeper." Lauren grins. "She was mighty impressed with you for bringing over a tutor."

"Oh." I glance down at the floor. "Well, hopefully whatever he has to say will be . . . something I can handle."

"Of course you can handle it," Lauren says encouragingly. "Maybe it's something good—maybe you've inherited a billion dollars!"

I burst out laughing.

"Well, if that's the case, I can't imagine why the Marinos wouldn't want me to know about it. We could all be loaded!"

At that moment, the doorbell rings. My smile remains frozen on my face.

"He's here. What do we do?"

Lauren gently pushes me toward the door.

"Answer it. I'll be waiting for you guys in the living room."

Gathering my courage, I step forward. *Don't chicken out, Imogen,* I instruct myself. *You know you need to talk to him.* I take a deep breath and open the door.

A bespectacled middle-aged man stands before me, his graying hair slicked back and his posture proud and straight. His eyes widen behind his glasses at the sight of me.

"Do I have the honor of meeting Lady Imogen Rockford?"

I stare at him, my skin prickling with shock, as I realize I know that voice. It's the man who called last night; the same man Keith claimed was his legal rival. *Keith lied to me.* Even though I know he and Carole are hiding things, the blatant lie has me momentarily speechless.

"I'm—I'm sorry," I say when I've recovered. I'm just a little confused by all this. No one calls me Lady Imogen. Well, no one except you and your assistant." I hold out my hand. "But anyway. Nice to meet you, Mr. Morgan."

"Please, call me Harry."

"Oh. Okay." I open the door wider to let him in, lowering my voice as I say, "This is my best friend's apartment. If you see her parents here at any point, please tell them you're my science tutor. Okay?"

I expect him to be thrown off by this, but he nods calmly.

"I can do that."

I lead him into the living room and find Lauren already perched on the loveseat, leaving the couch free for us. Three cans of Diet Coke and a box of Cheez-Its sit on the coffee table, and in this bizarre moment, I feel myself on the verge of giggles at the thought of prim and proper-looking Harry Morgan digging his fist into the box of cheesy crackers.

"Harry, this is Lauren Fox," I introduce them. "Lauren, meet Harry Morgan."

"Pleased to make your acquaintance," Harry says politely. "And thank you for offering your home for this conversation."

"Sure," Lauren replies, though her expression looks suddenly anxious—almost as anxious as I feel. "Nice to meet you too."

I sit on the couch and Harry follows suit.

"So, what is it?" I ask, my voice clipped. "What did you need to tell me?"

"Well. . . . This would be extraordinary news for anyone, but I suppose you might have always thought it possible, being that you were third in line," he begins, pulling a folder of papers from his briefcase.

I stare uncomprehendingly at him.

"Third in line for what?"

"Oh, my God. Was I actually right? Did she inherit a billion dollars?" Lauren blurts out.

Harry chuckles.

"Not nearly that much, I'm afraid. But you have indeed inherited something."

He hands me the folder in his lap, opened to a page that reads *The Last Will and Testament of the eleventh Duke of Wickersham.* I can't look past the heading.

"My grandfather is dead?" I cry.

Harry stares at me, aghast.

"I—I wrote to you right after he passed. I called Mrs. Marino about it. Did you not know?"

"No. I didn't," I say faintly, my head spinning.

"I'm terribly sorry for the shock," Harry says, lowering his eyes. "I'm afraid the duke's health steadily deteriorated after his stroke six years ago. But he's in a better place now. We can comfort ourselves with that."

My cheeks burn with shame as I realize it isn't just his death that I've been in the dark about. I never knew he was so sick—I never called or visited. How could I have been such a coward? And *why* didn't the Marinos tell me what they knew?

"I'm so sorry," I whisper.

"That brings me to the business at hand," Harry says, clearing his throat. "Your grandfather's death means you inherit . . . everything."

For a split second the world freezes. There is no sound or movement beyond my frantic heartbeat.

"What? I'm—I'm not—I shouldn't be next in line," I manage to stammer. "That doesn't make sense."

I watch as the color drains from Harry's face.

"Did you also not receive my messages about your cousin, Lucia?" he asks haltingly.

I gasp at the sound of her name on his lips. For years she's existed only in my memory, and it rattles me to hear someone else speak of her. And then it dawns on me what he might be about to say, and I shake my head, because it's impossible—impossible.

"What messages?" I whisper.

Harry winces, clearly dreading what he has to say.

"I am so—so very sorry to have to tell you this." His voice wavers. "Lucia is—she's—well, I'm afraid she's . . . dead."

IV

"**N**o."
I jump off the couch, scrambling away from Harry in horror. Lauren tries to comfort me but I push her away, swallowing the bile I feel rising in my throat.

"It's impossible. She—she's only two years older than me! She was stronger than me, better than me. There's no way she could be dead."

"Please, Your Grace, I understand it's a shock, but I—"

"Don't call me Your Grace!" I explode. "I'm not anyone's *Grace*."

"But you are. That's what I've come here to tell you, what I've been trying to convey for weeks now." Harry leans forward, gazing at me with an almost reverential expression. "Your grandfather's passing means that you inherit not only Rockford Manor, but his title and dukedom. Hence, you will from now on be addressed as Her Grace, the Duchess of Wickersham."

"That's—that's insane!" I look wildly around the room. "Lauren, where's your phone? I need to call England. This has to be a joke. My grandfather and Lucia will be there and we'll all have a good laugh—"

"Imogen," Lauren interrupts me. "I don't think he's kidding."

I look from her to Harry Morgan and back again, feeling as though the wind has been knocked out of me. My once-closest friend, the cousin who so often intimidated me with her larger-than-life presence, *can't* be dead. But the pained expression on Harry's face is enough for me to realize it's true. And I'll never again have the chance to make things right between us.

I sink numbly into an armchair.

"How did she die?" My voice is barely audible.

Harry briefly shuts his eyes.

"There was a violent storm last fall, the worst I've ever seen in Britain. That night Lucia told the staff she was retiring to bed early, but when the housekeeper went to her room the next morning, she wasn't there. Her bed hadn't been slept in, and there was an empty bottle of vodka by her dresser, leading us to believe that she'd been drinking—again. The Rockford staff searched the grounds and found her body later that day." Harry takes a shaky breath. "Her head had struck one of the stone pillars just outside the Maze."

I struggle to comprehend his words.

"So—that was it? How do you know for sure what killed her?"

"Between the dangerous weather and her inebriated state,

the police concluded she must have fallen in the rain and hit her head against the stone. The autopsy confirmed the cause of death as a blow to the head from a blunt object, and while they offered to do further testing, your poor grandfather was too distraught and unwell to be put through anything more. For his sake, we asked for the case to be closed and dear Lady Lucia put to rest."

"I'm—I'm going to be sick," I blurt out. I cover my mouth with my hand, stumbling into the guest bathroom.

Afterward, I lean my head against the cold tiles of the wall, the room spinning as my mind fills with the image of Lucia's beautiful face—soaked in blood. I'm half conscious of Lauren joining me, rubbing my shoulders soothingly, but nothing gives me any comfort. The story has a horribly familiar ring to it. An innocent accident, a sudden death, the Maze—it's like losing Mum and Dad all over again.

It twists up my insides, knowing that she's gone and I never apologized, never made up for the years I stayed away. All my guilt bubbles to the surface as I wonder what might have happened if we'd kept in touch, if I had been there for Lucia. Maybe she wouldn't have been drinking that night—maybe somehow, in some way, I could have prevented her accident.

After what feels like ages, I manage to stand. Holding on to Lauren for support, I slowly return to Harry.

"Are you all right, Your Grace?" he frets, jumping to his feet as soon as I enter the room. I sink into a seat facing him.

"I should have been there for them," I whisper. "Not just at the funerals, but long before that. I'm so sorry I didn't get your messages, and that I was out of the picture all this time.

I handled everything all wrong, and I—I don't know if I'll ever forgive myself for it."

I can't hold back the tears any longer; it's like a dam has burst. I bury my face in my hands, letting the tears fall and soak into my palms. I usually feel relief after a hard cry, but not this time. There's a painful silence as Harry and Lauren watch helplessly. Then Harry takes a deep breath and begins to speak.

"You can't fault yourself for anything. You were just a child at the time of the fire, and I was told that you were treated for post-traumatic stress disorder afterward. It's no wonder you had trouble returning to Rockford or seeing anyone who reminded you of that night." He clears his throat. "But so many people are now counting on you to come back, to take your place at the helm of Rockford Manor."

I feel a shiver of trepidation at his words.

"I don't understand. Why *me?* Isn't there someone else?"

"I'm afraid that with the fire, and Lucia's passing, you are the late duke's closest living descendant and last in the line of inheritance. Rockford Manor is tied up in entail, which means that if there is no direct heir to take ownership of the estate, the house and all the land will be taken over by the British government," he explains. "In that event, the staff, who have been at Rockford for decades, would lose their jobs and their home. They need you."

"Can't I be the owner or heir without actually living there? You have to understand, I haven't been since . . ." My voice trails off. "I just—I'll never look at Rockford the same, after everything that's happened. I can't imagine being there without my family."

Harry gives me a compassionate look.

"This is an awful lot to take in, I know. But unfortunately, the estate law requires the owner and heir of Rockford to live on the premises and run the property. Additionally, the people of Wickersham have always had a duke or duchess to lead local charities, host events for the townspeople, and most importantly, provide jobs. We also give tours of the estate during summer months and holidays. Rockford Manor and its family are an integral part of the lives of our local community, and that's something—if you don't mind my being direct—you really should consider."

"Wow. He kind of has a point," Lauren says under her breath.

I anxiously tug on a lock of hair.

"But—but I know nothing about running an estate or being the face of a town. I'm not sure I'm the right person for the job."

"You're the only person," Harry says firmly. "No one is expecting perfection, least of all from a seventeen-year-old. You'll have plenty of help and instruction along the way. All that matters is that you're willing to learn."

"But Lucia . . . she was born for that type of life, and I'd be taking it from her. She would hate me for it." I shudder inwardly.

"Lucia wasn't necessarily intended to be heir either," Harry says carefully. "Her father was next in line, and if he and his wife had lived and produced a son, that boy would have taken Lucia's place in the line of inheritance. The fire changed everything; it reshuffled all the cards. And now we have to make do with the hand we've been dealt."

I can't sit still anymore. I restlessly pace Lauren's living room, racking my brain for a solution. But instead, my mind fills with images of my younger self—turning my back on Lucia at the Rockford Cemetery, refusing my grandfather's invitations. If I decline my inheritance and let Rockford Manor fall to pieces, it will be the same cowardice all over again. But this time it would affect more lives; it would be a betrayal to my parents. I won't, *can't* do that. And in that moment, my mind is made up.

I will move to England; I will do all that is asked of me. I owe the Rockfords—my family—that much.

"Okay," I say simply. "I'll do it."

I feel strangely lighter as soon as I've said the words. There won't be any more worrying or wrestling with my future, debating with the Marinos about NYU versus a gap year. My future has been decided. It's not one I would have ever chosen, but the idea of fulfilling a duty to my father's family gives me a sudden sense of purpose—something I've been missing since I lost him.

Harry lets out a sigh of relief while Lauren gapes at me.

"You're doing the right thing," she says after a pause, squeezing my hand. "But . . . this is all so weird. I can't picture us living in different cities, much less different countries. What will I do without you?"

"What will I do without *you*?" I shake my head sadly. "We'll just have to talk on the phone or email every day, and visit each other as much as possible."

"Maybe you can make one of the rooms in your new mansion the Official Lauren Fox Guestroom?" she says with a small smile.

"Of course. If anyone could brighten that place for me, it's you."

"Let me speak for everyone in Wickersham when I say how thrilled I am that you've agreed to assume your title and estate," Harry says grandly. "Now, I have some papers here for you to sign, primarily the deed of inheritance and ownership. We also need to book your travel. How soon can you leave? The earlier the better, as it's not customary for Wickersham to be without a duke or duchess on site for this long."

"Um . . ." Although I've made my decision, I'm still floored by how swiftly everything is moving and changing. "Well, I have to graduate from high school first. That's only two weeks away. And if I plan to leave any earlier than my eighteenth birthday, which isn't until October, then I probably have to get my guardians' permission first. Right?"

"Actually, no," Harry clarifies. "Your parents' wills state that if ever you should inherit the title and estate, you may be considered emancipated and thereby live at Rockford, running the property under a co-regency until you turn twenty-one. After that, you retain sole control."

I stare at him, my mouth falling open.

"Why . . . why would my parents think to include something like that in their will? Before the fire, there was no chance of me ever inheriting anything."

"It's customary to have a clause like this for all immediate family members of someone on the level of a duke," Harry answers. "In the past, wars could wipe out multiple heirs within a year. Fifth and sixth cousins had to be prepared to assume inheritances. Since then, the precaution has stuck."

I nod slowly.

"Okay. But what's a . . . a co-regency?"

"It's another authoritative figure who shares control of

decision making with the heir until he or she comes of age. In this case, as estate manager, I am your co-regent." Harry smiles. "But I promise, you won't see too much of me. I'll be there to help you manage the tenants and staff and so on, and we'll make decisions about the property together, but aside from that you're free to do as you wish."

"Jeez, and to think just yesterday your only prospect was being an undeclared major at NYU," Lauren marvels. "Talk about your life changing overnight!"

"You're not kidding," I say quietly. "I—I should probably go home and talk to the Marinos about all of this. I have no idea how the conversation with them will go down, but I have a feeling it won't be pretty. Everything would have been so different if they had just been *honest* with me."

"Would you like me to come speak to them with you?" Harry offers.

"I can be there too, for moral support," Lauren adds.

"Thanks, both of you. But I think I need to do this alone. I'll call you tomorrow to go over any other arrangements we have to make," I tell Harry.

"One more thing," Harry says, rising to his feet. "Since you'll be arriving in England around the start of the social season—meaning you'll be expected to make public appearances and entertain guests at Rockford—you need to undergo a bit of study. Duchess training, so to speak. We can fly in an etiquette expert and put him up at a nearby hotel, if you'll make time for lessons after school."

"Um . . . what?" I squeak. "You really want to spend a fortune sending an etiquette expert to America to give me *duchess* lessons? This is too weird."

"I'm not the one spending it," Harry says with a grin. "You're an heiress now, don't forget. These papers you're about to sign will transfer the Rockford bank accounts into your name. As your co-regent, I'm tasked with giving you an allowance so that you don't burn through your inheritance as so many young people do. But if I may be so blunt, an etiquette expert will hardly break the bank. And it's rather necessary."

Lauren and I turn to each other, eyes wide.

"It's like . . . like you're a whole new person now," Lauren says awkwardly.

I shake my head.

"I'm not. They can call me a duchess, but I'm still me."

I return home to find Carole putting the finishing touches on dinner while Zoey sets the table. For a moment I just stand in the doorway watching, knowing this will be my last glimpse of normalcy before I drop my news on them—before life changes forever.

"Hi," I call out. "I'm home."

"Good. You're on dishwashing duty tonight," Zoey replies, giving me a smirk.

Carole comes out of the kitchen to greet me, and from the way her eyes keep nervously darting back and forth, I can tell she's read Harry Morgan's letter—and she doesn't want me to know about it. My anger at their secrecy flares anew, but I force myself to stay calm for Zoey's sake.

I wait to speak until Keith returns from work and we're

all seated around the dinner table, preparing to dig into a roast chicken.

"I have some news," I begin, my voice sounding funny and high-pitched to my ears. "It's a good thing you're all sitting down."

Carole's fork drops to her plate with a clatter and Keith frowns at me in concern. Zoey claps her hands together in glee.

"You and Mark are together!"

"Um, no. But I love how you think my having a boyfriend would be groundbreaking news."

"I'm just saying, it's about time." Zoey shrugs.

"*Any*way," I continue. "It has to do with my family. The Rockfords."

"Zoey, can you give us a minute alone?" Keith quickly interjects.

"What?" Zoey looks at him incredulously. "Are you seriously banishing me from dinner right when Imogen is about to make a big announcement?"

"Let her stay," I tell Keith. "She's going to find out anyway."

He pushes his plate to the side, his frown deepening. I clear my throat awkwardly and turn to Zoey.

"Zo, I'm not sure how much of this you know, because we never really talked about it, and you were only eight when I came to live with you guys. But my parents who died in the fire, they . . . they were part of a noble family in England. The family has always owned Rockford Manor in Oxfordshire, which is a mansion that includes acres of land, plus a local village where people live and farm—"

"Wait, noble? Do you mean like royalty?" Zoey interrupts, her eyes wide.

"No, no. But in England there's a system called the peerage—dukes and duchesses, earls and countesses—and they're ranked just below royalty. My dad was the younger son of the Duke of Wickersham, which made him a lord and my mom a lady."

Carole and Keith sit frozen, listening to me with a look of dread in their eyes.

"So what does that make you?" Zoey asks breathlessly.

"Well, when my parents were alive, it meant that I was treated a certain way just because I was part of this family of dukes and duchesses. But then after the fire, the line of succession changed—everything changed. My first cousin, Lucia, became next in line to inherit Rockford Manor and the title. So she would have been the Duchess of Wickersham." I swallow hard. "But she died in an accident last year—which I didn't even know about until today." My hands shake as I speak, and I can't look at Keith and Carole, unable to grasp how they could have kept this from me.

"That's awful! But what does it mean for you?" Zoey presses.

"Her death left me next in line after my grandfather. And he passed away last month—which I was also unaware of." This time I'm able to look at Carole and Keith, shooting them a withering glare.

Zoey's mouth hangs open.

"That means you're . . . you're a . . . ?"

"Yeah. You're looking at the new Duchess of Wickersham and owner of Rockford Manor." I try to lighten the mood with a jokey tone, but instead sound almost as terrified as I feel.

"Oh. My. God."

Zoey, at least, seems to love this. She gapes at me as though

I've turned into a celebrity straight from the pages of her favorite magazines.

"Are you serious? This is unbelievable! Don't tell me I have to bow to you now, though, do I?"

"Of course not!" I laugh. "I mean, people bowed to my grandfather, but I'd feel ridiculous if anyone bowed to me. Like I said, I'm not royalty."

"But you're close to it," Zoey marvels.

"Well . . . I guess, sort of. The Duchess of Wickersham usually serves as a lady-in-waiting for royal ceremonies like coronations and weddings and stuff like that." I realize how completely full of it I sound, and I cough in embarrassment. "Sorry. I know this is all so sudden and unreal, but I signed the deed of inheritance, so there's no going back."

At my words, Carole and Keith simultaneously snap out of their state of shock.

"You signed what?" Keith bellows.

"How did any of this happen? How did you speak to Harry Morgan? He wasn't supposed to contact you!" Carole frets.

"And that's the part of the story I understand the least." I grip the sides of the table in fury. "How could you keep everything a secret from me? I should have known that my grandfather was sick, and that he and Lucia *died*. I should have been at their funerals. And, Keith—you lied to me about who called last night. I trusted you both, my parents trusted you, and here you've been lying to me for ages! How *could* you?" My voice breaks, and I turn away, gulping a breath of air.

Carole's face crumples, tears brimming in her eyes. Zoey is stunned into silence, glancing around the table as if she no longer recognizes any of us. Only Keith keeps his composure. When he speaks, his voice is firm and even.

"I'm sorry you feel that way, Imogen. But the reason we've kept everything from you is simple—to protect you. Maybe you don't remember how you were when you moved in with us, but Carole and I will never forget the state of distress you came to us in. For a year, you'd wake up in the middle of the night crying from nightmares; you barely spoke or ate or left your room. Whenever you received a letter or any kind of correspondence from Rockford Manor, your nightmares and panic worsened. Finally, more than two years after the fire, you became yourself again, the girl we remembered. We finally got to see you smiling and happy. So Carole and I promised ourselves we would do everything in our power to keep you that way, which meant shielding you from the people and places that triggered your trauma. We owed it not only to you, but to your parents."

I stare at him, speechless. I don't remember being in such bad shape when I first moved in with the Marinos. I've tried to block those years out, and now they're mostly a blur.

"But—but—" I stammer. "My parents would have *wanted* me to know about Lucia and my grandfather. And my dad would have expected me to take care of Rockford Manor. It was his childhood home. He would never want me to just turn down my inheritance and let the place be left to the government. I might have been . . . broken from what happened, but that doesn't mean you can make decisions for me about what's rightfully mine."

"There's more to it than that," Carole says slowly. Keith

shoots her a warning look across the table, but she continues. "Your father loved Rockford Manor, that's true. But not long before the fire, when your mother was preparing for the annual summer trip, she confided in me that she wasn't comfortable at Rockford anymore. She said that she'd seen strange things at the house, and that she sometimes felt afraid there."

"What?" I blink in confusion, trying to reconcile this description with my memories of Mum cheerfully reading to me in the Rockford library and taking tea in the gardens. "She never seemed afraid."

"Well, I imagine she wouldn't have wanted to show it."

"So what was she scared of? What were the things she saw?" I press.

Carole shrugs helplessly.

"I don't know. When I asked, she just brushed it off and said she was probably being silly. But I could tell there was more to the story. Then when I found out another tragedy had taken place there, when your cousin died, it confirmed my fears that something isn't right about Rockford Manor. For five people to die right there in the gardens—it's . . . it's . . ." She can't finish her sentence, her expression growing all the more urgent. "You can't go. We can't lose you too."

"You won't lose me. . . ." My voice trails off as I fidget with my napkin. Carole's words have me rattled, returning my mind to the confusing, frightening place where a flower grew and sparks flew out of nowhere. But there's no way to know if Rockford Manor had anything to do with all that—and Carole's theory about the fire and Lucia's accident being linked to some kind of macabre conspiracy in the house sounds far-fetched even to my own overactive imagination.

"I think we need to show it to her, Keith," Carole says abruptly.

My head snaps up.

"Show me what?"

Keith hesitates.

"It'll help her understand," Carole urges. "It's time."

"Seriously, what are you guys talking about?" Zoey demands.

Keith nods slightly, and Carole pushes her chair back, leaving the room. The three of us wait in silence, my heartbeat picking up speed, until she returns holding a piece of paper.

"We received this letter a year and a half ago," Carole reveals. "Keith and I talked it over, and since we didn't know who sent it or what to make of it, we decided not to share it with you—we didn't want to cause you unnecessary worry or fear. But after you read this, I think you'll have a better grasp on why we were so vigilant in keeping you away from the Rockfords."

I swallow nervously and take the letter from Carole. Zoey scoots her chair closer to me to read over my shoulder, and her sharp intakes of breath coincide with my own shock at the words, written in an unfamiliar cursive hand.

January 21, 2013

Dear Mr. and Mrs. Marino,

I trust that you and your family are well. I write to you as a friend, with knowledge of a plot that concerns your goddaughter, Lady Imogen, should

*she ever return to Rockford Manor. I can't tell you
more, nor can I go to the authorities. They wouldn't
believe me.*

*The one thing I know is that Lady Imogen should
be safe so long as she stays with you in America.
Don't let her return.*

*Sincerely,
A Friend*

I stare at the letter, rereading it until the words blur together. Who could have sent this? What kind of plot were
they talking about? My legs begin to tremble under the table
and I shift in my chair, trying to steady them.

"Maybe it's a joke, or a trick?" Zoey says hopefully. "For all
we know, the person who wrote the letter was just jealous of
Imogen's getting to be a duchess and wanted to keep her away
from it all."

"But Imogen wasn't a duchess—or even next in line—when
this was sent," Keith objects.

"Still, Zoey might be right," I say. "People who follow all
that British society stuff know about me, and whoever wrote
this letter must have realized I was third in line for the title
at the time. Maybe there's some distant cousin out there who
was jealous and wanted my place?"

Even as I speak the words, I know my theory doesn't make
much sense—but then, how could I be at the center of some
vendetta in England, when I haven't been there since I was ten
years old? Another thought occurs to me.

"Did you ever show this to anyone else? Like Oscar at Rockford Manor? Or the police?"

"We didn't share it with anyone from Rockford, but we did make a copy for the Wickersham police," Keith replies. "They ran a handwriting check but couldn't find any local matches, and they conducted an investigation, though they dismissed it a little too quickly for our liking."

"If it was a legitimate threat, they wouldn't have dismissed it." I feel a surge of relief. "I'll show the letter to Harry Morgan tomorrow and send a copy to Oscar. I know I can trust both of them. If they feel I have something to worry about, then we'll deal with it, but otherwise . . . let's just treat this as a prank. Okay?"

Carole stares at me, the color draining from her face. I realize then that she must have been certain the letter would change my mind.

"You're so determined to do this," she says shakily. "How can you brush aside the danger you might be in?"

"Because we don't *know* that I'm in danger. The police didn't seem to think so—and I can't make major life decisions based on an anonymous letter that could be someone's idea of a good joke." I take a deep breath. "I know that the easier and safer move might be to just stay here and let the manor and my inheritance go. But I've only done the safe thing since the fire. And every time I took the easy way out, by avoiding my cousin and acting as if the Rockfords didn't exist . . . I ended up full of regret. Especially today, when I found out Lucia and my grandfather are gone, and I can never apologize or make things right. So this time, I'm going to be brave. I'm saying yes. And I'm really sorry if it upsets you, but . . . there's nothing you can say to change my mind."

A heavy silence falls over the table.

"You're still a minor," Keith finally says. "You do need our permission."

I wince, unsure how to say what I need to without hurting them further.

"Um. The estate manager, Harry . . . he told me my parents' will states that if I ever became heir to Rockford Manor as a minor, I'd be considered emancipated. Meaning, technically—I don't need permission. I have the paperwork, if you need to see it."

Zoey's expression is beginning to match her parents'.

"Wait a minute, are you saying you're moving to England *forever*?"

"I wish I could say no, but yeah. I have to. We'll visit regularly, though, all four of us. The place is huge, you can have your own wing if you want—" I stop midsentence at the sight of Carole crying silently and rush over to her chair.

"Please, tell me what I can do to make this a little better," I beg. "I don't want to upset any of you, but I need to do this."

"You'll stay till graduation and my birthday, right?" Zoey asks in a tiny voice.

"Of course," I promise. "I won't leave a day before you turn sixteen."

"If there's nothing we can do to stop you, then—then there is one thing you can do for us," Keith says quietly. "You'll go to school at Oxford. Just like Edmund and I did."

I stifle a laugh.

"Keith, you know I hate to disappoint you, but my odds of

getting into Oxford are, like, one in a million. It doesn't matter if I have legacy there. Nowadays you pretty much have to be valedictorian to get in. And we all know I'm not."

"It might not be as hard as you think. The third duke made quite the sizable endowment to Oxford in the eighteenth century, and the Rockfords have continued contributing to the school ever since," Keith divulges. "So long as your grades are respectable, which they are, I see no reason why you wouldn't get in."

"But even if I did get in, how would I keep up with all the super-smarties? You've always said how insanely hard the coursework was there," I remind him.

"You could specialize in the subject you're best at. Maybe English literature? You love reading."

"Oh, I've heard about Oxford's English program. Apparently you have to give three-hour presentations on your reading material in Latin." I start to feel a case of the sweats coming on. But as I look at Keith, I know I have to find a way to appease him. It's bad enough that I'm leaving them. "What if I take a summer course? If I survive it and pass, then I'll apply for a full term next year."

Keith hesitates for a moment, but then he gives a slight nod. Carole shakes her head angrily at Keith and rises to her feet.

"A summer course at Oxford in no way changes the fact that you're going to be living on your own at seventeen, with immense pressure on your shoulders and the very real possibility of a threat to your life. I can't give you my blessing on this."

"I'll hardly be alone," I try to reassure her. "I'll be living with a staff of a dozen people, including the butler who practically raised my dad, plus full-time security."

"Butler?" Zoey echoes, her mouth agape.

Carole wipes her eyes with the back of her hand.

"I know I can't talk you out of your inheritance. What young girl wouldn't want to be a duchess and live in her own palace? But I've always had a bad feeling about that place—and you might think the letter is just a joke, but it only strengthened my suspicions. So no, I can't be happy about this."

"I don't expect you to be happy about it now. But I hope one day you will be, and that you'll see I did the right thing," I say. "And I promise, if I get there and I sense anything wrong, I'll come home right away. Please, just . . . try not to worry. Everything is going to be okay."

Zoey reaches for my hand across the table.

"You have my support," she says, forcing a smile. "My sister, the *duchess.*"

V

I toss and turn in bed that night, Lucia's face coming to mind every time I drift off to sleep. When I close my eyes, I see her as she was at age twelve—but her beautiful face is marred with blood. The dark red spills from her eyelids onto her cheeks; it streaks her hair crimson. I'm desperate to get away from the terrifying sight, and yet I am frozen in place.

"How could you let this happen to me?" she sobs, shaking her pale arms toward me. *"How could you let me turn into this?"*

My eyes snap open just before she gets close enough to touch me. I'm back home in New York—and she is gone. But the weight of my guilt is heavier than before. I should have been there for her, and instead . . . I am taking her place.

"Forgive me, Lucia," I whisper into the darkness.

I lie there for hours, not sleeping or moving—but remembering the two little girls who used to play together, sharing secrets and sleepovers in the Rockford boathouse. I know that when morning comes, I'll be forced to grow up fast. And sure enough, as daylight breaks, the two little girls from my memory vanish with the moon.

❧

My new reality begins with Harry Morgan arriving at the apartment to escort Zoey and me to school. He warned me at the end of our meeting yesterday that the news of my succession to the dukedom would be public knowledge by morning, what with the UK being five hours ahead.

"Just in case the press should set up camp outside your school, I'd really prefer that I chauffeur you and Miss Marino," he said.

I relented, but only because the word "press" freaked me out. Now, as I make my way into the living room and find Carole and Keith staring Harry down as if he's from an opposing faction, I wonder if maybe this wasn't such a great idea.

"Morning!" I call out in a fake-cheery voice. "I see you guys have already met."

The three of them nod stiffly. Only Harry offers a smile.

"Are you ready, Your Grace?"

Carole and Keith exchange a look of shock as they hear my title used for the first time.

"Just a sec." I rifle through my backpack and pull out the anonymous letter. "What can you tell us about this?"

Harry Morgan's eyebrows shoot up as he reads the letter. He scans it a second time before shaking his head and handing it back to me.

"I can tell you one thing—it isn't from any of the staff. I have each of their contracts in my office, and I'm familiar with everyone's handwriting. Not to mention I know all your employees and tenants quite well. I am very confident that no one inside Rockford Manor is plotting anything against you," he reassures me.

I nod with relief.

"That's what I needed to hear."

"What about outside Rockford?" Keith interjects. "Just because this wasn't written by someone who lives on Rockford grounds doesn't make it any less of a threat."

"Actually, it does. The fact is, anyone who possesses a great title and wealth finds him- or herself in the hot seat." Harry shrugs nonchalantly. "Take the Duchess of Cambridge, for example. For all her legions of admirers, she has her share of detractors writing nasty things about her online or sending letters that make this one look like a love sonnet. That's simply life in the public eye, and that's why we take our household staff and security so seriously. I assure you, Mr. and Mrs. Marino, that Lady Imogen will be extremely well protected at all times." He leans forward intently. "No one will be able to touch her."

Zoey chooses that moment to bound into the room.

"Ooh! Are you Harry Morgan? I'm practically the duchess's sister." She shakes his hand before turning to look at all of us. "So, what'd I miss?"

"Just Harry telling us we don't need to worry about this wacky letter." I stuff it back into my bag. "C'mon, let's go."

⁓

Thankfully, I'm not a big enough story in New York to warrant more than a few straggler journalists outside Carnegie High. Zoey and I are able to slip inside unnoticed—but I should have known she wouldn't be able to keep the news to herself. By the time lunch rolls around, I find myself adjusting to a bizarre new social sphere in which people who barely acknowledged my existence are now dropping by my lunch table as if they do so every day, gushing about England and asking when I'll get to meet William and Kate.

"Why didn't you ever say you were a soon-to-be duchess?" asks Jenna Carvel, one of the überpopular girls crowded around Lauren and me.

"Um . . . because I wasn't supposed to be," I say glumly, my mind on Lucia. "But either way, it would have been pretty lame for me to go around announcing it, right?"

Lauren nods in agreement, but the other girls stare at me in confusion.

"What do you mean, lame? And how did you manage to keep it a secret that you're even part of that family?" Jenna raises an eyebrow. "I mean, your grandfather was the prince's *godfather*!" Those last words elicit an excited hush from the rest of the girls.

"Well, he does have a couple other godfathers too," I clarify. "But yeah, everyone knew when my parents were alive. After I moved in with the Marinos, and then started middle school, I just . . . I don't know . . ."

"She preferred to fly under the radar," Lauren chimes in.

"Yeah. That."

For the rest of the lunch period I keep quiet, listening to the chatter of our table's new arrivals. It's not that I was *un-*

popular before, but I definitely wasn't in the "it" clique, nor am I a social butterfly like Zoey. I have Lauren and a handful of good friends from over the years, but we aren't exactly storming the halls and turning heads. So this sudden influx of attention is just . . . weird. But the most surreal part of the day comes when the bell rings. Relieved to have the awkward lunch period over with, I hastily grab my tray and am headed for the door alongside Lauren, when I'm nearly plowed into by head cheerleader Tyra Ward, who waves a piece of paper in the air.

"Imogen, look! You're one of the top stories on the *Daily Mail*!"

Oh, God. I take the printout from Tyra and cringe at the sight of my goofy Facebook profile photo filling the center of the article. The headline reads "American Commoner Revealed to Be Duchess of Wickersham!"

"Someone really needs to strike the word 'commoner' from the dictionary," I remark to Lauren.

"Hey, Duchess."

I turn around at the sound of Mark's voice.

"Please don't call me that," I say with a sheepish grin.

"Can you believe Imogen is leaving us?" Lauren says mournfully.

Mark shakes his head.

"And here I thought we were finally going to hang out."

He throws his arm around my shoulder, and I feel myself stiffen. He's so cute, and it's not as if I haven't imagined what it would be like to get closer to him—so why does his touch feel wrong somehow?

Another face fills my mind. I touch my cheek, feeling the

phantom sensation of his kiss. *Sebastian.* The crush that won't quit. What is my *problem?*

I'm relieved when we enter our classroom and Mark is forced to drop his arm back to his side, then annoyed at myself for being such a weirdo. Any girl would be lucky to be the center of Mark's attentions. But . . . maybe it's for the best that I can't seem to let him in. Saying goodbye to the Marinos and Lauren is going to be hard enough. I don't need to add "first boyfriend" to the list of people I'll miss.

A few days after my fateful meeting with Harry Morgan, I arrive at a conference room in the Tribeca Grand Hotel, where Basil Crawford, the esteemed etiquette expert, is waiting for me. He looks like some kind of Victorian gentleman off to the races, with his navy suit over a pale blue vest and silk ascot, topped off by an actual top hat.

"Your Grace," he says, drawing out the words as he lowers into a bow. "It's an honor to be at your service."

"Um, wow. Thanks," I answer lamely, embarrassed by his over-the-top greeting.

Basil immediately stands upright, the simpering smile wiped off his face.

"No, that won't do at all. 'Um, wow, thanks'? The people expect their duchess to be proud, to own her position with confidence!" He stamps his foot for emphasis. "Let's try that again. This time you will smile and reply, 'Thank you, Mr. Crawford. How do you do?'"

"Okay, but . . . do people really have to bow to me?" I ask timidly. "I feel ridiculous. I mean, I'm not a princess."

"Dukes and duchesses are traditionally bowed to; however, there is quite a difference between a bow to them and to a member of the royal family. A bow or curtsy to a duke or duchess is slight, whereas for the royal family, you dip much lower."

"It feels so *Godfather*-esque. 'Come, kiss my ring,'" I joke in a bad Marlon Brando impression.

Basil gives me a dead serious look.

"Your Grace, surely you don't mean to compare the British aristocracy to the Italian Mafia?"

And so begins my first day of duchess training, during which Basil crams my brain with everything from forms of address for people of different ranks ("Your Majesty" for the sovereign, "Your Royal Highness" for princes and princesses, "my lord" or "my lady" for peers below dukes and duchesses, "sir" for baronets and knights) to seating arrangements at dinner parties (the gentleman of highest rank sits at my right hand, with everyone else following according to their title and station). By the end of the day, I am convinced England is one giant web of snobbery.

"I mean, why do they rank everything?" I complain to Basil, hunched over my furiously scribbled notes. "The way you're talking, I can barely share an elevator with someone without knowing their rank. You have to admit it's crazy."

"The British peerage has existed for centuries, and might I add that it's worked quite well for the most part," Basil says, arching an eyebrow. "We British like to have a purpose, a role to play, on the great stage of society. Everyone from a duchess to a housekeeper has her own important place in this world, her own unique set of superiors and inferiors. Categories and titles are simply what we're accustomed to, and we've found that they help society run smoothly."

"If you say so."

"Now, for your final lesson of the day, it's essential that you know why your title was created. Do you have any idea?"

I shake my head sheepishly.

"One of your ancestors, Randolph Henry Rockford, proved to be one of England's greatest military heroes at the turn of the eighteenth century. After he won a number of crucial battles for England, King George I expressed his gratitude by granting him a dukedom over the settlement of Wickersham, along with the massive funds to build a palace worthy of such a hero," Basil explains. "Of course, the papers scoffed that King George was cruel to choose Wickersham, for the land was notoriously barren, especially in comparison to Oxfordshire's other, far more verdant towns. But eventually the fifth Duchess of Wickersham, Lady Beatrice, changed all of that."

"What did she do?" I ask.

"I suppose you could say she was the ultimate green thumb. Within a year, ugly old Wickersham was transformed into one of the most beautiful, frequently painted landscapes in England."

This is the first moment of our lesson where I feel a flicker of interest.

"How did she do it?"

Basil hesitates.

"It's hard to separate truth from fiction on that account. I suppose we'll never know."

I open my mouth to ask more, but Basil claps his hands together and rises.

"That's all for today, Your Grace. I'll see you at the same time tomorrow, for a crash course on the high points of the London season."

The week flies by in a frantic whirl of final exams, duchess training with Basil, and packing for the big move. I find myself so busy that every time my mind wanders to Sebastian—wondering what he's like nowadays, if he and Lucia were still close when she died, if and when I might see him again—I'm able to settle the inexplicable butterflies in my stomach by focusing on one of the many overwhelming tasks at hand. And before I know it, it's the night before graduation.

Too antsy to sleep, I throw on a sweatshirt and head onto the fire escape. It's a perfect, balmy evening, and as I listen to the symphony of New York—the endless sweep of taxis, snippets of music floating up from apartments and restaurants, the chatter and laughter of passing pedestrians—I realize how fortunate I've been to grow up here, and how much I'll miss it. I feel a fresh wave of terror as I imagine boarding the flight to London in just one week, leaving behind my country and everything I know. What am I *doing?*

"This was always your favorite spot."

I turn around at the sound of Carole's voice. She is still dressed, her eyes red-rimmed under the moonlight.

"Sit with me?" I pat the step beside me.

We sit silently for a few moments, looking up at the stars. And then she says softly, "I'm really going to miss you."

My heart constricts.

"I'm going to miss you too. You've been the mother I needed all these years."

She reaches out to touch my cheek.

"I always knew you were never truly mine, and that I might have to let you go someday. I just didn't think it would be this soon."

"You're not losing me," I assure her. "I may be living in another country, but we'll always be connected."

She smiles wanly.

"I hope so."

I squeeze her hand. "I can never thank you enough for all you guys have done for me."

"You can thank me by taking care of yourself," she says intently. "Be on guard over there, and promise to come home the second anything seems . . . amiss. That's the best way you can thank us—by keeping yourself safe."

Her grave tone sends a foreboding shiver up my spine.

"I—I will. I promise."

"We're the class of 2014, the bright and the brave,
As we grow and find our way, roads to greatness we shall pave!"

Lauren and I stand in a circle of adrenaline-crazed class-mates, yelling our class cheer while tossing our graduation caps in the air and giggling as we fail to catch them. Cipriani restaurant is all decked out for Grad Night, with a dance floor and DJ, photo booth, buffet spread, and sundae bar. The air is thick with heightened emotion, as everyone surrounding us is either beaming and cheering or hugging someone in tears. The most important chapter of our lives thus far has come to a close, and I feel myself swinging wildly between celebrating finally being done with school, and trepidation over what comes next. In less than a week, I'll be on a plane to England. But standing here in downtown Manhattan, surrounded by the people and friends I've known since the sixth grade, I can't imagine being anywhere else.

The DJ transitions from an up-tempo song into a ballad, just as I catch sight of Mark Wyatt heading my way—looking extra cute in his formal wear.

"Hey, Imogen, Lauren."

"Hey. Fun party, right?" I say awkwardly. My flirting skills always suffer when I have an audience.

"I'm going to get a refill," Lauren says, raising her plastic cup with a little smirk. "See you guys later."

"Want to dance?" Mark asks after Lauren leaves.

"I'd love to," I say with a smile.

As Mark takes my hand and leads me to the dance floor, I'm overly conscious of my body—wondering if I'm too sweaty, if my heartbeat is as loud as it feels, if my hairdo is intact. We assume slow-dance position, his arms around my waist, mine draped across my shoulders. And then he takes me by surprise with his words.

"I like you, Imogen. You already know that, though, right?"

"Oh! Um. I like you too," I say with a nervous giggle,

though the words come out of my mouth sounding a bit more like a question than a statement.

"That's good to hear. But I know you're leaving and I won't have another chance to do this. So . . ."

And before I realize what's happening, he bends down and brushes his lips against mine. The kiss is quick, so quick that I don't really feel . . . much of anything. I mean, I know we're in a restaurant filled with our classmates, so I didn't expect a long, sweeping make-out session or anything, but I can't help feeling a twinge of disappointment that the kiss isn't quite the heart-melting occasion I imagined whenever I thought about taking our friendship to the next level.

And then I awkwardly overcompensate with too much enthusiasm.

"That was *great!*" I blabber, wanting to smack myself in the head as soon as the words are out of my mouth.

Mark looks pleased.

"I'm glad you liked it."

"Um. Yeah." I'm not sure if it's my imagination, but I can feel our classmates' eyes on us, and I'm way too self-conscious to attempt a repeat performance. "I should go find Zoey. I'm her chaperone tonight, you know."

"Oh," Mark says, disappointment flickering across his face. "Bummer."

"I'll see you around!" I call over my shoulder, before scurrying off to rejoin Lauren. I find her and Zoey by the buffet, practically collapsing in giggles. I have a feeling I know what they're laughing at, and I make a concerted effort to ignore it.

"Shouldn't you be with your date?" I ask Zoey.

"I can't believe you did a kiss-and-run!" she screeches, ignoring my question.

"You guys, stop," I hiss. "We don't want Mark to hear. And thanks a lot for spying on us."

"It's not spying when you guys had your big moment in full view of everyone," Lauren retorts.

"So what the heck happened? I thought romance was blooming," Zoey says.

"I don't know. Maybe it was just too public to be romantic. Besides, what does it even matter?" I fill a plastic cup with punch before glancing back at the two of them. "It's not like I can date him from England."

At the mention of England, the two of them fall silent.

"Maybe you'll find a hot British guy," Lauren says halfheartedly, forcing a smile. "Like a Prince William type."

An involuntary image flashes through my mind: a grown-up version of Sebastian, no longer just a cute boy, but now a tall, muscular, handsome man. I shake my head to rid myself of the daydream.

Zoey suddenly holds up her manicured hand, distracting me from my thoughts.

"Please—just for tonight, let's not talk about England," she says quietly. "Let's pretend you're not going anywhere, like everything is normal."

I wrap one arm around her and the other around Lauren.

"Okay. Tonight, I'm not going anywhere."

❧

The following week finds me, Zoey, Carole, and Keith standing numbly at a check-in counter at John F. Kennedy International Airport. We watch my luggage get tagged and sent on its way, knowing that each checked suitcase brings us closer to the moment of goodbye.

"You're all set!" the woman behind the Virgin Atlantic counter says cheerfully, oblivious to our bleak expressions. "Security is up the escalator to your left."

I swallow hard. "Thanks."

Zoey clutches my hand, and the four of us slowly make our way to the security checkpoint.

"I guess . . . this is it," I say, struggling to keep my voice steady as I look at my second family. I will never forget this image of them: Keith's eyes so protective, Carole forcing a brave smile, and Zoey nervously playing with the gold heart necklace I gave her for her sixteenth birthday. My tears spill over as I pull them into a group hug.

"I love you all so much."

"You'll always be a daughter to us," Carole whispers into my hair.

"Call us if you need anything at all," Keith says, kissing my cheek.

"I know. And you'll visit me before school starts up again, right?" I ask. "All three of you?"

"You won't be able to get rid of us," Zoey says, wiping away a tear.

We hug one last time, and then I know I have to walk away while I still have the courage.

"Goodbye . . . just for now."

I blow them a kiss and force my feet to move in the direction of security. I want desperately to look back for one last glimpse of them, but I know I shouldn't. My new life in England is waiting, whether I like it or not—and there's no turning back.

Harry Morgan booked my flight to London, so I had no idea I'd be sitting in first class until I glanced at my boarding pass. Luckily, the surprise of walking past a real bar on the airplane and finding my seatmates happily sipping champagne jars me out of my melancholy mood. Each seat takes up its own row, consisting of a lounge chair and ottoman. As I settle into my ridiculously comfortable seat, I have a feeling this might be the first flight on which I manage to fall asleep.

As the spiffy flight attendants come around offering drinks and dinner menus, I pull out my "Preparation: England" folder. It includes maps of the Rockford Manor estate and grounds, as well as the newest issues of British papers and magazines, from the *Observer* to *Tatler* magazine. I'm anxious to be up-to-date on current events and Brit slang—the last thing I want is to be the clueless girl who has no idea what it means if someone says something like "And Bob's your uncle!" Which does not, as one would expect, mean that I have an uncle named Bob, but is apparently a jovial way of ending a sentence when giving out instructions. Clearly, I have a lot to learn. But as dinner arrives and the flight attendant conjures a cloth-covered table from the side of my chair, I feel myself sinking into a relaxed lull. My eyelids grow heavy by the end of the four-course meal, and the observant attendant hurries to my seat, instructing me to get up as she converts it into an actual *bed*. With sheets and a duvet. Somewhat in disbelief at the idea of getting into bed on a plane, I crawl under the sheets and close my eyes.

I toss and turn in my sleeping bag inside the Rockford boat-house as voices outside flood my subconscious.

"Look," I hear Dad say, his voice tinged with excitement. "It's happening! I always guessed it was Imogen."

"Don't, Edmund!" Mum cries. "I just want her to be safe. Please, let's take her home."

"This is her home . . . in more ways than you know."

From another direction comes Lucia's furious hiss.

"I'll never forgive you for this. Never!"

I frown, shaken by Lucia's voice. Why is she so angry? But before I can give it another thought, I hear a fire engine's siren drowning out every other sound.

I wake with a jolt. What in the world was up with that dream? I've never heard those words spoken before, but I can't help wondering—did my parents really have that conversation all those years ago? Did they know something about me that I was unaware of? That I'm still unaware of? I shift nervously in the airplane bed. My subconscious is obviously more than a little freaked out about returning to Rockford.

Sunlight is streaming through the airplane cabin, and I quickly check the time, amazed to discover that I slept a full four hours. We'll soon be landing at London Heathrow Airport.

I watch the journey map on the TV screen in front of me, and as the little plane on the screen inches closer to London, my pulse begins to race. Am I ready for this? Ready for the onslaught of painful memories, and all the expectations people have of me as an overnight duchess?

As my panic grows, I hear the captain announce that we're beginning our descent. I lean back in my newly transformed seat, squeezing my eyes shut. It doesn't matter how unprepared I am. We're landing. My new life is beginning. And there's no pause button to press.

PART II

When Her Grace Beatrice the Duchess of Wickersham arrived at Rockford Manor, she created an international stir. Her marriage to the fifth duke in 1830 was the first of the transatlantic alliances between an English nobleman and American heiress, and the idea of a nineteen-year-old American girl as chatelaine of Rockford Manor provoked much interest. But far greater controversies were to follow her. It wasn't long before rumblings could be heard in the staff quarters and throughout Wickersham Village, with talk of frightening occurrences at the manor since the beautiful young American's arrival. This was the beginning of Beatrice's characterization as a member of the "occult."

—"THE ROCKFORD DYNASTY: PERCEPTION VS. MISCONCEPTION," *THE ISIS* MAGAZINE

VI

After making it through the slow-moving customs line, I head toward baggage claim, nearly bumping into a man in a black suit who holds a sign bearing my name, complete with the Rockford coat of arms: a winged-back lion surrounded by Union Jack flags and a coronet. I quickly recognize the man from the photo Harry Morgan sent me. This must be the new Rockford driver.

"Hi, Alfred?" I approach him. "I'm Imogen."

I catch a flicker of surprise as the driver takes in my sweatpants and Nikes—was I supposed to dress up for the flight?—but then he gracefully takes my hand and dips into a bow.

"Welcome, Your Grace. Feel free to call me Alfie."

"Thank you . . . Alfie." The nickname seems more fitting for a toddler than this balding middle-aged gentleman, but I decide to go with it.

Just then, a group of middle school girls stops in front of us, staring from me to the HER GRACE, IMOGEN ROCKFORD sign.

"*You're* the new duchess?" one of them asks in apparent disbelief, her mouth hanging open to reveal a wad of bubble gum.

"Um. Yeah," I answer awkwardly.

"Can we get a picture with you?" her friend asks, pulling a sparkly iPhone out of her pocket.

I'm too surprised to reply, but luckily, Alfie is there to take control.

"Our apologies, but Her Grace just landed from a long journey abroad and is quite tired. I'm afraid she can't pose for photos just now." And with that, he takes my arm and leads me toward the luggage carousel.

"I'm sorry," I call timidly over my shoulder. When the girls are out of earshot, I turn to look at Alfie. "That was weird. I guess people here are more interested in the family than I thought?"

"Yes, Rockford is rather a household name here in the UK. But there's always extra interest when a young person holds a title. It's such a rare occurrence, and of course it's more exciting for the public to have an appealing young duke or duchess instead of the usual crusty old folk." He chortles merrily, then looks alarmed. "Not to speak ill of your dear late grandfather, of course."

"Oh, I know what you mean," I say automatically, my mind still digesting his words. *Household name.* Yikes.

I point out my three heavy suitcases, which Alfie runs after and collects with ease, despite my offers to help with *at least* the lightest one. We navigate the maze of London Heathrow until we reach the exit to the parking lot, or the car park, as Alfie calls it.

My first breath of London air is perfectly crisp and cool. I look up at a sky dotted with clouds and zip up my sweatshirt as a gust of wind sweeps through my hair.

"Beautiful day, isn't it?" Alfie remarks.

"Yeah, but it's a lot colder than I remember June being," I reply.

"This, cold?" Alfie chuckles. "Oh, you're in for it when winter comes!"

"I probably shouldn't have packed my New York summer wardrobe," I say wryly. "Oops."

"Don't you worry about that," Alfie says. "Oscar figured you might not be prepared for our weather, so he had me take your maid up to London to do a little shopping for you."

"What?"

So many things are wrong with that sentence. Personal maids still exist in the twenty-first century? And *I* have one, who's forced to do my shopping?

Alfie glances at me worriedly. "I hope you don't mind. We just thought you'd need time to settle in at Rockford before going up to London—"

"No, it's not that," I interrupt. "Of course I appreciate it. I just feel bad for the . . . maid having to do that. I didn't even know I had my own—I assumed the maids were just house-keepers for the whole estate."

"You're the duchess; of course you have your own maid," Alfie says with a grin. "Her name is Maisie Mulgrave. You'll like her—she's only a couple of years older than you."

I draw a sharp breath.

"I remember Maisie from . . . before, when we were little. So she stayed at Rockford, then?"

"Oh, yes. And you mustn't ever feel uncomfortable on her behalf. Maisie considers it a real treat to shop for her mistress. She told me on the way home that it was the best day she'd had in a long while."

Well, that just makes me feel worse. What kind of life does Maisie have if doing someone else's shopping is such a source of excitement? My misgivings must be written all over my face, because Alfie hurriedly adds, "It's true. I used to drive Maisie into the city to do Lady Lucia's shopping all the time. In fact, she saved her best clothes for you. Maisie felt it would be a shame for them to go to waste."

His words stop me in my tracks. How can he so casually say Lucia's name, so easily mention her abandoned clothing? Maybe Alfie and the others at Rockford Manor have come to accept her being gone, but Lucia's name still feels like a sucker punch every time I hear it—a stinging reminder of why I'm really here, and of the tragedy that took her away.

Alfie pauses in front of a dark silver Aston Martin, and I quicken my pace to catch up to him.

"The Rockford vehicle," he says proudly when I reach him. Though my knowledge of cars is minimal at best, even I can tell that this one is special.

Alfie opens the door for me, and I sink into the smooth leather backseat. As he takes the wheel, I roll down my window and peer outside. The view is a flurry of industrial-looking buildings broken up by long stretches of grassy fields.

"Are we going to see any of the classic London sights on the way?" I ask. "Like Big Ben or Parliament?"

"'Fraid not," Alfie says apologetically. "The route to Oxford doesn't pass through Central London."

We stay on the highway for the next hour and a half, the scenery continuing in nondescript fashion, until Alfie exits at High Street and the view transforms, as if we've jumped back in time from a modern-day city to a medieval town. I gaze out the window at an ancient-looking village filled with ivy-covered stone buildings, inns, and pubs. A storybook cityscape of towers and steeples looms overhead.

"Here we are," Alfie announces. "Central Oxford."

He continues through the winding streets, pointing out the different impressive-looking colleges that make up Oxford University, and pauses at an especially magnificent fortress-like building crowned with a soaring bell tower.

"That's Christ Church college, where I hear you'll be starting summer school next month. You must be excited."

"Um, nervous is more like it," I confess. "But it sure looks incredible."

"Quite," Alfie agrees, gesturing to the tall steeples of Christ Church. "We call these the dreaming spires. Oxford is famous for them."

"It's beautiful here," I remark. "I hardly remember it from when I was little."

"This is also the most cosmopolitan area you'll find within a half hour of Rockford," Alfie says. "Whenever you'd like to be around friends your own age and visit a pub, or do a spot of shopping, just let me know and I'll drive you. It's only eight miles from the manor."

I wonder if I'll even *have* any friends here. I guess I'd better hope I hit it off with someone in summer school. The thought of having to form an entirely new social circle makes my stomach churn, and I try to refocus on the scenes outside my window.

The narrow streets give way to the countryside as Alfie drives past the Oxford border into new terrain marked by green rolling hills and lofty hedgerows. We pass an antique-looking sign that reads WELCOME TO WICKERSHAM, and I feel a prickly sensation at the back of my neck: the feeling that someone—or some*thing*—is waiting for me.

"This is all yours," Alfie says grandly. "The town of Wickersham."

The picturesque village is nestled among hills and dales, its elegant little houses like something straight out of a history book. As I look around, I feel the sudden tug of a memory.

The three of us file into church on Christmas morning, me in the middle, with one hand in Mum's and the other in Dad's. My face wears the glow of a child who has never wanted for anything, a girl secure in the knowledge that she is adored.

Cousin Lucia and her parents are already seated in the Rockford pew, and I can't contain my smile when I see who is sitting across the aisle: the Stanhopes. I gaze up at my parents, silently thanking them for bringing me here, for bringing me to Sebastian—even if I am just a little kid in his eyes. One day, I'll be all grown up and maybe then he'll look at me differently. . . .

As we pass the rack of votive prayer candles on the way to our pew, an unlit candle suddenly bursts aflame. I gasp, and Mum and Dad exchange a glance. But by the time we're in our seats, the incident is nearly forgotten. Surely it must have been my imagination.

Though I know what I'm about to see, I'm still unprepared

for my visceral reaction to the church. The medieval structure stands in Wickersham's central square, flanked by stone statuary.

"I've been there," I blurt out.

"I'd imagine so." Alfie smiles at me in the rearview mirror. "Your family has belonged to this church since Rockford Manor was first built, and the family members who aren't buried on Rockford grounds were interred here."

"What about Lucia and my grandfather? Are they buried here?" I ask softly, feeling a stab of guilt at the fact that I don't know, that I even have to ask.

"No. They were buried at the chapel in Rockford," he says somberly.

I swallow hard. "Oh."

I am the last surviving heir. And in mere minutes, I'll be entering the house that used to be filled with my family—the house where they are now all buried.

"I think I'm going to be sick." I clap a hand over my mouth.

Alfie swerves to the side of the road, and I fling open my door. I make it to the bushes just in time, and then burst into tears—partly because throwing up is my least favorite thing in the world and today marks the second time I've endured it in the past month, but mostly because I have the feeling that I've made a terrible mistake. *I shouldn't have come back.*

"Are you all right, Your Grace?"

I hear Alfie approach and crouch down beside me. He hands me a bottle of water, which is somehow ice-cold even though we've been in the car for almost two hours. I gulp it down gratefully.

"I'm—I'm okay. Sorry about that."

"If you don't mind me saying so, Your Grace, I think what you're doing is very brave," Alfie says gently.

I wipe my eyes. "You do?"

"Yes. And I know how grateful Rockford Manor's tenants and staff are to have you here. Your arrival means that life as we know it can continue."

I raise my eyes to the sky.

"Okay. Let's go."

ॐ

"Are you ready for this, Your Grace? May I roll down the windows?"

I suck in my breath at the sight of hundreds of strangers crowded together outside the black iron gates of Rockford Manor. They wave flowers and Union Jack flags and hold up banners reading WELCOME, OUR IMOGEN, DUCHESS OF WICKERSHAM! and LONG LIVE THE DUCHESS!

"This is all . . . for me?" I ask. Rhetorical question, I know, but I've never been made such a fuss over in my entire life, and it has me a little dumbfounded.

"It sure is." Alfie meets my eyes in the rearview mirror. "Ready to greet your public?"

"As ready as I'll ever be."

Alfie rolls down all four windows, and a deafening cheer erupts. I smile shyly at the men and women flourishing their banners, and I wave to the children jumping up and down alongside the car.

"Those are your townspeople and tenants," Alfie tells me. "On occasions like weddings, or a new duke or duchess stepping into the title, they gather for a formal welcome to pay their respects. It's tradition."

"It's really sweet," I remark, a blush still reddening my cheeks.

After a chaotic few minutes, Alfie presses a button next to the steering wheel and the manor's gates open on cue. The cheers reach a fever pitch as we pull through the entrance, not quieting until the car passes the crowd. Now it's just me and Alfie again.

I peer ahead nervously, my eyes automatically searching for the Shadow Garden and the Maze, even though they're the last places I want to see. I quickly remember they're both tucked behind the estate, hidden from my current view, and I breathe a sigh of relief.

A lump rises in my throat as the car sweeps past my favorite childhood surroundings: the lake, the grassy parkland, and of course, the castle-like manor itself. Everything looks the same as when I was here all those years ago, and for a moment it seems impossible that I won't find my parents or relatives inside.

Alfie drives forward into the Great Courtyard, and I feel a rush of emotion at the sight of the dozen figures waiting for me on the front steps . . . just like when I was little. As Alfie slows to a stop, a tall, slim young man in a black suit rushes to open my door while his nearly identical counterpart hurries to the trunk to retrieve my suitcases. *Footmen,* I remember.

"Good afternoon, Your Grace," the footman says, dropping to a bow before helping me out of the car.

"Thank you. It's nice to meet you, Mr. . . . ?"

"Carter, Your Grace. The pleasure is all mine."

This "Your Grace" stuff is starting to feel pretty silly. I wonder how long it'll take for everyone to feel comfortable just calling me Imogen.

The staff remains lined up in perfect form, and for a moment I'm at a loss as to what I'm supposed to do. Are they waiting for me to call out "At ease" or something? But as I approach the front steps, a familiar figure hurries down toward me, his eyes shining as he lowers into a bow.

"Your Grace," he says softly. "My, has it been a long time."

I'm speechless as I look at Oscar. He has changed from the dapper butler I remembered into . . . someone who looks twenty years older, and troubled. He's grown bald, his face is creased with countless lines, and his eyes have lost their sparkle. It occurs to me now that Oscar is a visual representation of the tragedies that have befallen Rockford Manor. It must have nearly killed him to stand by as he lost the family that he cared for so deeply, and once again I'm overcome with a heart-wrenching sense of regret.

"Oscar," I whisper. "It's so good to see you."

"And you as well, Your Grace. I often wondered when I would see you again." His eyes fill with emotion. "You've grown into such a beautiful young woman. Just like your mother."

I can feel the tears pricking at the back of my eyes, and I throw my arms around him, like I used to as a little girl. His scent reminds me of my father—a subtle English cologne mixed with the woodsy smell of Rockford Manor—and I hold on tighter before finally letting him go.

"Sorry," I say with a half smile. "I just . . . missed you."

"I missed you too, Your Grace," he says warmly. "Allow me to reacquaint you with the staff."

We turn around to face the steps, where eleven pairs of eyes watch us intently.

"You of course know Harry," Oscar says, nodding to Harry Morgan, who steps forward and bows with a broad smile.

"Wonderful to see you on home turf, Your Grace."

"You too, Harry." I grin back at him. "Thanks for getting me here."

"And the housekeeper, Mrs. Mulgrave." Oscar directs my attention to the tall, skeletal-looking figure dressed in an ankle-length black skirt and matching blouse. "She's been at Rockford for more than twenty years now. You probably remember her from before?"

My smile freezes on my face.

"Yes, of course. I remember."

She's changed too, but the difference is far more chilling than what I see in Oscar. Maybe it's because I was so hopelessly intimidated by her as a child, maybe my past feelings are coloring my present view—but as I look at Mrs. Mulgrave now, my blood turns cold. She makes me think of a living corpse, with her skin-and-bones frame and the deadened look in her eyes. What happened to her? She was always a stern, humorless character when I was a child, but I don't remember ever seeing her like this—like someone only half present among the living.

"Good afternoon, Your Grace."

Mrs. Mulgrave lowers into a slight bow, her mouth setting in a thin line that just barely resembles a smile. She holds out her hand, and it feels cold and limp in mine.

"Good afternoon," I echo.

"Mrs. Mulgrave will help you manage the day-to-day

affairs of the house, and she is indispensable when it comes to planning parties and hosting visitors," Oscar says.

I glance at Mrs. Mulgrave uncertainly. I can't picture her in any sort of festive scenario.

"She also manages the household accounts, and will review them with you weekly," he continues.

I force a smile in her direction. "Great."

"And now Mrs. Findlay, our esteemed cook." Oscar nods to the stout fifty-something woman with graying blond hair.

"It's an honor to serve you, Your Grace," she says in an Irish accent, dropping into a curtsy and giving me a kind smile.

"Oh, I remember you well, Mrs. Findlay, especially—" I stop midsentence, not wanting to recall her treacle tart or any of the other treats she used to make for me and Lucia before everything changed.

"Mrs. Findlay prepares a full breakfast, dinner, and afternoon tea every day, plus lunch on the weekends," Oscar says, filling the awkward pause. "Whenever you host guests or parties, she'll create the menus with you."

Just then, I notice Mrs. Mulgrave giving the younger woman beside her a slight push in my direction.

"This is my daughter, Maisie. She will be your maid."

"Maisie?" I can't help blurting out in astonishment.

I hardly recognize her. The past seven years have transformed Maisie from a plain preteen into a beautiful young adult. I didn't expect her to be so . . . pretty. She wears a black tee with black pants, but the simple clothing and lack of makeup only enhance her looks. She has heavy-lidded deep brown eyes, clear skin with the hint of a tan, the kind of plush pink lips that housewives in my New York hometown would pay good money for, and long brown hair highlighted with strands of gold. Her only adornments are a thick wristwatch and a rectangular pendant hanging on a chain around her neck.

I feel a pang of sympathy as I look from mother to daughter. If Maisie's luck had been different—if she'd been born to parents like the Marinos—she could have had the world at her feet, instead of being shut up in a house working as a maid.

"Maisie, it's really nice to see you again. I have a feeling we'll be good friends," I say warmly.

A peculiar expression crosses her face, a vaguely familiar look I feel I've seen before. Though she's still smiling, her eyes cloud over, and I wonder if I said something wrong. Did I come across as patronizing? Or maybe . . . maybe she remembers the last time I visited, and the way Lucia and I ignored her. Maybe she never liked me to begin with.

But I don't have time to analyze her reaction any further as Oscar continues the round of introductions. I meet Mrs. Findlay's kitchen assistant, Katie, and two other housemaids, Betsy and Elena, who are tasked with the upkeep of the public rooms open to tour groups and guests. And then I come face to face with someone I remember all too well.

"Max," I say, my throat dry.

He smiles gruffly, and I am momentarily transported to that day in the Shadow Garden seven years ago, when he handed me the seeds that sprouted at my touch. I wonder if he ever thinks about that afternoon, or if the memory was lost in the wake of the fire.

"Your Grace," Max says, taking off his cap as he bows. "I'm ever so pleased you're back."

"Thank you, Max. I'm glad to see you too."

"Well!" Oscar claps his hands together purposefully. "I imagine you must be hungry. Mrs. Findlay has prepared a welcome lunch for you, if you'd like to eat shortly. Carter will bring your suitcases up to your rooms."

"I can unpack for you," Maisie offers.

"Oh, no, thank you," I say hastily. "I mean . . . you don't have to do that."

Oscar gives a signal to the staff, which sends them dispersing in different directions. Carter and the second footman, Benjamin, lug my suitcases up the stairs and through the front doors, while Mrs. Mulgrave, Mrs. Findlay, Maisie, and the other maids all walk in steady formation to the back of the house. Alfie hops back into the Aston Martin, Max disappears into the gardens, and soon Oscar and I are the only ones left.

❧

"Welcome back to Rockford Manor, Your Grace," Oscar says, before opening the front doors.

"Holy—"

I bite down on my lip to keep from letting an expletive fly in front of Oscar. I forgot how overwhelming and magnificent the Marble Hall is. In the years I've been away the gigantic foyer must have shrunk in my mind, but now I stand dwarfed by the seventy-foot-high ceiling, gaping at the stone carvings, classical paintings, towering potted palms, vases bursting with flowers, and white marble sculptures surrounding me.

I step back to gaze at the main entrance archway with King George I's coat of arms carved into the center, framed by imposing Corinthian columns. A balcony lies beneath the arch, and I envision an orchestra stationed there, playing for guests as they saunter through the Marble Hall below. I look up and find that even the ceiling is a work of art, covered in its entirety by a painted scene that would have been at home in the Louvre. This place is completely over the top.

"There you are. Come along, Imogen darling."

My head snaps up at the sound of Mum's voice. I stumble forward, eyes searching desperately for her, even though I know deep down that she won't be found. My heartbeat picks up speed, the adrenaline of longing flooding my insides—and from out of nowhere, a gust of wind swirls around my body, nearly hurtling me off my feet with its force.

"What was that?" I cry out.

Oscar hurries to close the windows.

"Awfully strange, our English weather. I don't think I've seen a breeze quite like that before."

It's only a breeze, just like he said, I tell myself, taking a deep breath. *I didn't . . . do anything.*

The sound of a dog's high-pitched bark is a welcome distraction. I glance down to find a tiny gray-and-white furball at my feet, looking up at me with big brown eyes.

"Teddy, over here!" Oscar orders.

The dog scampers in his direction and I follow.

"What kind of dog is he?" I ask, bending down so Teddy can sniff my hand.

"Teddy's a shih tzu," Oscar replies. "He was Lucia's dog, so he's been a little out of sorts since . . ."

The weight in my chest returns as I look upon the ownerless dog. I find myself on the verge of tears yet again.

"How would you like a tour of the first floor before lunch?" Oscar suggests, his welcoming smile lightening the mood. "I imagine you might have forgotten your way around, after all this time."

I blink away the moisture behind my eyes.

"A tour would be great. Thanks, Oscar."

I follow him through a long red-carpeted corridor, lined with white marble busts of past dukes and duchesses. The corridor grows more ornamented as we approach the first drawing room, with gilded glass cases displaying fine china from past generations of Rockfords. I stop to glance at them before stepping into the Blue Drawing Room.

"I don't remember this," I murmur, looking around in awe.

"Rockford children don't normally spend time in the formal rooms, with the exception of the library, and of course, the dining room for Christmas dinner," Oscar says. "So I suppose you wouldn't remember the Blue Drawing Room. This is one of the spaces you will use for entertaining guests."

I try to imagine hanging out with Lauren and Zoey in here, watching our favorite shows while noshing on junk food, but I can't picture anything so casual taking place in this grandiose room. Especially considering there isn't exactly a TV or a couch for vegging out. The room is instead filled with dainty chairs upholstered in blue silk and decorative mahogany tables, with an elaborate Persian carpet spread underneath. Artwork fills every inch of wall space, and Oscar points out the different pieces to me now.

"That's the third duke in the painting above the fireplace, while this portrait on the south wall depicts his wife and baby," he explains. "And of course, the two paintings on the north wall are of the first duchess."

I nod, catching my reflection in the pier glass mirror hanging above a gold Louis XVI clock. I look small and younger than my age, overwhelmed by my surroundings.

"Now, on to the Red Drawing Room," Oscar says, leading the way through dark wooden doors bordered by massive marble casing.

"We really needed a second one of these?" I joke.

Oscar grins. "I suppose having only one drawing room was considered rather paltry back in the day."

I follow him into a high-ceilinged room upholstered in crimson damask and decorated with bronze sculptures and potted palms. A massive crystal-and-gold chandelier sparkles from the ceiling, sending a glittery ray of light over the matching red chairs, ottomans, and—finally!—a couch, although it looks far more formal than comfy.

The Red Drawing Room is just as rich in art as the Blue, and Oscar proudly points out portraits of my ancestors painted by John Singer Sargent and Giovanni Boldini—names I know from my junior year art history class.

"And now to the dining room," Oscar announces. "Only holiday and state meals are eaten here; the rest of the time you'll eat in your private dining suite upstairs."

"What are 'state meals'?" I ask.

"That's when you host one of the royals, a titled member of the British peerage, or a member of Parliament," he says nonchalantly.

I can't help laughing.

"Um . . . you do realize I don't know any of those people, right?"

"Oh, that doesn't matter. The royal and titled families have been acquainted with the Rockfords for more than three hundred years, so the current titleholders will expect to socialize with you. And considering your position, you will also be expected to introduce yourself to members of Parliament."

The more he talks about my terrifyingly public future, the more I long to catch the next flight back to New York. I take a deep breath and push myself forward, into a room I remember.

The dining room soars forty or fifty feet high, up to a glorious ceiling painted with scenes of the first duke triumphant in battle. The walls are covered in hand-painted murals and frescoes, flanked by bronze columns. A long mahogany table stands in the middle of the room, and as I look closer—I catch a glimpse of a pale *hand* resting on the edge of the table. But Oscar and I are the only two people in the room.

The hairs on the back of my neck prickle as I take another step forward. And then a flash of blond hair whips against the back of one of the red-and-gold dining chairs.

"Your Grace? Are you all right?"

I'm only half conscious of Oscar speaking to me. I creep around the other side of the table to face the chair—and I let out a bloodcurdling scream.

A skeleton's face stares back at me, with empty sockets where her brown eyes should be. She wears her emerald dress from eight Christmases ago, and her colorless hand inches its way across the table toward me—

"Your Grace!" Oscar grabs hold of me. "What on earth is the matter? Why are you screaming?"

"I saw her," I gasp. "L-Lucia."

Oscar falls silent.

"You must have imagined it. Lucia is gone."

And as I blink and look back at the chair, I realize he is right. She is no longer there. Did she disappear? Or is the combination of guilt and grief causing me to lose my mind?

"Perhaps it's the jet lag. You must be exhausted," Oscar says hastily, steering me out of the dining room. "We can save the rest of the tour for later. I'll show you up to your room, and Maisie will bring your lunch on a tray whenever you'd like to eat."

"Thanks," I say faintly, glancing back one last time at the empty chair.

VII

By the time the dinner hour approaches, I'm too drained to make my way downstairs. I lie splayed out on the bed, staring numbly at the world's most beautiful bedroom. I've been given the Duchess Suite, a relic from the days when husbands and wives slept in separate rooms.

The bedroom's damask walls are painted robin's-egg blue, the same shade as Tiffany's famous little boxes, with matching curtains framing the French windows. The ceiling above my bed is gilded in a mosaic pattern, and impressionist paintings grace the walls. Delicate white-and-gold furniture softens the room's edges, and the freshly cut peonies in a vase on my bedside table lend the air a sweet smell. It's the kind of bedroom any girl would dream of, and I find myself wondering how many times Lucia peeked inside, eagerly waiting for it to be hers.

When Oscar showed me up to the room, I couldn't help

asking if it used to be Lucia's. He said no, Lucia stayed in a west wing bedroom and wouldn't have moved into the Duchess Suite until she took the title—something she would now never get to experience.

I roll over with a sigh; I used up all of my energy Skyping with the Marinos earlier. Zoey squealed over my room, but the sadness evident in Carole's and Keith's faces left me with the heavy weight of homesickness. I wonder if I'll always have this feeling of being torn in two.

I hear a rap at my door and reluctantly sit up.

"Come in."

Maisie stands in the doorway.

"I was wondering if Your Grace is coming down to dinner?"

"Please, call me Imogen," I tell her. "And I'm actually really sleepy. Do you mind saving my dinner for tomorrow?"

Maisie gives me a blank look. Do they not *do* leftovers at Rockford Manor? Based on her expression, the answer seems to be a definite no.

"Or . . . give it to someone else?" I suggest. "I'd just hate to see the food go to waste."

She nods. "As you wish, Your Grace. Would you like me to turn down the bed for you?"

"Oh, that's okay," I say awkwardly. "I'll see you tomorrow, Maisie. Thanks for everything."

Maisie gives the room a lingering glance before wishing me good night, and I wonder if she's thinking the same thing: *what a beautiful room, and what a shame that it was never Lucia's.* And suddenly, I find myself stammering a question.

"Maisie, wait. I . . . well, it's been so long since I saw my cousin and I've been wondering so much about her. I don't know what she was like when . . ."

"When she died?" Maisie finishes my sentence.

I flinch.

"Yes."

Maisie's unspoken reply, and my own conscience, taunts me. *Why didn't you ever call if you actually cared about her?* But if that's what Maisie is thinking, she's at least nice enough to hide her scorn.

"Lady Lucia was brilliant," Maisie says simply, straightening her back and adopting a more formal tone. "You might say that her mind worked a beat faster than everyone else's. She was outgoing, with a wild sense of humor, and she had the gift of walking into a room full of people and instantly holding them under a spell. Of course, she was beautiful, too." Maisie pauses, as if considering something. "Her best portrait is in the State Room. Have you seen it?"

I shake my head, my heart constricting as I imagine my cousin—a dazzling light, flickering unthinkably toward oblivion. I take a deep breath and refocus on Maisie's question. "No, I haven't been to that room yet."

"Would you like me to show it to you?"

I nod breathlessly. "Yes, thank you."

My sleepiness forgotten, I follow Maisie out of the bedroom and down the stairs. A strange surge of adrenaline courses through me as we near the State Room. Am I actually *excited* to see this portrait of my dead cousin? No . . . it definitely isn't excitement, but I am eager, anxious, to see her face after all these years, and I hope that her familiar features will replace the terrifying skull's face in my mind from earlier today.

Maisie opens the door and we step into the most lavish room I've seen thus far, decorated in the rich colors and furnishings of the Louis XVI era, with gilded ceilings and crown moldings, sparkling Baccarat chandeliers, and a sumptuous hand-woven tapestry covering an entire wall, illustrating yet another of the first duke's victorious battles. Above the white marble fireplace, the life-size portrait of a modern beauty hangs in a place of honor.

I walk forward in slow motion until I am inches away from her painted face. The twelve-year-old Lucia was remarkably pretty, so I shouldn't be surprised to find her even more gorgeous in her late teens. But it's Lucia's expression that catches me off guard and sends a shiver through me. Her face has no trace of the sparkle and curiosity I remember. Instead, she wears the gaze of someone who's seen and done . . . too much. I search her expression for a glimpse of my old friend, but of course, the cousin I knew was a child. I don't know this older, aloof Lucia. And suddenly, a cry escapes my throat. I cover my mouth, mortified at a near stranger witnessing my tears, but Maisie places a tender arm around my shoulder.

"It's all right," she says soothingly.

I turn to give her a grateful smile, but as our eyes meet, the moment breaks—as if we've both realized how incredibly awkward this is.

"Did anyone really watch over Lucia? After the fire, I mean?" I ask, wiping my eyes with the back of my hand. "I know our grandfather wasn't well, so I can't imagine he was able to be a full-time parent."

"The late duke was her official guardian, but my mother was the one who really looked after her," Maisie replies. A moment later she adds, "That was Lucia's favorite dress. She wore it on her last birthday."

"It's beautiful. She looks stunning."

And she does, with her halo of blond hair, sultry brown eyes, high cheekbones, and porcelain skin. A strapless, floor-length cream-colored dress hugs the curves of her tall, slender frame, and her bow-shaped mouth tilts upward in a secretive smile—like a twenty-first-century Mona Lisa.

"I wonder what she was thinking about when this was painted." I reach forward, gently touching the canvas.

"Her boyfriend, I'm sure," Maisie says softly. "He was her favorite topic."

I hold my breath, turning to face Maisie.

"What was he like?"

Her eyes cloud over, just as they did when I suggested we become friends.

"He was a good chap, and devoted to Lady Lucia. He lives in an estate less than ten miles away, so he came to the house all the time to see her. He loved her terribly."

I feel my heart pounding in my chest, so loudly that I'm sure Maisie can hear it.

"What's his name?" I ask, even though I already know. Only one person fits Maisie's description.

"Lord Sebastian Stanhope."

I nod quickly, turning back to Lucia's portrait before Maisie can look into my eyes and see the effect his name produced. It was so long ago that my silly, childish self loved him, but . . . did I ever really stop? Isn't he the reason I was so unsure about Mark Wyatt, and every other guy who has ever paid me any attention? I've never forgotten him—I couldn't if I tried. But none of that matters now. He belongs to Lucia. He always has.

I am now desperate to get away from this room, away from her smoldering portrait.

"Thanks for showing me, Maisie," I murmur, heading toward the door. "I think I'm ready to go now."

I wake shivering in the middle of the night. The temperature seems to have dropped a good ten degrees since I went to bed, and even my thick bedspread can't ward off the chill.

Suddenly I hear a voice. I sit bolt upright, my heart racing. It sounds like singing—faint and far-off, but the words are clear.

> *"I know dark clouds will gather round me,*
> *I know the road is rough and steep.*
> *But golden fields lie just beyond me,*
> *Where weary eyes no more will weep. . . ."*

I can't breathe. It's Lucia's song—the one she sang that day in the Shadow Garden. Am I dreaming? Where is it coming from?

> *"I'm just a poor, wayfaring stranger,*
> *Traveling through this world alone.*
> *There's no sickness, pain or danger,*
> *In that fair land to which I go. . . ."*

The voice continues, seemingly moving closer, growing louder. My hands shake as I switch on the bedside lamp and climb out of bed. Holding my breath, I creep to the door and fling it open, my fear nearly paralyzing me in the doorway.

The singing stops. Nobody is there. Yet I can hear the unmistakable sound of footsteps.

Get a grip, Imogen, I tell myself. *It's all in your head again.*

But as I crawl back into bed, I could swear a new scent has followed me into the room—an unfamiliar, jasmine-tinged perfume.

༒

The next day begins with breakfast in the Bow Room, the private dining chamber named for its bow-shaped windows. Despite my fitful sleep the night before, my spirits lift as soon as I enter the room, with its cheerful cream-colored wall panels and damask curtains pulled back to reveal views of the lush French garden below. Ornamented gold mirrors hang in between the windows, highlighting the matching gilt console tables and china underneath. In the center of the room, a round table covered in a crisp white tablecloth is set for breakfast. I slip into the inviting velvet-backed chair and lift the lid on my dish, sighing in contentment at the over-easy eggs, sizzling bacon, and breakfast potatoes. I'm about to dig in when a perky, twentysomething redhead waltzes into the room with Oscar.

"I'm sorry for the intrusion, Your Grace, but I wanted to introduce you to the social secretary we've just engaged for you. This is Ms. Gemma Montgomery." He holds up his hand as I start to stand. "Please, don't get up."

Gemma drops into a curtsy, then takes the seat across from mine at the table.

"Lovely to meet you, Your Grace. How do you do?"

"Fine, thanks." I glance from her to Oscar. "Sorry to be so clueless, but what exactly *is* a social secretary?"

"I'll be running your public schedule," Gemma explains. "As a duchess, you'll make numerous appearances per year, from lending your support at charity dinners and Oxford events to hosting festivities for the Wickersham locals at Rockford Manor, and potentially following in your grandmother's footsteps by serving as a lady-in-waiting at royal ceremonies. You'll certainly be at the next royal wedding, whenever Prince Harry decides to get himself hitched!" She giggles.

"Wow. I never imagined . . . all this. Do I have anything coming up soon?" I ask, crossing my fingers under the table that she'll tell me I have a good month to get over my nerves before braving the public.

"Yep!" she answers cheerily. My heart sinks. She must sense my anxiety, as she adds reassuringly, "It's a very low-pressure first appearance, which is why we chose it. You'll be attending the Oxford versus Cambridge Varsity polo match this Saturday."

"Okay . . . do I need to know anything about polo, or can I just cheer when everyone else does?"

Gemma laughs.

"Polo is pretty important on this side of the pond. I'll make sure you're schooled in the finer points before the match."

And school me is exactly what she does, though I can't say I absorb much of it. Once she launches into her spiel about polo sticks, chukkas, and "the line of the ball," I find my mind wandering hopelessly. I'm not exactly the sporty type. When she asks if I'm all clear on the game, I nod confidently rather than subject myself to another lecture. As long as I can follow along well enough to smile and feign frustration at the right times, I figure no one will be the wiser to my cluelessness.

"Now, the biggest event we'll need to prepare you for is the annual Rockford Fireworks Concert," Gemma says, once the discussion has finally shifted away from polo.

"Oh, God." My stomach lurches in panic as I recall the social event of the season, which my parents used to cohost along with Grandfather, Uncle Charles, and Aunt Philippa. I close my eyes briefly, remembering hundreds of guests dancing in the gardens while the orchestra played classic British tunes, the staff dashing to and fro as they served enough food to feed a small army, and the dazzling display of fireworks at the night's end. "Is the party actually still happening this year, even though . . . I'm the only one left to host?"

Gemma nods, her eyes sympathetic.

"I'm afraid it's tradition. The event has only been canceled once in the past fifty-some years, when Wickersham was in mourning right after the fire of 2007. The concert is such a high point for the locals, it would be a shame to cancel it."

I take a shaky breath, fiddling with the tablecloth.

"So . . . what do I have to do?"

"The good news is, Oscar tells me he and Mrs. Mulgrave have the planning and setup down to a science, since they've worked together on this very event for twenty years now. So you won't have to trouble yourself with too many details," Gemma reassures me. "Your main duties will be social—receiving the guests and leading the evening's entertainments."

I nod, pushing away my half-eaten breakfast. The idea of hosting the concert without the rest of my family seems to magnify how very alone I am.

Once Gemma leaves, my thoughts return to a darker place. I pull the map of the Rockford grounds from the pocket of my cardigan, studying the spot I marked with a circle: the Rockford Cemetery, where my parents, my grandfather, and Lucia are all buried. I have to visit their graves; I've already waited one day too long. But my eyes flick back and forth from the cemetery to the Shadow Garden and the Maze, which lie along the same route. Visiting their graves means coming face to face not just with death, but with the very setting where my parents and Lucia died. And I can't—not yet.

Saturday morning finds me fidgeting in front of the full-length mirror as Gemma arranges an odd little hat on my head at an even odder angle.

"This thing looks ridiculous on me," I complain. "I still don't see what was so wrong with my first outfit."

"No one wears a tank top and jeans to a polo match, least of all the Duchess of Wickersham," Gemma chastises me. "I'm surprised Maisie didn't already tell you."

"I didn't mention it to her," I say with a shrug. In truth, I've been avoiding Maisie since our moment in front of Lucia's portrait. There's something about the memory that gives me a prickle of discomfort. Maybe it's the way Maisie looked at me as she spoke, or the tone of her voice when she talked about Lucia. As if they had some kind of connection, or sixth sense, that I'll never understand. Or maybe I'm still reeling from the discovery that Lucia and Sebastian were together all this time—and embarrassed by my own reaction.

"Well," Gemma continues, "at least she had the good sense to fill your wardrobe with the right British designers."

She smoothes the shoulders of the pale lilac floral-print Jenny Packham dress we found among my closet's unexpected treasures. The dress hits just above the knee, and nude platform pumps elongate my not-quite-tanned legs. I have to admit, the dress and heels combo looks pretty good. But the hat is all wrong.

"I can't wear it." I gently swat Gemma's hand away from my head. "I've never been a hat person to begin with, and this one is maybe the most unflattering I've ever tried on."

"It's called a fascinator, not a hat," Gemma corrects me. "It's what British ladies of your station wear to polo matches."

"Well, I'm British American. So I'm never going to look or be exactly like them, anyway."

Gemma sighs in defeat. "All right, then. No fascinator, but you'd better give your hair a good brushing."

Once Gemma is satisfied with my look, we head down the grand staircase to meet Alfie. On the second landing, we come across Mrs. Mulgrave and Maisie heading upstairs.

"Your Grace, I was just about to check to see if you needed anything," Maisie says. She gives my outfit a once-over. "I wasn't aware you had any special plans today."

"Nothing too special, just a polo match," I say with a grin.

"What match?" Mrs. Mulgrave asks, her empty dark eyes flickering with sudden interest.

"The Jack Wills Varsity, of course," Gemma answers for me.

Maisie and her mother exchange a rapid glance full of meaning but impossible for me to understand.

"If I may—" Mrs. Mulgrave begins, but Gemma cuts her off.

"I'm sorry, I'm afraid we're quite late as it is and should have been in the car five minutes ago. Her Grace will return for tea at four o'clock."

"Bye!" I give them a little wave before following Gemma down the stairs, leaving the two of them standing there, watching me go.

❧

As we pull up to the Oxford University Polo Club, Gemma turns in her seat to scrutinize me.

"Your face is a little shiny; take these blotting papers. Now, make sure to walk with your shoulders back and neck extended, like Basil taught you. Aim for the posture of a ballerina. I'll get out first and lead the way."

"Good luck, Your Grace," Alfie says warmly, slowing to a stop in front of the polo field entrance.

I peer out the window, my palms growing sweaty at the sight of what appears to be hundreds of spectators in the stands.

"Thanks. I'll need it," I say under my breath.

Gemma steps out of the car, and after one nerve-racking second, I follow. But no one warned me about the perils of wearing heels on a grassy polo field, and my legs immediately buckle beneath me. Gemma grabs my arm while I'm mid-flail, hoisting me upright, and of course that's when a multitude of flashbulbs go off, as the reporters in the stands suddenly seem to figure out who I am.

"Great. My first public appearance is me almost falling on my butt," I say through gritted teeth.

I can tell this isn't exactly the grand entrance Gemma envisioned for me either, but she squeezes my arm comfortingly.

"It doesn't matter. Just hold your head high and smile."

My smile ends up looking more like a paranoid grimace, but at least we make it to the stands without another stumble. As we settle into an empty bench at the top of the stands, labeled ROCKFORD ROW, I feel eyes boring into me from all sides; I can't stop blinking as cameras continue flashing in my direction. I look down at my lap, fiddling with my jewelry, until an escalating cheer from the audience signals the start of the action.

The sight of the four young men on horseback galloping onto the field and wielding their polo sticks in unison sends a ripple of excitement through the crowd. The players wear the Oxford uniform of dark blue shirts, white jeans, knee-high black riding boots, and heavy black helmets. As they ride up to their cheering section, lifting their helmets in greeting, my eyes fall on the player riding slightly apart from the other three, somewhat removed from the jubilant scene. I lean forward in my seat, peering closer, my heart beginning to race. Something about the half smile playing on his lips, the tousled golden-brown hair, reminds me of . . . someone I used to know, someone who once meant the world to me.

Look up, I plead silently. *Let me see your face.*

I wonder if my thoughts did in fact reach him—because it is at this very moment that he chooses to glance up and meet my eyes. And under his gaze a rush of emotions comes flooding over me with abandon, until I am a little girl again, both giddy and tormented as I look upon him. I can no longer hear the stampede of hooves from the Cambridge team entering the fray, or the sound of Gemma's voice in my ear. I can no longer feel the sun's heat or the cool breeze; I can't see anything in my line of vision but him. Sebastian Stanhope—near me again after all these years.

I sit up straighter as Sebastian stares at me, his eyes narrowing in recognition. Does he see his childhood friend when he looks at me? Or is he just tipped off by the fact that I'm seated in the Rockford row? I smile tremulously, lifting my hand in a shy wave—but he quickly looks away. Does he *not* recognize me, then?

I feel Gemma nudge me in the ribs.

"You know Lord Sebastian Stanhope?"

"We were friends when I was little," I say quietly. "And . . . he was my cousin's boyfriend until she died."

"I knew he was dating Lady Lucia," Gemma says. "But I didn't realize you two were acquainted. I'm sorry, I suppose I should have warned you he'd be playing today? I hope I haven't made things uncomfortable."

"No, of course not. We always got along so well when we were younger. I don't see why it would be different now."

Before Gemma can respond, the umpire's whistle signals the beginning of the game. I watch, mesmerized, as Sebastian and his Thoroughbred fly back and forth across the vast field, sending the little white ball soaring into the Cambridge goalpost. Based on the boisterous cheers whenever Sebastian makes a play, it's clear that he is the star. And suddenly, without warning, my mind flashes back to a summer afternoon when I was six.

My father is teaching Sebastian the game of polo on the Rockford Manor riding grounds while Lucia and I look on with interest. Dad rides a full-size horse, but the three of us sit atop ponies.

"Can't you teach us now, Uncle Edmund?" Lucia whines. "Why are you spending so much time with Sebastian?"

Dad smiles at her but keeps his eyes on his young charge.

"You'll have your turn, don't worry. But your friend Sebastian shows great promise. I've never seen such aim and skill in someone so young."

Sebastian beams, and I watch him with awe. I always felt Sebastian was special—and now my dad has just confirmed it.

The memory has been buried for so long that it catches me off guard as it surfaces, nearly bringing tears to my eyes as I watch Sebastian's winning plays on the field all these years later. If only Dad had lived to see that his early lessons with Sebastian would be the start of a career.

At the end of the game's first period, known as "chukka," the spectators file out of the stands, congregating and mingling on the field.

"What are they doing?" I ask Gemma.

"It's called divot stamping," she explains. "It's a polo tradition. Between each chukka, spectators are invited to hang out on the field, and their footsteps help replace the mounds of earth that the horses' hooves tear up during the game."

"Interesting. Should we join them?"

"The Duchess of Wickersham doesn't participate in divot stamping," Gemma says with a chuckle.

"Oh. Too bad."

Just then, footsteps approach our bench. I look up to find a cute guy about my age, tall and lanky, with sandy brown hair and hazel eyes. An adorable dimple appears in his left cheek as he smiles at me.

"If it isn't Her Grace, Imogen Rockford! I'm awfully glad to see you again."

I stand up, my hand flying to my chest. *"Theo?"*

"That's right." He holds out his hand but I ignore it, instead throwing my arms around him in a hug.

"Oh, my God, I didn't recognize you! You're so different and grown-up and you don't—" I stop myself before I can finish my sentence. "You don't have a nose full of snot anymore" probably isn't the thing to say to a long-lost friend.

"You're looking pretty tidy yourself," Theo says, giving me a little wink. I don't quite know what he means by "tidy"—my outfit is well ironed?—but I sense a compliment there.

"Thanks. So . . . your brother's a polo star? I had no idea."

"He's the pride of Oxford. I won't be surprised if he turns pro after uni. But tell me about you. I—I didn't think I'd ever see you again," Theo admits.

I can tell just by looking at him that his thoughts have drifted to the dark place where mine so often reside—the garden where my parents died, the last summer we were all together. I look away.

"I know. I didn't think I'd ever come back. But . . . well, things happen." I shrug as if this is all no big deal, when in fact it's overwhelming in its enormity.

Theo moves closer, resting his hand on my shoulder. I notice Gemma burying her face in a magazine, trying to give us a semblance of privacy.

"How are you getting on at Rockford? There must be so much to learn, or relearn, about the place."

"Yeah, and about being a duchess. Everything is new and bizarre right now," I confide in him. "But I'm learning and hoping I'll fit into this role eventually."

"Well, I'm here if you need any advice or anything," Theo offers. "I know Rockford Manor pretty well, and growing up with Sebastian has taught me all the dos and don'ts for English heirs." He grins wryly.

I smile back, grateful at the thought of having a real friend here.

"Thanks, Theo. I'd love that."

The umpire's whistle blows, and I watch as the divot-stamping crowd hurries to their seats.

"I should get to my parents, but let's meet up on the field after the match, yeah? My family will want to see you too, I'm sure."

Sebastian. A shiver runs up my spine at the thought of being one short hour away from standing beside him and hearing his voice. Just as quickly, a flush of shame blazes across my cheeks. What is *wrong* with me, getting so excited about seeing my dead cousin's boyfriend? It doesn't matter that I loved him first—I can't look at him that way again.

"Imogen?" Theo is looking at me expectantly, and I shake off my thoughts, finally raising my eyes to meet his.

"Yeah, sounds great. I'll find you after."

VIII

Oxford takes the win, and Gemma and I jump to our feet with the rest of the fans, clapping and joining in on the cheer. As the spectators rush the field, thrusting pens at the players and requesting autographs, I hang back in my seat, my pulse racing with a mix of nerves and adrenaline.

"Are you ready, Your Grace?" Gemma asks, typing a text into her phone. "Alfie just arrived."

"Not yet. I want to say hi to the Stanhopes. I'm just waiting for the crowds to thin out."

Gemma raises an eyebrow at me. "All right."

After a surreal half hour spent watching Sebastian sign autographs, and wondering if I'm better off just ducking out unseen, the owner of the polo club comes onto the field and herds the fans toward the exit, until the players and their families are the only people left.

"Let's go," I tell Gemma.

We climb down from our seats and I hold on to her arm to steady myself as we hit the field. A flock of butterflies seems to have taken up residence in my stomach, but as nervous as I am, I realize I've been waiting years for this moment. I cannot wait to see him again.

"There she is!" I hear Theo call out. "Right here, Imogen."

Theo and his parents surround Sebastian, who is in mid-conversation with a teammate, his back toward me. As Theo says my name, Sebastian's body seems to tense.

Lord and Lady Stanhope turn around first, an unsettling expression in their eyes as they face me. They look almost . . . afraid. But I too feel a chill as I look up at them, remembering the sound of Lady Stanhope's wails and the feel of Lord Stanhope's arms pulling me back from the fire. Seeing them brings that night back with a startling freshness.

I lower my head to the Stanhopes in a quasi bow, just as I used to do when I was little. But then the two of them drop into a deeper bow and curtsy, reminding me that, unbelievable as it might seem, I am technically their superior now. I am the duchess.

"Welcome back, Your Grace," Lord Stanhope says formally.

"It's lovely to see you again," Lady Stanhope adds with a smile.

"It's nice to see you too," I return. "Congratulations on the game."

I glance past them to Sebastian, who still appears immersed in his conversation.

"Hey, Seb." Theo nudges his brother. "Did you see who's here?"

After a moment's pause, Sebastian finally turns away from

his teammate and looks toward me. My breath catches in my throat as our eyes meet, and he lowers his head in the most graceful bow I've ever seen.

He is even more than I imagined him growing up to be. His body is taller, stronger, his eyes are a deeper and richer green. He carries himself with a sense of confidence and maturity that leaves me feeling ten years his junior, instead of just two.

"Hello, Your Grace," he says quietly.

His voice has changed since I last saw him. It is low and husky now, with a musical quality that brings goose bumps to my bare arms.

"Hi," I nearly whisper.

For a moment all I can do is gaze up at him. There is so much to say after all that has happened, after all the years that have passed, but no words feel adequate. So I go with the easiest topic.

"That was a really great game. Congratulations."

He gives me a fleeting half smile.

"Thanks."

I wait for him to say more, to ask me something, but instead he looks away. Why is he acting so distant? Doesn't he remember the summers we spent together, all the laughter and secrets we shared? But it's my fault, of course. I'm the one who disappeared; I should have expected he'd forget me— especially when I was never his favorite to begin with. Lucia always filled that role. And now I represent the girl trying to take her place.

I look away and try to focus on Theo, the one person in the family who seems legitimately happy to see me. He smiles broadly as our eyes meet.

"We ought to have a welcome dinner for Imogen," Theo says, turning to his parents. "A classic English supper, with her neighbors and ours all invited."

Lord and Lady Stanhope exchange a funny look, while Sebastian remains poker-faced. I feel a wave of embarrassment at the thought of them forced into throwing me a dinner party.

"That's so sweet, Theo, but totally unnecessary," I say hurriedly. "It's too much. But I'd love to have you all over to Rockford sometime."

"Nonsense. That's a lovely idea, Theo, and we'd be delighted to give a dinner in Your Grace's honor," Lady Stanhope says. "Will next weekend do?"

"Oh—sure, that would be great. Thank you so much," I say as I give Sebastian another glance.

"Wonderful. I'm afraid we have to get going—the team is having a do at the Savoy—but we look forward to seeing you next weekend. Theo will call with the details." Lady Stanhope gives me another slight curtsy, and then she and Lord Stanhope air-kiss each of my cheeks. Theo gives me a friendly hug, while Sebastian simply presses my hand for a brief second—not quite a handshake, but no more affectionate either. Still, the touch of his hand sends a tingle through my fingertips and a flutter in my chest.

"Cheers, Imogen," Theo calls as the four of them turn to leave.

"Bye," I call back.

I slowly make my way to the exit, where Gemma is waiting, my mind racing with questions. Why were Sebastian and his parents so aloof, yet Theo so friendly? Why are they going ahead with this dinner party that they so clearly don't want to host? And most of all, *why* does Sebastian still have this hold on me—as if no time at all has passed?

❧

I return alone to Rockford Manor, conscious of how cold and quiet the house seems after the warmth and chaos of the polo match. My legs feel heavy as I climb the stairs, and when I open the door to my room, I have the eerie sensation that another presence is with me.

"Hello?" I call out tentatively, flicking on the light switch. "Maisie, is that you?"

No one answers or stands before me—but I hear the unmistakable sound of breathing; a repeated sigh that comes from no particular direction and seems embedded in the room, echoing across the walls.

"Who is it?" I whisper. "Who's doing that?"

Suddenly a fierce gust of wind hurtles against the window above my desk. I watch in openmouthed astonishment as the window rattles violently, the latch coming undone from the strength of the breeze, until the window loses the fight, swinging open *all by itself.*

I open my mouth to scream but only manage a faint cry. As I scramble backward toward the door, I could swear I see a face in the windowpane, the hauntingly beautiful face from the State Room painting. *Lucia.*

"Your Grace? What's the matter?"

I gasp as Mrs. Mulgrave comes toward me from the other end of the hallway. Her sunken eyes look red, her face more pallid than I've ever seen it.

"I—I thought I saw something in the glass, and—and then the window opened all by itself," I babble.

A strange flicker of understanding . . . or curiosity lights up in Mrs. Mulgrave's eyes. She moves past me into the bedroom, her hands coming to rest on the windowsill. I follow her, watching in confusion as her face registers disappointment.

"It's only a faulty latch," she says curtly. "I'll send Carter to repair it at once."

"But—but—"

I don't know how to explain that it isn't just the latch, that there's something in here, breathing, watching me. But Mrs. Mulgrave is already on her way out the door, and besides, she's hardly the person to soothe my frayed nerves.

I sit down on the bed, taking in a shaky breath. Maybe this is just my hyperactive imagination, stirring up drama over an innocent window latch. After all, I *was* keyed up from seeing Sebastian. Or . . . I could be sharing my bedroom with a ghost. This is the second unnaturally fierce breeze I've encountered since arriving at Rockford Manor, and I can't help wondering if it means something.

"Did you meet Sebastian Stanhope after the match?"

For a moment, I'm sure I misheard. Mrs. Mulgrave already left the room, or so I thought, and she's never spoken to me about anything beyond the most basic of household topics.

I glance up and find her standing still as a statue in the doorway, watching me unblinkingly. I look away.

"Yes," I say slowly. "I saw him and his family, but only for a little bit."

Her shoulders stiffen.

"How did he seem?"

"Um, good, I guess. His team won," I answer, completely bewildered by this turn of conversation.

Mrs. Mulgrave's eyes seem to implore me for more, but her voice remains soft and controlled.

"He's distracting himself, the poor boy. He was head over heels for Lucia, you know." Her gaze flicks from me to the open window.

I shrink back, unsure what to say. The room feels oppressively cold.

"Will that be all, Your Grace?" she asks, returning to a businesslike tone.

"Y-yes. Thanks."

I watch Mrs. Mulgrave stride out of the room, with the disturbing feeling that she was trying to convey a message in her carefully chosen words. But what the message was, I don't know.

❦

Carter assures me that he's fixed the window and it can't possibly open by itself again, but I still enlist Lucia's dog, Teddy, to sleep at the foot of my bed. Even though his ten pounds of fur won't be much help fending off malevolent forces, I somehow feel safer with the cuddly little creature keeping me company overnight.

When I wake the next morning to sunlight streaming through the curtains and the sound of Teddy's soft snores, my fears of the previous night seem like a faraway dream. I feel slightly awkward when I see Mrs. Mulgrave at breakfast, but she is perfectly polite, leading me to wonder if I could have read too much into her comments.

After breakfast, I find Max waiting for me in the Marble Hall.

"I thought we might go over the state of the grounds," he explains. "Is now a good time?"

"Sure."

But even as I agree, I have the sinking feeling that I'll be forced to revisit the garden I never again wish to see. I'll just have to be honest and tell Max that's the one place I can't return to.

The rear doors of the Marble Hall open onto the sprawling Fountain Terrace, decorated with statues and topiary. A promenade curves southward from it, lined with yew trees that resemble giant gumdrops, and banks of daffodils and bluebells. Multiple gated gardens snake outward from the grassy lane.

"This is the first of the gardens that we allow visitors to tour," Max says, leading me through a gate with a plaque above it reading THE FRENCH GARDEN. "We just planted new pink roses for the summer season."

"They're beautiful."

I can feel Max watching me intently as I wander the perimeter, taking in the blooming flowers and lush orange trees.

"Do you approve?" he asks.

I can't help giving him a funny look. *He's* the Rockford's landscape gardener—what does he care what I think? But then, as I constantly have to remind myself, he and everyone else on the staff now answer to me. If I wanted him to plant cacti instead of roses in this garden, Max would likely have to bite his tongue and do it. How strange, to be in a position of power when I'm such a novice, so out of my element.

"Everything's perfect," I say with a smile.

"I thought you might say that." Max looks at me questioningly. "What's strange is . . . nothing looked perfect until you arrived."

His words don't make any sense, but I still feel a shiver of foreboding.

"What do you mean?"

Max shakes his head, perplexed.

"This land was once so easy for me to cultivate. But after the fire, the earth seemed to—to go into a depression. Flowers struggled to bloom, the grass yellowed, and even when the grounds looked presentable from afar, you could see when you looked closely how they were a shadow of their former self. The Rockford Manor gardens used to be our number one tourist draw, but it hasn't been that way for years. Now most visitors bypass the grounds in favor of the house." He fixes his gaze on me. "But since the day you arrived, it's been as if . . . as if the land was waking up. I haven't seen such beauty in seven years."

My throat is suddenly dry. I inch away from Max.

"It's obviously a coincidence." I force a lighthearted chuckle. "What could *I* have possibly done?"

"Sometimes I wonder," he says softly, "if you might be like . . ." He stops himself before finishing his sentence.

"Like who?"

"Never mind." Max shakes his head and his face relaxes into a smile. "Forgive me, I'm being a foolish old man. I'm just so terribly glad that the marvelous land I love is . . . back. Now, let me show you the Rose Garden."

I stare at Max's retreating figure as he moves forward. What was he about to say? He clearly suspects something about me, but . . . what? I'd give anything to disappear, to get away from Max and the unnamed fear he is filling my mind with. But I have no other choice than to follow him into the next plot of land. As I gaze at the bowers of red, white, and pink climbing roses and at the little swing beneath the vine-covered pergola, I am distracted by a memory.

"This was my mother's favorite garden. She used to sit here and read on the bench while I played in the grass. We always ended the day with her pushing me on that swing. . . . I loved it here."

I am so immersed in thought, I don't realize I've been speaking aloud until I hear Max reply.

"That's right. You were so little, I wasn't sure you would remember."

"I remember almost everything," I answer. "I just choose some memories over others."

A hollow ache settles in the pit of my stomach as I look around. This garden is radiant, just like my mother once was. But without her, it seems forlorn, like a great home emptied of its inhabitants.

While Max inspects one of the plants, I make my way to the bed of roses at the center of the garden, encircled by the long brick bench Mum used to occupy. I sit down, my hands absently skimming the flowers as I let myself remember her. And then I freeze, my body seizing with terror, as the same vibrating energy from long ago fills my fingertips.

I cry out, springing off the bench in alarm. But I can't stop myself from glancing back at the flower bed, and what I see renders me speechless.

Little cracks are forming in the dirt where my hands just were, *moving* before my eyes and creating space in the flower bed. From the cracks a new rose suddenly bursts forth, more vivid and more frighteningly beautiful than all the others.

I jump in front of the rose, shielding it with my back. Whatever it takes, I can't let Max see it. But he already heard my yell.

"What's wrong, Your Grace?" He hurries toward me, and I hold up a hand to reassure him.

"I'm fine, I just—scraped my knee on the bench," I fib.

"Are you sure? Let me check the brick—"

"No, no!" I interrupt, my voice a little too loud. "I'm actually ready to get out of here, if you don't mind. I'm . . . eager to see the other gardens."

Max looks perturbed, but he doesn't question me further. "Of course."

I wait for him to move toward the exit first, keeping my back in front of the unearthly rose until he is out of sight. That freak flower is all I can think about as Max shows me around the rest of the grounds. I'm oblivious to the waterfalls surrounding the Rockford lake and bridge; I barely notice the animals grazing on the home farm. I just nod and smile at Max on autopilot, while the entire time I'm wondering *What the hell is wrong with me? Who am I?* What *am I?* My touch didn't create anything or cause anything remotely out of the ordinary while I was in New York these past years . . . so why now?

As we head back in the direction of the house, we come

upon the plot of land I've been dreading. I know, as soon as my feet hit the gravel leading toward it, that we are on our way to the Shadow Garden. I stop in my tracks.

"Max, I—I can't," I blurt out. "I don't want to see it."

He looks at me in confusion.

"You don't want to see what?" And then his brow clears as he realizes what I meant. "Oh, no, I certainly wasn't planning to take you there. That garden, and the Maze, haven't been in use since . . . then."

"What?" I stare at him. I should be relieved, but I feel oddly unsettled. "Why not?"

He hesitates before admitting, "It's been the biggest puzzle of my career. The Shadow Garden of course burned in the fire, but then, when I tried to restore it, I simply . . . couldn't." He looks at me with wide eyes. "The rest of the grounds fell into decline after the fire too, but I was still able to produce some semblance of a presentable landscape. In the Shadow Garden, however, nothing I planted grew. The earth refused the water and the seeds. After two years trying, I finally gave up, told His Grace that it was no use. He didn't push further—I don't imagine he wanted any more to do with it after that awful tragedy." He wipes a bead of sweat from his forehead and gazes at me. "Although perhaps . . . perhaps now the Shadow Garden might be different—just like the rest of the grounds."

"I don't know what you mean," I say, although I have a distinct idea. "And I have no desire to ever reopen the Shadow Garden."

My stomach lurches as a crazy thought enters my mind. Is it possible for gardens to be . . . *possessed?* Could that be the explanation for my hands causing flowers to suddenly bloom on the Rockford grounds? Is there something *enchanted* about this land? Could the gardens be responding to me, bringing my unwanted abilities out from hiding?

"What about the Maze?" I ask, my voice wobbling.

Max shakes his head in bewilderment.

"I can no longer get through it."

"What?"

"I mean, I can enter the Maze, but I used to know the entire outline of it, all of its twists and turns and how to get through to the end. But something . . . changed. And now whenever I go in, I get lost." He laughs nervously. "You must be thinking I'm too old for this job, that I've gone senile."

"No." I struggle for breath. "That's not what I'm thinking at all."

"If I can't figure out the Maze, then it's not safe to allow children and tourists in. And after the dear late Lucia died right outside of it . . . well, we had to close it up," he says sadly.

"There's something hidden in the Maze."

My father's words automatically return to me, filling me with fear. If I ever want to discover what he meant that day, how can I—if the Maze is impenetrable?

"Max, I'm not ready to go back to the house just yet," I say abruptly. "I want to see my parents. I mean . . . I want to visit their graves."

In all the madness of the past hour, I've somehow gained the courage to face my pain. Now I'm filled with longing—to be near them, to ask them what's happening to me, and to know I'm as close to them as I'll ever be.

IX

I slowly climb the grassy hill toward the small, picturesque Rockford Chapel and Cemetery, holding a bouquet of geraniums in my trembling hands. I asked Max to cut them for me, to avoid touching the earth myself and creating another phantom flower. He left after that, handing me a map to find my way back, understanding that I needed to be alone.

My feet move forward of their own will, my eyes hurriedly scanning the names on the gravestones, bypassing ancestors—until I see them.

Two marble headstones lie side by side, rose stone for my mother and gray for my father. They link in a carved heart.

I sink to my knees in front of them, the geraniums I brought falling to the ground as I wrap one arm around my father's grave, the other around my mum's. I no longer care if my touch sparks or conjures anything—this is the closest I will ever come to hugging my parents again.

The hollow pit in my stomach deepens, and I can feel the force of my pain pulling me down, drowning me in the darkness I've been running away from. But I can't fight it anymore.

"I miss you," I whisper through my tears. "And I'm sorry . . . so sorry."

I look up, murmuring aloud the words carved on their headstones and breaking down again as I read FATHER & MOTHER TO THEIR BELOVED IMOGEN. I rest my head on my father's grave, and as a breeze ripples through my hair, I imagine that it is Mum, stroking my hair the way she used to when I was a little girl. I raise my face, my hands still pressed against the marble, and watch in amazement as a forceful gust of wind carries the fallen geraniums, lifting them into the air and gracefully placing them at the feet of my parents' graves. It seems my unwanted gift is resurfacing at full strength—but in this one instance, it doesn't scare me. I find it beautiful.

Hearing the sound of shoes crunching on leaves, I wipe my eyes and hurriedly stand up. Before leaving, I lean over to kiss both headstones.

"I love you. I'll be back."

Turning around, I come face to face with the person I least expected to see. Sebastian Stanhope stands under the cemetery's archway entrance, his green eyes watching me with surprise. I walk toward him as if in a trance, wondering how much more surreal this day can possibly get.

"Hi. What are you doing here?" I blurt out. As soon as the words leave my mouth, I realize. "Lucia. God, I'm—I'm sorry."

"That's okay," he says. As he looks at my tearstained face, his eyes soften. "Are you all right?"

I manage a smile.

"Yeah. Thanks. . . . What about you?"

Sebastian merely shrugs. Our eyes meet, and for a split second, we are connected in our grief.

"Where—where is her grave?" I ask timidly.

"I'll show you."

I follow Sebastian to the other side of the cemetery, across from where my parents lie. He stops in front of a rose-colored marble gravestone, just like Mum's. Only this one reads:

LADY LUCIA ROCKFORD
THE MOST HONORABLE MARCHIONESS OF WICKERSHAM
FEBRUARY 11, 1995–OCTOBER 25, 2013

"Isn't it strange," Sebastian says as I stand motionless in front of her grave, "how this is the last place the three of us were together?"

I cover my face with my hands. The memory is unbearable, and I hear myself gasping for breath in an effort to hold back my sobs. Suddenly Sebastian's arms are around me, my face pressed against his shoulder. The odd combination of grief and comfort at being in his arms has me dizzy, my knees trembling.

"I'm sorry, Ginny," he says, his voice hoarse. "I shouldn't have said that."

I glance up, looking into his eyes while still in his arms.

"I'm still Ginny to you?"

He nods slowly.

"I'm the one who should be sorry." My words tumble forth. "The last time I saw you both, I was . . . scared and stubborn and all messed up. You don't know how badly I wish I could go back in time and do things differently—stay in touch with you both, be there for Lucia . . ."

Sebastian gently releases me, his face tensing. I wonder if my apology came out wrong, if I made a misstep, but as I watch his eyes drift back to her grave, I realize he simply wants to be alone with her.

"I—I should get back to the house. Do you want to come in after, for tea or something?" I ask, my cheeks flushing as I make the offer.

"Thanks, but I can't stay long." He gives me a fleeting smile. "I'll see you soon, though, for dinner at our house this weekend."

I nod.

"See you then."

"Take care, Ginny," he says quietly, before moving closer to Lucia's grave.

Ginny. Hearing Sebastian call me that gives me a sprig of hope, makes me feel that somehow everything will work out. But as I descend the hill back to the gardens, I remind myself that I shouldn't—*can't*—indulge in any of these romantic feelings. Not when Sebastian is standing in the cemetery, mourning my cousin.

When Lauren's face pops up on Skype that night, I couldn't be more relieved. It's been less than two weeks since I arrived in England, but I feel changed already, and I need my best friend to remind me what my world used to be like.

I feel a pang of homesickness as she fills me in on the start of her summer in New York, from the downtown party scene to weekends in the Hamptons. I used to be a regular fixture in her stories, and now it's strange, listening to them as an outsider.

"I really wish you were here," I say wistfully, after she finishes cracking me up with her tale of a bikini-shopping trip gone wrong.

"So I can embarrass myself in person?" she jokes.

"I just miss you," I admit. "I know I won't ever find another friend like you, especially not in England."

Lauren gives me a perceptive look.

"You okay, girl? You seem more . . . down than I'd expect for a newly minted duchess."

"I'm not down, it's just been a long day."

I ache to tell her about visiting my parents' graves, seeing Sebastian, and discovering my reawakened gift—if you can even call something so undesired a "gift"—but I can't find the words. The experiences feel too personal, too close to discuss, especially over Skype.

"When do you start your summer class at Oxford? Maybe you'll make some friends—or meet a hot British guy," Lauren suggests with an impish grin.

"Not for another few weeks," I reply. But my mind is miles away from summer school, and I find myself blurting out the question I've been asking myself all day—despite how crazy I know it will sound.

"Lauren, do you think it's at *all* in the realm of normal for someone to have a seriously green thumb? Like, able to grow flowers at the touch of a hand?"

She stares at me.

"Uh, what? Where did *that* come from?"

And just like that, I chicken out of telling her everything.

"Oh, it's nothing." I force a breezy tone. "I've just discovered some serious . . . gardening skills here."

"Growing flowers at the touch of a *hand* isn't a skill. That sounds supernatural," Lauren says, giving me a strange look. "You're not, like, on drugs, are you?"

"No." I roll my eyes. "I was exaggerating, it's not at the touch of my hand. I just have this ability to grow things . . . kind of fast."

"O-*kay*." She laughs. "Well, then I expect to see some bad-ass gardens when I come to visit."

I quickly change the subject, asking for the latest on her brother, Anthony, before I can let slip anything else that makes me sound like I'm taking hallucinogens. But her words keep echoing in my ears. *"That sounds supernatural."*

As soon as we hang up, I Google "Growing flowers from your hands." If I expected to find an online support group for people with my same freakish talent, I'm sorely disappointed. Most of the links that turn up are New Age websites, where growing flowers from your hands is apparently a metaphor for self-improvement. I find a dozen different dream forums with people asking what it means to *dream* of growing flowers with the touch of their hands—but no one has actually done it. In every link I click, the idea is treated like a fantasy.

So how could it happen to me?

The night of the Stanhopes' dinner, I find myself obsessing over what to wear. I need to make the right impression without looking like I'm trying *too* hard. I finally settle on a formfitting, knee-length pale blue dress by the British designer Reiss, with a pair of nude pumps by another British designer, L. K. Bennett. I'm still in awe over the wardrobe Maisie picked out for me, and I hope I can do justice to these beautiful clothes.

A knock sounds at the door, followed by Maisie stepping into my room.

"I just wanted to see if you need any help getting ready for tonight," she offers, giving my dress an approving glance. "That looks perfect on you."

"Thanks, Maisie." I smile at her, feeling an involuntary flutter of excitement at the thought of Sebastian seeing me in it. "You picked out the most gorgeous things for me. I can't thank you enough."

Her cheeks flush. "I rather enjoyed it."

"Well, I'm definitely grateful, especially considering I don't have your fashion sense. Where did you *get* it from?"

I cringe as soon as the words are out of my mouth; I didn't mean to sound so condescending. But I do wonder—how does a girl who's been raised as a maid know so much about high-end designers?

"Lady Lucia taught me everything I know," she says, meeting my eyes.

"Oh. Of course." I swallow hard. "Do you—do you miss her?"

Maisie doesn't answer, turning the question on me instead. "Do you, Your Grace?"

"Well, I . . . I unfortunately lost touch with her, so it's been years since I really knew her," I admit. "But yes, I miss Lucia and the friendship we once had. I spent every summer with her until I was ten, and I guess . . . she was my best friend in those days."

"She missed you too," Maisie says, her voice level.

"Really?" My breath catches in my throat. "She told you that?"

Maisie nods. I want to know more, but before I can ask another question, she picks up the hairbrush on my vanity table and motions for me to sit down.

"Let me do your hair. I used to always fix Lady Lucia's before she went out, and that was when she would tell me everything—all about where she was going and what she'd done the night before," Maisie confides.

"She told you everything?" I echo.

Maisie's eyes meet mine in the mirror. "There wasn't anything she could hide from me."

I fall into silence. Maybe I'm reading too much into it, but something in Maisie's tone gives me pause. What kind of secrets might Lucia have entrusted her with?

"Would you like me to wrap your gift for the Stanhopes?" she asks abruptly as she runs the brush through my hair.

"What gift?"

Seeing my confusion, she explains, "It's a tradition in the country. At a dinner party, the guest of honor always brings a gift for their hosts."

I look at her in alarm. "Oh, no. I only planned on bringing a bottle of wine. Is that not enough?"

"I'm afraid not, Your Grace," she says solemnly.

"I don't have time to go shopping," I fret. "What should I do?"

Maisie hesitates. When she speaks again, her voice is tentative.

"My mother and Oscar keep an assortment of hostess gifts on hand. In fact, there's a beautiful statuette that Mother has been saving for such an occasion. It would look lovely on a desk or mantelpiece. Should I wrap it for you?"

I breathe a sigh of relief.

"Maisie, you're a lifesaver. That sounds perfect."

An hour later I sit in the backseat of the Aston Martin as Alfie drives through the nearby town of Great Milton, toward Stanhope Abbey. I've been there before, on long-ago playdates with Sebastian and Theo, but my recollections of their house are hazier than those of my early years at Rockford Manor.

I draw in my breath as we pull through the gates and continue up the winding road to an Elizabethan mansion, set against a backdrop of rising hills and lush green parkland.

"Here we are," Alfie says. "Stanhope Abbey."

"Is it strange to be back?" I ask timidly. "You must have driven Lucia here all the time."

"Not so often. After she got a license and her own car, she was thrilled to be rid of me." Alfie smiles sadly.

"I'm sure that's not true," I tell him.

Alfie's expression changes.

"The car made Lucia so independent, I think she forgot I was there for her. And I often wonder . . . Well, if she had only entrusted me to do my job that night and take care of her, if she wanted to go out so badly, I would have driven her anywhere she wished to go. She didn't have to walk out into that storm, when the pouring rain and winds made it impossible to see where you—" He breaks off midsentence. "My apologies, Your Grace. I have forgotten myself. You shouldn't be burdened with an old man's regrets."

"No. You can't blame yourself," I say gently, realizing I'm repeating the words that have been said to me so many times about my parents' deaths. "There's no way you could have known she was planning to go out in that storm. And if she was determined to walk to the Maze alone . . . well, I don't see how you or anyone could have stopped her."

"Thank you, Your Grace." He pauses. "If you don't mind my saying so, you're . . . very different from Lady Lucia."

"From what I've seen, I don't think anyone could compare to her," I agree. "She was unbelievably gorgeous, and if her personality was anything like what I remember, then she was a real force to be reckoned with."

"Please don't misunderstand me," Alfie says hurriedly. "I wasn't making an unfavorable comparison. On the contrary, actually. I loved Lady Lucia, we all did, but—well, she never would have cared to speak to me the way you just did."

I don't doubt him. Even as a little girl Lucia had an imperious streak, treating the staff as her underlings. But it throws me to hear any criticism of my cousin, who up until now loomed in my mind as the Perfect Predecessor, with shoes too large to fill.

"I'm sure she did care. But I know what you're getting at, and . . . thank you."

"Have a wonderful night, Your Grace," he says as the Stanhopes' footman opens the car door.

"Welcome to Stanhope Abbey, Duchess," he greets me, dropping into a bow. "The family is expecting you in the drawing room."

He leads me up the front steps and into the house, which is smaller than Rockford Manor but just as lavish, complete with frescoed walls, painted ceilings, and halls lined with awe-inspiring sculptures and family portraits. I'm beginning to realize that for English aristocrats, the home is the place to show off all their precious assets, with no corner left unadorned.

"The Duchess of Wickersham," the footman announces as we approach the drawing room door.

I watch from the doorway as the Stanhopes and four other guests rise to their feet. My eyes instantly meet Sebastian's. He is a vision in his dark suit, and I feel a familiar swooping in my stomach as we look at each other. His gaze is friendly, like the Sebastian I remember from before, and I wonder if we've moved past the awkwardness of my return—if we've reached some unspoken understanding since meeting in the cemetery.

Lord and Lady Stanhope step forward to greet me, followed by their guests: Viscount Warren and his daughter, Lady Cecily Warren, who looks around my age, and a Mr. and Mrs. Blythe from London. Once the formalities are out of the way, Theo comes up to me with a big grin.

"Imogen, you look cracking," he says, draping an arm over my shoulder.

"Cracking?" I repeat dubiously.

"He means you look good," Sebastian says with a brief smile. His words set off a flock of butterflies in my stomach, but then I remind myself that he's only relaying what his brother said. If anyone here is flirting with me—and that's still very much an *if*—it's Theo, not Sebastian.

"Thanks, Theo. You look cracking yourself," I say, my nerves beginning to settle. And as I study him, I realize Theo *is* pretty darn cute. Anyone in this room would be overshadowed by Sebastian's movie-star looks, but Theo is adorable, the kind of guy I can picture Zoey going nuts over.

I suddenly remember the gift in my hands, wrapped to perfection by Maisie.

"I have something for you all. Let me give this to your mom."

The three of us approach Lady Stanhope, who is chatting with the viscount and his daughter.

"Lady Imogen, you must get to know Cecily here," she says as we join them. "I think you two will be fast friends. Cecily is starting Oxford this fall."

"Oh, cool. I'm about to start a summer class there, at Christ Church college," I tell Cecily.

"So am I," Sebastian says, eyeing me in surprise. "Which class are you taking?"

"Classical Literature and Mythology. What about you?" I hold my breath as I wait for his reply.

He smiles, but his voice has a slight edge to it when he speaks.

"The same. I needed an extra few credits for my degree. What made you choose the subject?"

For a moment I'm speechless, thrilled at the idea of us in the same class, but I regain my composure just in time.

"English is my best subject, and my guardian back in New

York insisted that I give Oxford a try this summer. If I can manage to do well, then I'll apply for next fall's term."

"Well, this is too lovely!" Lady Stanhope says, smiling brightly. "All three of you at Oxford! Theo, you're next."

"We'll see." Theo laughs.

I hand Lady Stanhope the gift.

"This is for you."

"Oh, you *shouldn't* have," she demurs as she begins unwrapping the package. I watch in anticipation, hoping she and the Stanhopes will love it as much as Maisie seemed to think they would.

Lady Stanhope holds up the unwrapped gift, an antique porcelain statuette of a striking woman. Theo's eyes dart nervously toward Sebastian, who stares at the statuette in shock.

"Um, it's a decorative piece," I explain awkwardly, bewildered by the reactions to my gift. "It's for a desktop, or a mantelpiece. . . ." My voice trails off, as I notice how pale Sebastian's face has become, making his green eyes look darker than I've ever seen them. He advances toward me, his hands clenching and unclenching repeatedly.

"Where did you get that?" he snaps, his voice so sharp it nearly makes me jump. "Why would you bring it here?"

"What?" I stare at him uncomprehendingly. "What are you talking about? It's just a present!"

"A present?" He lets out a short, mirthless laugh. "I should have known."

Theo springs in between me and Sebastian. "Let it go, Seb," he says, looking at his brother worriedly.

Theo takes the statuette from his mother, but Sebastian reaches for it at the same time, knocking it out of Theo's grasp.

The figurine shatters on the hardwood floor, sending porcelain shards flying across the room. For one terrible second, we all freeze in place. Then Lady Stanhope yelps in alarm, Theo rushes to my side—and Sebastian slips out of the room without a word.

X

"What just happened?" I cry out. "What's *wrong* with him?"

"I'm sorry," Lady Stanhope murmurs, first to me and then to each of her guests. "I'm so sorry—I don't know what's gotten into him."

"I'll be back," Lord Stanhope says grimly, following Sebastian out the door.

Lady Stanhope nervously smoothes her hair and takes a few shallow breaths.

"Why don't we move into the library and let the maid clean this up?"

She leads the way into the corridor, but I hang back, unable to tear my eyes away from the shattered figurine. I don't know what disturbs me more—the fact that my gift provoked such a reaction, or that my sweet childhood friend has turned into someone capable of flying into a temper.

I feel a hand on my shoulder, and I turn around, looking into Theo's kind eyes.

"I . . . I don't understand," I say falteringly.

"Of course you don't. My brother is a prat for assuming the worst of you," Theo says, shaking his head. "You didn't know what you brought, did you?"

"What do you mean? It was just a silly gift!" I feel tears pricking at my eyes, and I force them back.

Theo takes a deep breath.

"It was a statuette of Lady Beatrice, the fifth Duchess of Wickersham, from the early 1800s."

The name is familiar.

"I think I've heard of her. My etiquette coach mentioned a Lady Beatrice as the person who supposedly tamed the Rockford land. But why would Sebastian be so mad about her statue?"

"Because he bought it for Lucia two years ago. I'm not sure where you got it, but it was hers. I remember Sebastian saying it was an original."

I can't believe it. Nausea washes over me as I realize what Maisie has done.

"I—I had no idea," I manage to choke out, staring at Theo in horror. "Maisie said it was a brand-new gift that Mrs. Mulgrave and Oscar had saved for a special occasion. She set me up! But *why?*"

Theo doesn't look surprised.

"Isn't it obvious? Lucia wasn't just Maisie's boss. She was her only friend and her whole life, really. I'm sure she has some resentment toward you for taking her place."

I sink into a chair, resting my head in my hands.

"I didn't ask for any of this. I didn't *want* to come back—it just seemed like the right thing to do. I made a big mistake, didn't I?" I give him a sidelong glance. "My maid is out to get me, and the friend I couldn't wait to reconnect with hates me."

Theo pulls up a chair beside me, placing a gentle hand on my shoulder.

"Sebastian doesn't hate you. I'm sure he's going to feel like a right arse when he finds out none of this was your fault. And why don't you just sack Maisie?"

I groan.

"I wish, but I can't do that. I have a co-regent who runs the estate with me until I turn twenty-one, and I highly doubt he'd be willing to fire Maisie over a gift gone wrong when her mom is the housekeeper and they've both been at Rockford a whole lot longer than me."

"I guess you're right," Theo concedes. He reaches for my hand, and I feel a flicker of surprise—both at his actions and the way I warm to them. "Look, I'm not stupid. I know I'm not the brother you were excited to see tonight. But let me be the friend you need. I want to be here for you."

I flush with embarrassment. Have I really been so obvious?

"I— It's not that I *wasn't* excited to see you. I was, honestly. But when we were younger, I spent more time with Sebastian. I knew him better—"

"You don't have to explain," Theo interrupts. "I get it. I'm just . . . stating my intentions, I guess." He grins, his cute dimple reappearing.

I squeeze his hand, touched.

"Your English directness is *very* refreshing. I don't think

I've ever heard an American guy our age say anything so eloquent . . . or sweet."

"That's good to hear," Theo says with a wink. "Well, we'd better join the others before my mum gets even more bent out of shape."

We walk together into the library, our hands brushing against each other. And I wonder—could I have feelings for Theo? I've never thought of him like that, but I have to admit he's surprising me . . . in a good way.

Just before we reach the rest of our group, I ask the question that has been nagging at the back of my mind since Theo told me about the statuette.

"Why Lady Beatrice? What made Sebastian choose that as a gift for Lucia?"

"Lucia had this . . . obsession with Lady Beatrice," Theo reveals. "It started out as an essay she and Sebastian had to write for university, but then she became fixated on her, especially on the myths surrounding her life."

"What myths?" I ask, my heart rate picking up speed.

But I'm too late. Lady Stanhope spots us outside the library door and gestures for us to join the others. My questions will have to wait.

Despite Lady Stanhope's best efforts, the dinner is pretty much a disaster. Lord Stanhope arrives in the dining room with the news that Sebastian is nowhere to be found, and his empty place at the table serves as the elephant in the room, resulting in stilted conversation and awkward pauses throughout the meal. When the after-dinner tea service wraps up and the Blythes, the viscount, and his daughter all stand to leave, I finally have my exit opportunity.

"Thank you so much for a lovely dinner," I say, forcing a smile for the Stanhopes.

"We're so sorry about what happened earlier," Lord Stanhope says in a low voice. "My son hasn't been at all himself since Lucia died."

"I understand," I say quickly.

After a sweet goodbye hug from Theo, I hurry into the night, where the Aston Martin is waiting. I can barely carry a conversation with Alfie when he asks about the dinner, my mind racing a hundred miles a minute as I wonder how I will confront Maisie.

Anger floods my veins as I throw open the front doors of Rockford Manor. Where is she?

I search through the numerous rooms of the first floor until I'm out of breath, but she is nowhere to be found. I run back to the Marble Hall, stopping short at the sight of Mrs. Mulgrave slinking down the staircase.

"Where's your daughter?" I hear myself shout.

Mrs. Mulgrave flinches.

"She set me up!" I fume. "Where is she?"

"What do you mean, she set you up?" Mrs. Mulgrave asks. Her face is illumined by a silver candelabra on the wall, casting her in a ghostly glow.

"She gave me a *gift* for the Stanhopes that turned out to be one of Lucia's belongings—a present from Sebastian. She made me look like a total bitch, trying to hurt him by reminding him of Lucia. What kind of person does that?" I shake my head in disgust.

Mrs. Mulgrave's eyes sharpen.

"I don't believe Maisie meant any harm. I'm quite sure she will have an explanation. And besides, when a man loves the way Sebastian loved Lucia, anything can and will remind him of her. There's no use hoping he will forget." Mrs. Mulgrave's voice takes on the soft, worshipful tone she uses whenever she speaks of Lucia, and tonight it gives me the creeps.

"The only thing I'm *hoping* is that the people I live with won't stab me in the back. And if that kind of betrayal ever happens again, I'm going to have a serious talk with Oscar," I warn.

Mrs. Mulgrave doesn't look the least bit worried on her daughter's behalf. She simply raises her eyes to the top of the stairs.

"Why don't you speak to Maisie yourself? The last I saw her, she was going to make up your room."

"Thanks," I mutter, before thundering up the stairs.

I fling my bedroom door open, finding Maisie looking like the picture of innocence as she turns down my bed.

"How could you?" I burst out, resisting the urge to throttle her. "How could you do that to me? I trusted you!"

Maisie stands perfectly still, looking at me with doe eyes.

"And don't play dumb. You said yourself that Lucia told you everything. You knew that stupid figurine was hers. Your plan was obviously to make me look completely evil and ruin the whole night." I fold my arms across my chest. "So why don't you tell me to my face why you hate me enough to do that?"

"I don't hate you," Maisie says simply. "I did that because I had to. And you needed to know, anyway."

"Needed to know what? That Sebastian is still heartbroken over losing Lucia? I figured as much. You didn't have to hammer the point home and hurt him like that!"

"Not just about that. I needed you to know about Lady Beatrice."

I throw up my hands in exasperation. "You caused an awful scene just to give me a history lesson about an ancestor from the 1830s? Yeah, right."

"Listen to me!" Maisie's voice rises, and I am shocked into silence as she drops her usual deferential manner. "Why do you think Lucia was so obsessed with the legend of Lady Beatrice? What do you think her legend *was*?" Maisie leans in closer to me, until I can feel her cold breath against my ear. "She was rumored to have a *power*—the power to summon the elements with her hands. She could create fire and water and make flowers grow . . . with nothing but her touch."

I freeze. This isn't real. I have to be dreaming this conversation; it can't be happening.

"That's just a . . . a stupid old myth," I say, my quavering voice giving me away. "Lucia might have believed in it, but I don't. Lady Beatrice was just some duchess who died ages ago."

Maisie continues as if she hasn't heard me. "Lady Beatrice's husband, the fifth Duke of Wickersham, accused her of sorcery, and she was put to death by hanging. When she was on the gallows, she threatened to return one day . . . through a descendant."

I wipe my sweaty palms against my dress.

"This is a very creepy story and all, but I don't see what—"

"I told you, didn't I, that Lucia couldn't keep anything from me?" Maisie stares at me, her eyes unflinching. "She told me about you, Imogen, about what she saw you *do*."

I feel the ground beneath me sinking. And I'm falling, falling.

"She didn't know what she was saying," I whisper.

"If I were you, I would talk to Sebastian Stanhope and find out exactly what he and Lucia discovered about Lady Beatrice at Oxford," Maisie says. "He might be able to help you in a way that I can't." She turns toward the door, then glances back at me. "Will that be all? My mother is waiting for me to help her downstairs."

How can she stand there so calmly, as if she hasn't just disrupted my entire world and confirmed the dark suspicions I never wanted to address?

"Why didn't you just *tell* me all this instead of ruining my dinner with the Stanhopes?" I ask angrily.

Maisie raises her eyes to the ceiling.

"I didn't have a choice," she says softly. "I owed her."

"Owed who?" When she doesn't respond, I add incredulously, "Lucia?"

Maisie gives the slightest of nods.

"Um, excuse me? Lucia is *dead*." My voice catches on the word.

Maisie's face inches closer to mine, her expression suddenly frightened.

"Ghosts never really leave, though, do they?" she whispers. "You feel her here too, don't you? There may be more to why you came back, Imogen. Never forget that."

I shudder, both at her words and her overly familiar tone.

"No!" I back away from her. "I have no idea what you're talking about. Just—just go!"

As soon as Maisie is gone, I lock the door and fling myself onto the bed. My legs are trembling violently, my mind racing with thoughts of ghosts, of what might happen if people find out what I can do. *Am I really just like Lady Beatrice?* Maisie has to be wrong; there can't be more to my return here. I came back to fulfill my title—wasn't that supposed to be it?

I can leave tomorrow, I think, remembering my promise to go home to the Marinos if anything is amiss. But would it even be possible to find peace at home, with this frightening question mark hanging over my head? As much as I dread it, I know I have no choice but to finish what I've started.

My dreams that night are a kaleidoscope of chilling images, from Mrs. Mulgrave's skeletal face sneering at me with contempt, and Sebastian smashing the porcelain figurine, to my cousin's lifeless, beautiful body lying in its coffin. I wake from the last nightmare with the sensation of someone's hand brushing against my leg, and I scramble against the headboard. The shadow of a woman's figure stands at the foot of my bed.

A scream rises in my throat, but my vocal cords are paralyzed, I make no sound. My fingers manage to switch on the light . . . but no one is there. The figure is gone.

I don't bother going back to sleep after that. Instead, I grab my laptop from the desk and sit up in bed, propping myself against pillows. Skype opens automatically, and my heart constricts at the sight of Zoey Marino's name lit up in green font. She's online—I can see my sister and hear stories from home, or I can stick with my original plan of researching a frightening ancestor.

I click on Zoey's name, but just as I do so, her name turns gray. She must not have seen me, and signed off. My decision has been made.

I sign out of Skype, and then type "Duchess Beatrice Rockford" into the Google search window. My eyes widen as the screen fills with dozens of links, most of them from supernatural conspiracy websites. They all look a bit dodgy—to borrow a British term—so I choose the Wikipedia link.

Lady Beatrice's left eye stares boldly at me through the opening of a mask that she holds up to her face. Her light hair is piled half onto the top of her head, the other half arrayed around her shoulders. An unusual ring adorns her right hand, and I zoom in on the portrait to see it more clearly. The ring is a diamond in the shape of an icicle.

I return to the Wikipedia article and click on the next image—a painting of Beatrice on the night of her hanging. She is older in this painting, but her blond hair is styled the same as in the earlier, youthful portrait. The painting depicts screaming townspeople snatching at the skirts of her heavy gown as she attempts to flee. Leaves and flowers are woven through her hair, and a long garland drapes across her dress, giving her the appearance of nature itself.

I look closer. There is no doubt that I resemble her; our blue eyes, high cheekbones, and ivory skin are all a match. We could be sisters from different eras.

Well, I am *related to her. It makes sense that we'd look alike,* I tell myself. *Stop reading into it.*

I close the picture and return to the article's sparse text. The bio skims her childhood and adolescence as a New York heiress in the early 1800s, her arranged marriage to the fifth Duke of Wickersham in 1830, and the discovery of her "supernatural skills" and "dalliance with the occult."

> After a bitter argument, the fifth duke reportedly witnessed his wife set fire to Rockford Manor's Shadow Garden, using nothing but her hands. She then rebuilt the entire garden from scratch— all in the span of mere minutes. The duke went mad at the sight, never again regaining his full sanity. The Duchess of Wickersham was tried and hanged for witchcraft, though she repeatedly insisted she was not a witch. She called herself an Elemental.

So she too revealed herself in the Shadow Garden. It's yet another unwanted link between Beatrice and me. Could this connection be the reason my touch only seems to affect the elements when I'm on Rockford grounds?

I reread the article, shuddering at the realization that if someone finds me out, or if Maisie ever repeats what Lucia told her about me, I could meet the same fate as Beatrice. Maybe not hanged—I'm pretty sure people don't do *that* anymore—but I'd no doubt be locked up somewhere. I'll have to do a better job of hiding my skills from now on, no matter what it takes.

I reach the bottom of the Wikipedia page, where article

sources are listed. In this case, there is only one—*The Un-earthly Duchess: A Biography,* by Humphrey Fitzwilliam, published in 1865. I feel a rush of adrenaline at the thought of reading an actual book about Lady Beatrice, written by one of her contemporaries. I quickly type the title into the Google search window—but all links lead to the same place, Oxford's Bodleian Library. The text reads:

> Humphrey Fitzwilliam's *The Unearthly Duchess: A Biography* is one of the Bodleian Library's historic treasures. Our copy is the only known volume still existing in print. Due to the book's fragile condition and historic significance, it is held in our preservation storage facility. If you wish to view this title, you will need to place a hold on the item, and it will be delivered to you in the Bodleian reading room of your choice. Please allow a minimum of three to five business days.

"Three to five days?" I groan. Deflated, I type in my information and place the library hold, all the while wondering how I can get my hands on the book sooner. And then Maisie's words ring in my ears.

"If I were you, I would talk to Sebastian Stanhope and find out exactly what he and Lucia discovered about Lady Beatrice at Oxford."

The two of them were studying the fifth duchess; they must have read her biography. I know now that I have to follow Maisie's advice, whatever her motives may be.

I have to talk to Sebastian.

By eight a.m. I'm dressed and ready, forgoing my fancy British clothes in favor of jeans and a gray hoodie. Thankfully it's Sunday, Alfie's day off, so I can call a taxi without arousing suspicion.

I creep down the stairs and through the corridors, praying not to run into Oscar or either of the Mulgraves. As soon as I make it past the front door, I break into a run, alternating between jogging and sprinting the mile-long path from the house to the front gate. When I finally reach the gate, panting and sweaty, the black cab is already parked and waiting for me.

"Are you Maisie?" the cabdriver asks as I jump into the backseat.

"Yes," I lie, adopting a British accent. "I need to go to Stanhope Abbey. I'm running an errand for my mistress."

"Of course." He turns around in his seat to glance at me. "Might I ask, what is the new duchess like?"

"She's very . . . normal," I say dryly. If only.

With no traffic on a Sunday morning, we reach Stanhope Abbey in no time—too soon for my liking. I've barely begun to get my nerves under control when we pull up to their gate, with the cabbie announcing into the intercom, "Maisie Mulgrave on an errand for Rockford Manor."

"Should I go around back to the servants' entrance?" he asks me as the gates open.

Uh-oh. Not knowing where the servants' entrance is will definitely blow my cover.

"No, they told me to come through the front," I fib.

After handing the driver his fare, I step out of the cab and slowly make my way up the Stanhope Abbey steps. I squeeze my eyes shut and take a deep breath before ringing the doorbell.

The footman who answers the door does a double take when he sees me, narrowing his eyes as he looks from my face to my casual outfit.

"It's me, Imogen Rockford," I say quickly. "I'm sorry I had the cabdriver say I was Maisie—I only told him that so he wouldn't ask questions. My driver is off today."

The footman stares at me with a combination of bemusement and delight, as if I am the juiciest piece of scandal he's come across in a long while.

"Your Grace," he says, a smile spreading across his face. "What a pleasure to welcome you back so soon. What can I help you with?"

"I need to speak to Sebastian. Can you tell him it's urgent? And please, don't bother the others. I know it's early, and I really only want to see Sebastian."

I realize as I tell him this that I'm probably giving him a lot more fodder for his imagination. But I'm past caring.

"Of course," the footman says smoothly. "Why don't you wait in the library while I go up and wake him?"

He leads me through the house, which seems colder and darker without the presence of the family or any guests. We arrive at the library, and the footman flips a switch that lights every lamp in the room.

The Stanhope library is just the thing to distract me from

my nerves, an oasis of leather-bound books packed into floor-to-ceiling shelves, accented by dark wood furniture and a crimson Persian carpet. Though not as gigantic and decorative as the library at Rockford Manor, this one is somehow more comforting. While the footman leaves to find Sebastian, I scan the bookshelves for my favorite titles. I easily find *Pride and Prejudice* and am hunting for *The House of Mirth* when I hear the sound of approaching footsteps.

Sebastian stands in front of me, dressed in jeans and a navy blue pullover that accentuates the green of his eyes. His golden-brown hair is mussed from sleep, and I feel a sudden urge to reach over and run my fingers through it.

"Hello, Your Grace," he says quietly.

"Sebastian." I try to smile. "You don't have to call me that, you know."

And then, at the same time, we both say, "I'm sorry."

I look up at Sebastian in surprise.

"I shouldn't have gone off on you like that," he continues. "Theo told me you had no idea about the statuette. I should have known Maisie was behind it. I'm really sorry."

I take a step closer to him.

"I'm sorry too. I was mortified when Theo told me it belonged to . . . to Lucia. I totally understand why you were so upset."

"Let's just forget it ever happened," Sebastian says, with a smile that doesn't quite reach his eyes. "Can we?"

"Well, that's just it," I say awkwardly. "I can't forget. Because I went home and confronted Maisie for setting me up, and she told me . . . some things. That's why I'm here."

Sebastian looks away.

"I hate to keep reminding you of Lucia, but I need to know if what Maisie said is true."

He gives a slight nod.

"Let's go outside. We can talk there."

As I follow Sebastian out of the library, I can't help noticing the outline of his tensed muscles through his shirt. *Not the thing to focus on, Imogen,* I admonish myself.

He leads the way out the front doors and onto a tree-lined path that curves to the left of the house.

"It's beautiful out here," I remark, trying to break the ice.

Sebastian doesn't seem to hear me.

"What did Maisie tell you?" he asks, an anxious glint in his eyes.

I take a shaky breath. "She said that you and Lucia were studying Lady Beatrice at Oxford and that Lucia was fixated on her story, because of Beatrice's supposed *powers.*" I try to laugh, as though I find the whole thing perfectly ridiculous, but my laugh sounds as false as it is.

Sebastian listens silently, his expression revealing little.

"Maisie also said . . ." I hesitate for a moment but force myself to go on. "She said Lucia had told her things about me, that *I* could be somehow connected to Beatrice and her so-called . . . abilities. The whole thing seems crazy, but Maisie wanted me to know about it for some reason. She wanted me to talk to *you* about it. I know I shouldn't trust her, but she freaked me out all the same. I spent last night researching Lady Beatrice online, and it seems there's only one legitimate biography on her, which I can't get my hands on until the Bodleian Library gets it in, and I thought maybe you've seen it. . . ." I realize I'm babbling and my voice trails off.

Sebastian turns abruptly, as he seems to wrestle with what to say.

"It's true," he finally answers. "The last year of Lucia's life, we worked together on a thesis for our mythology class. Lucia chose Lady Beatrice as our subject, and that's when we read her biography at the Bodleian and discovered that she was rumored to have been an Elemental—someone who can create and control any of the four elements, using nothing but their hands. Lucia became obsessed, both with the idea of this power and with Beatrice's final words the night she was hanged."

"What were they?" I ask, my throat turning dry.

"Her last recorded words on the gallows were *'When my true descendant shows herself, all others before her will be swept away, until she and only she controls my home, Rockford Manor.'*"

My heart leaps into my throat. *". . . all others before her will be swept away."* My grandfather, parents, aunt, uncle, and cousin—was it a ghastly coincidence that they all died in swift succession? Or was there more to it?

"I tried telling Lucia the whole thing was mad, that history had warped the story of the old duke murdering his wife and turned it into bloody folklore. But she insisted we had proof that the myth was real. *You.*" He looks into my eyes, and I find myself backing away, as if he can see through me. "She watched you create a flame with your own hands that night—and we both saw you conjure the flower. I tried to come up with another explanation for her, but what else was there? She ran with the idea, determined to find out all she could about Beatrice and then confront you, armed in some way with her knowledge. But she never got the chance, did she?" Sebastian closes his eyes wearily.

I shake my head in horror. I might have wondered all these years if something was wrong with me, but I never imagined anything like this; I never thought of myself as some kind of supernatural *thing*.

"You don't believe it, though," I say, my voice barely above a whisper. "You wouldn't be standing here with me if you thought I was some otherworldly Elemental, or whatever you call it."

Sebastian runs a hand through his hair, exhaling in frustration.

"I don't know what to think. I *saw* you, Imogen—I could never forget what I saw that day."

"But you weren't afraid in the garden," I remind him. "You didn't treat me differently, and you promised to keep my secret. Did Lucia so easily change your opinion of me? What did she want to confront me about, anyway?"

Sebastian looks away from me as he speaks. "At first, I thought it was because Lady Beatrice was referred to in our research as an aberration, a witch. The things she could do . . . well, people back then took it to mean that she was evil, that she needed to be kept away from innocent people she might hurt. I thought Lucia was worried about what you might be able to do. But the longer we worked on the paper, the more I realized what was really bothering her. It was the idea that *you* were the true descendant—and that if Lady Beatrice's prophecy came true, Rockford Manor and Lucia's inheritance could be taken away from her and turned over to you."

"What?"

I feel a sharp pang in my stomach at the realization that my cousin hadn't missed me or cared about me. She'd only thought of me as a threat.

Sebastian takes my arm.

"But listen—I didn't agree with her."

"She was your girlfriend. Of course you sided with her. You were probably just as freaked out by me, thinking I'm some kind of Elemental witch plotting to steal the family fortune. That's why you acted so distant when you first saw me again, why you didn't seem at all glad that I'd come back." I blink back tears, reeling from the betrayal of my two oldest friends.

"No. It's not that. Things are complicated for sure, but I never thought that about you. In fact . . ." Sebastian lowers his eyes. "I told Lucia how I felt, how I thought she was wrong about you. It was the one thing that came between us."

My breath catches in my throat. So then . . . he cared. He cared enough about me to stand up to his beautiful, powerful girlfriend.

"I thought what you did that day in the Shadow Garden was . . . incredible," Sebastian continues. "It was magic. Afterward, I kept waiting for you to come back. I wanted to ask you to show me more—but you never did."

"And now?" I ask, my chin quivering. "What do you think now, after everything you've seen and read?"

Sebastian touches my shoulder briefly, and I feel a tremor where his hand was.

"I've seen enough to know that you're still the Ginny I remembered from when we were kids. Open, honest, and incapable of hurting anyone. Maybe you are an Elemental, maybe not." He leans in closer. "But I'm not afraid."

Relief floods through me, and I find myself gratefully reaching for his hand. Our fingers lock for one brief second and I revel in his touch, until we simultaneously drop our hands to our sides.

"So . . ." I take a deep breath, regaining my composure. "Maisie said something mysterious about there being another reason why I'm here, something I should ask you about. Any idea what she could have meant by that?"

"I don't know." Sebastian pauses. "Maybe—maybe she's trying to get you to finish what Lucia and I started in the Maze."

"The Maze?" I repeat. "But it's been closed since the fire. Max said he can't find his way around it anymore."

"Yeah, the fire changed the layout somehow—I still haven't figured out how to make it all the way through to the center. But I was always able to retrace my steps and find my way back to the start when we needed to get out."

"And what were you guys doing in there?" I ask, the hairs on my neck standing up as my father's words come to mind again. *"There's something hidden in the Maze."*

"Lucia was looking for something, and she convinced me to help her," Sebastian says with a sad smile. "It was something called a water-stone. Lady Beatrice's biographer wrote that she hid it there for her chosen descendant to find after she died. Of course, no one has ever seen it." He rolls his eyes. "That part of the story always sounded like a load of codswallop to me—an excuse to get tourists buying tickets to treasure-hunt at Rockford Manor. But I wonder if Maisie believes in it too, and if that's why she urged you to talk to me. Lucia must have told her I know how to get through the Maze."

"But why?" I ask, my heart racing. "What's so special about a stone? Why did Lucia want it so badly, and why would *Maisie* want me to find it?"

He shakes his head. "I'm not sure about Maisie, and I don't even know if the stone exists. But I think the reason Lucia wanted it was because of her fear of losing Rockford . . . to you."

"She thought if she found the stone, then *she* could some-how be Lady Beatrice's descendant instead of me?"

"Something like that." He hesitates. "But once she realized we didn't see eye to eye on any of this, she stopped talking to me about it. I—I can only guess what she was thinking now."

"My father told me something the day he died. I've never told anyone else." My heart thuds loudly in my chest. "He said that something was hidden in the Maze, and that it was there for me when I really needed it. I never understood what he meant, and sometimes I thought it must have just been one of his games or riddles. But now I'm wondering . . . was he talk-ing about the water-stone?"

Sebastian stares at me.

"We're going into that Maze," he says. "I'm going to help you find it."

"No, really," I object. "I can look for it myself. I'm not scared of a garden maze."

"I know you're not," he says. "I know you don't need me there. But I want to be."

I look up at him, color flooding my cheeks. "Really? But

won't that be too painful since that's where she . . . ?" I can't bring myself to say the last word. *Died.* I watch as Sebastian's eyes darken, and then he looks down, studying a fallen tree branch.

"I've been through everything you can imagine already," he says. "I can handle this."

XI

That night, Lucia pays me a visit in my dreams.

I am standing at the top of the grand staircase, about to descend, when she appears below, a pristine figure on the bottom step. I freeze, staring at the back of her gauzy white dress and her cloud of blond hair. The intoxicating scent of jasmine bathes the air as she floats toward the Marble Hall, her hands possessively skimming the walls of Rockford Manor. A chill runs through me as I hear the sound of her light voice singing softly.

> *"I know dark clouds will gather round me,*
> *I know the road is rough and steep.*
> *But golden fields lie just beyond me,*
> *Where weary eyes no more will weep. . . ."*

She stops to brush her manicured fingers over a piece of artwork, her bow-shaped mouth turning up in a smile. I can't look away. My heart is in my throat; goose bumps prickle my arms. How can she be here?

Suddenly the front doors swing open. When Sebastian walks through them, I find myself involuntarily racing down the stairs, as though someone else is in charge of my movements. No one seems to hear or see me, so I sneak behind one of the tall pillars in the Marble Hall, a silent voyeur.

I watch her lips part at the sight of him, her eyes coming alive with an expression I'm unable to discern. And then her neck swivels in my direction. I can't breathe as her brown eyes fix on me, in a gaze thick with hatred.

With that one look, I understand. Lucia Rockford might be gone, but her presence is a permanent mark. The house— and Sebastian—still belong to her. I am nothing more than an unwelcome successor.

"Looking for this?" she whispers, dangling her pale hand in front of me, her finger adorned with an unusual, icicle-shaped diamond ring. And then she begins to laugh, a shrill, humor-less sound that echoes against the walls, until her voice seems to multiply.

"Sebastian!" I scream.

But he is gone. And now another blond girl joins Lucia, a girl who looks a bit like . . . me. Her blue eyes bore into mine as she creeps closer.

"Who are you?" I demand, my voice quavering. "Are you . . . Lady Beatrice?"

She merely smiles—a strange, incandescent smile.

ᖆᴏ

I jolt awake, my pulse racing. With trembling hands, I reach for the lamp on my nightstand. My breath returns as light floods the room, with no sign of Lucia or the other blond girl.

Teddy stretches lazily at the foot of the bed, oblivious to my nightmare. I reach over to stroke his back, wondering what the dream meant. Why was my cousin portrayed as an enemy? Is my subconscious guilty over my lingering feelings for Sebastian, and trying to *make* Lucia into the enemy? Or is it because I now know the dark thoughts she had about me? And who was that second blond girl in the dream—some alternate version of me? Or was it Lady Beatrice?

"Imogen, pull yourself together," I tell myself sternly. "You have some investigating to do."

Teddy looks up at me questioningly.

"Yeah, I know, I'm talking to myself." I sigh.

Teddy flops back onto his side, unimpressed. As much as I want to drop the whole thing and fall back to sleep alongside him, my mind is whirring, and I know I have to do something. I need to find out more about Lady Beatrice and our supposed connection, more than what Sebastian told me. And suddenly it occurs to me where I might find the most information— even more than online or at the Bodleian.

I haven't been inside the Rockford library since my return. It used to be my favorite room in the house, and I guess . . . I didn't want to face it without the person I used to spend the most time with there. My mother. But tonight I have no choice. The Rockford library possesses the vastest collection of our family history, and I have a feeling I might find what I'm looking for there.

I pull my robe tighter around my shoulders as I tiptoe down the grand staircase, nervously aiming a flashlight ahead of me. Stealing through the dark, I have the chilling sensation that ghosts are floating alongside me, that the portraits on the walls are following me with their eyes. With a pang of longing I think of the Marinos' modern apartment, far too bright and contemporary to house any spirits.

I recognize the door to the library by its familiar, towering marble casing. For a moment, I'm certain I can hear snatches of sound inside: the soothing hum of a woman reading aloud, the melodic giggling of two young girls. But just as quickly, the sounds fade. Holding my breath, I open the door, flick on the lights, and step into an enormous oasis of books.

I forgot just how long the library is; it must run the entire length of Rockford Manor's west front. With its vaulted stucco ceilings, decorative window arches, statues, busts, and paintings of past dukes and duchesses, the room is a seamless blend of art and literature. An eighteenth-century mahogany rolltop desk beckons the writer, while the carved white bookcases lining the walls hold books numbering in the thousands. A painful wave of nostalgia overcomes me as I move farther into the room, but I still smile at my surroundings. It is a book lover's dream.

I pace the bookshelves, which are ordered by subject, until I find *Rockford Family & History*. I quickly scan the titles, bypassing two shelves of volumes on the first duke and his battles, till I reach Lady Beatrice's period in history. But while there seems to be a record of nearly every duke and duchess in the family up until my grandfather, the fifth Duke and Lady Beatrice are missing from the shelves. I flip through three different books covering the entire Rockford dynasty, but none of them allow so much as a mention of Lady Beatrice. And then it all becomes clear as I open a coffee-table book about the Rockford gardens—only to find that a page has been torn out.

Someone has clearly tried to erase Lady Beatrice from our family records. And that only increases my desperation to find out more about her.

I drum my fingers against the bookcase impatiently, glaring at the volume in my hand. I'm so wrapped up in thought that it takes a few minutes before I notice the sticker on the book's cover: "Property of the Rockford Archives."

The Rockford Archives . . . I vaguely recall seeing the name on the map of the manor that Harry Morgan gave me weeks ago. The archives are a physical *place*—and while Lady Beatrice might not have been allowed representation in the public Rockford library, surely bits of her life must remain in the private archives.

I quickly stuff the book back into its shelf before racing upstairs, eager to retrieve the map and the ring of keys Oscar gave me upon my arrival. As I seize the keys from my desk drawer, I say a silent prayer: for one of them to unlock the door to the Rockford Archives.

Holding the map in one hand and a flashlight in the other, I quietly make my way up to the Rockford Archives, located in one of the manor's four towers. The map directs me to a door concealed within the Marble Hall's wall paneling, and my heart jumps as I open it and find a stone spiral staircase. I follow the staircase higher and higher, my thighs beginning to burn from the climb, until I at last reach a narrow stone door. My fingers fumble with the keys on my key ring as I try each one, and on my second-to-last attempt, the door finally creaks open.

I step into the tower room and look around in wonder. It is a nondescript little space, lined with identical file cabinets and a smattering of brown boxes. But the view out the window is the most incredible sight I've ever seen, revealing miles of Rockford parkland, the lake, and the bridge, all lit up by the night's stars. It's like a painting brought to life.

The only light in the tower is from an antique table lamp that barely casts a glow when I switch it on, so I keep my flashlight trained ahead as I investigate the file cabinets. My heart sinks as I realize they aren't in any particular order. It'll take me months to go through the endless supply of stuff in here.

I slump onto the floor, hugging my knees to my chest. It's past three o'clock in the morning, and I am mentally and physically exhausted, longing for the comfort of my bed. But how can I leave now, after all the effort it took to find the archives?

An idea occurs to me, and though I feel foolish for even considering it, I can't think of any other way to tackle the mountain of files in front of me.

"Lady Beatrice," I whisper. I clear my throat and try again, this time louder. "Lady Beatrice. If—if you're out there . . . somewhere . . . please, show me what I'm looking for."

I chant her name and repeat my request for what feels like

hours, until I've grown numb and the words have lost their meaning. And . . . nothing.

I peel myself off the floor. That was just stupid. No one else in their right mind would call on a long-dead spirit for help. I'm really beginning to lose it. Which isn't too comforting a thought.

A gust of wind blows into the tower, knocking the flashlight out of my grasp. I whirl around. The window is closed, so where did the wind come from?

And then my eyes follow the flashlight's glow. Its beam is pointed at a small box tucked between two file cabinets, bearing my name. I cover my mouth in shock.

Time moves in slow motion as I approach the box and lift the lid. I feel a tightening in my chest as I touch the contents, returning to a former life. My elementary school class pictures, old report cards, and baby photos mingle with letters from Mum to Grandfather, updating him on my latest milestones. A lump rises in my throat as I read Mum's handwritten words.

December 5, 1998

Imogen said her first word today! 'Dada.' Edmund was awfully chuffed! We just knew she'd be a daddy's girl . . .

October 23, 2006

Thank you, dearest, for Imogen's beautiful bracelet. She loves it. Birthday #10 was a success! Can you believe our little one is already in her double digits?

I drop the letter back into the box, tears blurring my vision. That was my last birthday with my parents. I remember the party, the gifts, and Mum and Dad beaming as they sang to me, none of us knowing we were about to be forever separated.

Only two sheets of paper are left in my box, which doesn't seem to have been updated since the fire. I pick them up, and discover that they are typewritten pages in the layout of an article. I quickly scan the heading and byline.

THE ISIS MAGAZINE
AN OXFORD UNIVERSITY PUBLICATION
MAY 21, 1988
THE ROCKFORDS OF WICKERSHAM:
PERCEPTION VS. MISCONCEPTION
BY LORD EDMUND ALBERT ROCKFORD

I sit up straighter, jolted by the sight of my father's name in print. I'm not sure what his magazine article is doing in my archive, but it's a welcome mistake. I eagerly begin to read my father's words from twenty-six years ago.

Every dynasty has its stain. The reprobate, the scandalous, the fallen—each great house of the English aristocracy can lay claim to at least one of these characters. We know their stories inside and out; we've read them in books, witnessed them in our neighbors, and maybe even lived them in our own homes. But what happens when the family stain goes *beyond* what we understand or know to be possible? How do we categorize someone as "good" or "evil" based on that which we've never seen before, and never knew existed?

How do we judge them at all?

When Beatrice, the Duchess of Wickersham, arrived at Rockford Manor, she created an international stir. Her marriage to the fifth duke in 1830 was the first of the transatlantic alliances between an English nobleman and American heiress, and the idea of a nineteen-year-old American girl as chatelaine of Rockford Manor provoked much interest. But far greater controversies were to follow her. It wasn't long before rumblings could be heard in the staff quarters and throughout Wickersham Village, with talk of frightening occurrences in the manor since the beautiful young American's arrival. This was the beginning of Beatrice's characterization as a member of the "occult."

For more than a century now, Lady Beatrice Rockford (1811–1850) has been known as "that wicked American" and her husband, the fifth Duke of Wickersham, the victim forced to send her to the gallows. But these roles are ludicrously reversed. The real ugly stain in my family history is my ancestor, the duke who murdered his wife simply because she was capable of something he had never seen. He feared what he didn't understand, and let his fear drive him to evil.

Is there anything inherently wrong in having a paranormal talent? More than likely, Lady Beatrice didn't wish for her gift, and with the exception of the burned garden, which she instantly restored, there are no accounts of her ever using her skill to cause any harm.

If we misconstrue that which we don't understand as frightening or criminal, then we are lost. But if we recognize differences in others as something beautiful or miraculous—even, or especially, differences as astounding as Lady Beatrice's—then we all win in the end.

By the time I finish my father's article, my cheeks are soaked with tears. *He knew.* That's the reason his pages ended up in my file. He wanted me to find them.

For the first time in seven years, I can feel my father's presence in the room with me; I can almost hear his voice. I shake my head in wonder at the realization that almost a decade before I was born, Dad wrote the very words he would have said if he were standing before me now—that I don't need to be afraid. My differences are what make me special. And there is no shame in being linked to Lady Beatrice.

The way Dad spoke to me so cryptically in front of the Maze, the look he and Mum exchanged in the church, the words he said to her in hushed conversation . . . I realize now what those long-ago moments meant. He suspected all along that I was different. Just like Beatrice.

I stand up, a smile spreading across my face. I wonder what

I can do with this gift if I'm no longer afraid of it. If I am an Elemental, like Sebastian said, then that means I can control the four elements. So . . .

I unlatch the window, my heart racing in anticipation. Keeping my eyes trained on the green leaves of the tree opposite me, I raise my arms in their direction. One of the leaves abruptly falls from its branch and, instead of blowing to the ground, drifts across the sky toward me. I gasp as a second leaf follows, and then a third, until a flurry of green is flying through my window, encircling me.

I drop my arms, and the leaves fall to my feet. Exhilaration floods through me. That was . . . amazing.

I bend down to pick up the leaves, and my flashlight's glow dances across another box. I freeze as I take in its label: LADY LUCIA ROCKFORD.

Do I dare to open it? I know I shouldn't—she would consider it trespassing. But I have no other way of knowing the person my cousin grew up to be. Her belongings are all I have left.

With trembling fingers, I open the box. I find a similar amalgam of class photos and report cards as in mine, and I feel myself deflate at the realization that her archive isn't updated either. Grandfather, or whoever was in charge of it, must not have had the heart to continue with the archives after the fire. The only difference I can find between her box and mine is that hers includes a stack of billing notices, with 2007 bills at the top.

PORT REGIS PREPARATORY SCHOOL
CHELTENHAM CHILDREN'S EQUESTRIAN CLUB

Dr. Archibald Heron, Clinical Behavioral Psychiatrist, Children & Adolescents

"Psychiatrist?" I read aloud in surprise.

I hold the bill directly under my flashlight. Maybe I read it wrong—after all, it's so dark up here. But no, there it is in bold print. The bill is dated one month before the fire, June of 2007. Scrawled in blue ink are the words

Still struggling with delusions and violent temper. Patient should see me on a more frequent basis.

I drop the paper in my shock. I remember Lucia's occasional temper tantrums, but delusions? If this is all true, how did she manage to keep her struggles so well hidden?

I suddenly feel dirty, like I've gone too far. I know well enough from my own therapy sessions that they're supposed to remain confidential—and here I am, delving into my cousin's records. I return the bill to her box and hastily close it.

"Ghosts never really leave, though, do they?"

I jump as Maisie's words echo in my ear. If there's any chance that she's right, and Lucia really is watching us . . . then she just saw me violate her privacy. With a shudder, I grab my dad's article and hightail it out of the tower. But as I descend the long staircase to the first floor, my mind spins with questions.

Lucia needing psychiatric help after the fire would make perfect sense, but Dr. Heron's notes were from *before*—when she had everything going for her. She was privileged and adored at home, popular at school, cool and confident in all settings, and she'd even managed to skip over any type of awkward stage. What was going on beneath my cousin's surface that caused Dr. Heron to write such things? How had I missed the signs that she needed help? And considering how close we were back then . . . why had she kept her struggles a secret from me?

I feel a pang of guilt as I ruminate about what I never knew, never guessed. It's becoming all too clear that our childhood friendship was never as honest as I'd thought. And I'm beginning to wonder if I truly knew Lucia at all.

I'm dying to share my father's article with Sebastian, but first I have a full day of duchess duties. Oscar, Mrs. Mulgrave, and I have a long meeting after breakfast to plan the annual Rockford Fireworks Concert, and I'm beyond relieved to have Oscar in the meeting. The idea of spending all that time alone with Mrs. Mulgrave makes me shudder. The two of them clearly have the affair down pat, so the purpose of the meeting is mainly to fill me in.

I squeeze in a Skype chat with the Marinos before another appointment with Gemma, and as always, seeing them is like breathing in fresh air. I'm relieved to find Carole and Keith looking a little less sad and pale, and Zoey her usual bubbly self. They want to hear everything, and as I give them a highly edited rundown of the polo match, dinner at the Stanhopes', and the happenings around Rockford, I realize just how much I'm forced to leave out.

After reviewing my "Summer Calendar of Events" with

Gemma, and another etiquette lesson with Basil Crawford, I'm free at last. Sebastian gave me his cell number the other day, and I feel a wave of nervousness as I type in his number. I deliberate over the text draft, finally sending a simple:

Hey there. Are you still up for the Maze? —Imogen

I now understand the expression "waiting on pins and needles" as I watch my phone, wondering when it will chime with a reply. I try picking up a book, then attempt to play a mindless game on my iPad, but nothing can draw my eyes away from the all-too-quiet phone. Just when I'm about to give up on a reply, I hear the ping.

Sorry, I was at polo practice. Should I come by now?

My breath catches in my throat as I type the word *yes*.

I stand at the entrance to the Maze, a massive labyrinth of green hedges rising at least ten feet high. The last time I stood in this same position was with my father all those years ago, and for a moment, I am frozen in time. Nothing looks any different. I could be ten years old again, and any minute now my dad will appear, slipping through the hedges.

"Imogen."

I turn with a gasp. *Have* I gone back? Is it him? But then I glimpse Sebastian walking toward me, and I experience the most confounding sensation of my heart both breaking and lifting at the same time. He isn't who I hoped to see in this moment—that person is never coming back. But the sight of Sebastian brings a smile to my lips, a flutter to my stomach . . . and I realize that my feelings for him are one of the only constants in my life since childhood. Even if it is a crush I shouldn't have, even if it is unrequited, how can it be wrong when it connects me to who I was before?

"Are you all right?" Sebastian asks, coming closer.

"I was just thinking about my parents," I admit. "The last time I was near the Maze was . . . that day. With my dad."

Sebastian's eyes soften.

"That's really rough. I'm so sorry." He pauses. "Do you remember them well?"

"Yeah, but unfortunately most of what I remember is that last day—because I've dreamed of it so often," I confide.

Sebastian places a comforting hand on my shoulder, and something about his touch makes me want to tell him more.

"The nightmare comes every few weeks. It starts innocently enough, tricking me into a state of happiness. And even though the dream takes a dark turn and I wake up in a panic, I never want to stop dreaming. Because that's how I know my last conversation with my dad by heart. That's how I can remember my parents' faces and smiles. The nightmare keeps me from forgetting them."

"Ginny."

Suddenly Sebastian is hugging me, his muscular arms warm and firm around my body. I lean my head against his chest, basking in his closeness. I know it's the comforting hug of a friend, nothing more. But in this moment, it's everything I need.

Out of nowhere, Lucia's face comes into sharp focus in my mind. I pull away from Sebastian, ashamed.

"I'm so sorry. I should be the one comforting you right now. This is where—the place where she . . ." I stammer, cutting myself off before I can say the last word. *Died.* "This must be so much harder for you."

Sebastian looks away in discomfort.

"I—I don't want to talk about it. Like I said before, I can handle being here. You don't have to worry about me."

I bite my lip as I study him.

"Okay. If you're sure . . . I have something to show you."

I pull my father's article from the pocket of my sweater and hand it to him. "I don't know if it was ever published, but I found the draft in the family archives."

Sebastian's expression changes as he reads it, and when he looks back at me, I can tell he is moved.

"Your dad was my hero ever since he taught me polo. After reading this, I think even more highly of him."

My eyes prick with tears, but I smile through them.

"That means the world to me."

Sebastian grins back, and then looks ahead to the Maze entrance.

"Are you ready?"

I nod. He leads the way, and I hear myself gasp as I enter for the very first time as the green hedges close in around us. The Maze is like a world unto itself—as soon as we're inside, it's impossible to see beyond its boundaries. All that exists now is an endless, narrow path bordered by tall evergreen walls, a twisting and turning labyrinth.

"It's obvious Max hasn't been here in years," I say to

Sebastian, after nearly tripping over a fallen branch. "This place looks totally overgrown and neglected."

Without thinking, I reach down to toss the branch aside. As my hand brushes the dirt, the fallen branches and dead plants disappear into thin air. Sebastian lets out a sharp breath.

"Sorry." I laugh nervously. "I didn't mean to do that."

I feel a light pressure on my hand, and I realize with a shock that he's taken hold of it.

"Don't be sorry. It's amazing."

I gaze at him gratefully. He can't know what a relief it is to see him witness the most secret part of me, and then look at me in awe rather than fear.

"Thanks." I smile. "I have to admit, I'm starting to become a little more intrigued by what I can do."

"You should be! By the way, I don't think I've ever seen Rockford Manor's gardens look so . . . alive."

"Yeah, apparently my talents have seeped into the grounds since I've arrived," I reply. "Max said the same thing to me last week. I think he suspects something."

Sebastian's eyes lock with mine.

"Can you trust him?"

"I think so," I say slowly. "I mean, I'm not going to volunteer any information. But I think he's okay."

"Good." Sebastian nods, and I feel strangely giddy about his protective stance.

We walk forward together, our shoes rustling against the overgrown weeds that litter our path. Every few minutes I reach down to touch the earth, and the obstacles in front of us disappear.

—

"What does it feel like when you do that?" Sebastian asks, watching me curiously.

"You can see for yourself if you want." I take his hand as casually as I can manage and place it over mine. Together, we reach for one of the hedge walls. I hear his breathing grow heavier; I feel my own breath stop as our fingers interlace against the evergreen. And then the electric sensation sizzles through my fingertips, through my whole body, stronger than I've ever felt it. I hear Sebastian whoop in amazement, and I whirl around. The hedge walls have transformed from green to a vibrant violet. It is the most beautiful color I've ever seen.

Sebastian and I turn to face each other at the same time, and nearly collide in our swift movement. His hand reaches for my hip to steady me. Heat fills my cheeks. His touch awakens something in me, something even stronger than my Elemental power. I glance up at him and find his eyes locked on mine. We inch closer, and it feels like anything can happen—

A clap of thunder bursts overhead. We spring apart. The spell is broken.

"We'd better get out of here before the downpour starts," Sebastian says, looking up at the sky. I nod, feeling slightly deflated.

He's memorized the way back to the entrance, and I follow silently. We reach the opening into the outside world just as rain begins to fall. Sebastian takes off his jacket and places it around my shoulders.

"Thanks," I tell him. "And thanks for going in there with me. You're a real friend."

He smiles briefly. Together we walk past the Maze, keeping

our eyes away from the gated Shadow Garden, waiting with all its haunting memories just steps away. When we reach the back entrance of Rockford Manor, I invite him inside for tea and dessert.

"Thanks, but I should get back," he says. "My car is parked outside the gate, so I'll head out that way."

"Okay. I'm sorry you have to walk another mile in the rain." I shrug off his jacket and hand it back to him. "Why didn't you just park in front of the house?"

"Oh, I . . ." He hesitates. "I guess I didn't feel up to seeing the staff."

"Of course," I say hurriedly. "I understand."

Going into the Maze with me is one thing, but entering the house where Lucia used to live, coming face to face with her maid and housekeeper and butler, explaining what he was doing there . . . I could see how that would be too painful, and I feel a stab of guilt.

Before we part ways, Sebastian says, "We can go back to the Maze whenever you're ready. Just let me know."

XII

Returning to the manor's front entrance, I notice a pair of second-floor shutters open—shutters that have remained closed ever since I moved in. The cold weight of fear sets in as I look up at the window. Someone is in Lucia's bedroom.

Filled with trepidation, I make my way up the steps and into the house. I find Oscar in the Marble Hall, and I feel a rush of relief at the sight of him.

"Good evening, Your Grace," he says with a bow.

"Hi, Oscar. Um, I don't know how to say this, but . . ." I pause. "I think I saw someone in Lucia's room. The window is open."

Oscar grimaces.

"That will be Mrs. Mulgrave, I'm sure. I hope she didn't give you a fright."

"Mrs. Mulgrave?" I echo. "Why would she be in there?"

"She was awfully fond of Lady Lucia," Oscar says,

awkwardly. "Her mother died so young that Mrs. Mulgrave took on the maternal role, and certainly loved Lucia like her own. It comforts her to make up Lucia's room every day, as if nothing has changed."

I feel slightly sick.

"What do you mean? She goes in there and pretends Lucia is still alive?"

Oscar lowers his eyes.

"I—I suppose so. I'll admit it makes me uncomfortable, but I don't want to be unkind. I believe she suffered the most of all of us when Lucia died."

"No wonder she doesn't like me," I realize with a sinking feeling. "She hates the fact that I'm the one living here, instead of Lucia."

"Please don't think that," Oscar says anxiously. "I'm certain she likes you."

"It's okay, you don't have to pretend," I tell him. "At least now I understand."

The following days are a strange blend of dreamy and chilling. Sebastian and I returned to the Maze three more times, and though we still can't find our way to the center, I have a feeling I'm growing closer—both to the water-stone and to him. But when night falls, I'm plagued by nightmares that become progressively more vivid and threatening. The Lucia who comes to me in my dreams is angry and vengeful, and every time I wake from one of the nightmares, I vow to stay away from Sebastian—but my resolve only holds for the first few minutes upon waking up. We can only be friends, I know that, but I can't give him up entirely.

As my feelings for Sebastian grow despite my efforts to stifle them, I find myself wondering about him and Lucia more often. What was their relationship like? Did he know about her problems, or did she keep them as well hidden from him as she did from me? Does he think about Lucia every time he looks at me? When those dark silences fall over him, is it because he's missing Lucia and wishing he were with her instead? But of course, these are questions I'll never bring myself to ask.

Two days before the Rockford Fireworks Concert, I get up early to make the trek to Windsor Great Park, where Sebastian is playing in a charity polo match and Theo and I are to be his guests. Gemma was practically giddy when I told her over the phone about the invitation. "That's Prince Philip's polo club! Don't forget the royal curtsy Basil taught you."

This time I have a better idea of what to wear, and I choose a casual white sundress with klutz-proof black flats. After getting dressed, I slip quietly out of the manor, holding my breath that I won't run into Mrs. Mulgrave or Maisie. They are the last people I want knowing where I'm going, and luckily I make it outside without anyone but Oscar seeing me.

Alfie is already waiting in the Aston Martin when I step outside. I settle into the backseat, leaning my head against the window as we begin the hour-long drive to Windsor. We make our way south along the river Thames until we reach a town that looks straight out of a Brothers Grimm fairy tale, with an enormous medieval castle looming high above cobbled streets and ancient storefronts below.

"There it is. Windsor Castle," Alfie says reverently. "Would you believe it's more than nine hundred years old?"

"That is seriously old." I whistle under my breath. "Is the Queen in there right now?"

"No, she's summering at Sandringham. But Windsor is one of the homes closest to her heart."

Alfie proceeds into Windsor Great Park, a breathtaking expanse of lush green meadow that stretches on for miles, bordered by horse trails and byways, and dotted with ancient oak trees, stone cottages, and exclusive gated estates. At last we arrive at the vast Smith's Lawn, home of the Guards Polo Club. Alfie insists on escorting me up the stands to meet Theo, and while I'm slightly embarrassed, I don't argue. This place is so huge, I can picture myself easily getting lost.

Alfie leads the way up the stands to Theo's row, and I keep my head down as flashbulbs go off in our direction. I should have expected them—Alfie's uniform with the Rockford logo is a dead giveaway. But I relax once I see Theo's dimpled grin.

"Hi there, Imogen!" he calls out, standing upon my arrival.

"Hey, Theo." I give him a quick hug.

"I'll leave you two to the game," Alfie says with a bow. "It's nice to see you again, Mr. Stanhope."

After bidding Alfie goodbye, Theo and I settle into our seats.

"It's been a minute since I saw you last," he says, stretching an arm across the back of my seat. "You've been spending your free time with my brother, I gather."

I glance down self-consciously.

"I know. We—we're taking the same summer class at Oxford."

"It hasn't started yet," Theo reminds me. There's a slight edge to his voice, but he flashes me a grin, as if saying, *Relax. This is just typical, easygoing banter.*

"Right, but Sebastian is helping me get caught up," I lie. "Since my curriculum in America was different."

I'm not sure what prompts me to make up the story; it just slips out.

"Can I ask you something?" Theo peers closely at me. "How is Sebastian?"

"What do you mean?" I ask, caught off guard. "Wouldn't you know better than me?"

"Yeah, I just . . . wondered what you thought. I guess because—well, it's been a tough year."

I glance down at the ground.

"Of course. He seems like he's handling it all pretty well, though."

Theo nods, a look of relief in his eyes. I wait for him to say more, but he shifts gears, chatting about the opposing team and filling me in on their high-goal players. I'm only half paying attention, the other half of me busy wondering what that exchange was all about.

The match begins. My stomach does a flip-flop as Sebastian rides onto the field, more handsome than ever in his Oxford uniform. I hear wolf whistles and cheers coming from a group of girls in the stands beneath us, and I exchange an amused look with Theo.

"They're called Stick Chicks," he explains with a laugh. "Polo groupies."

"Oh." I glance back at the girls, suddenly noticing how perfect their bodies are, how glamorous they look in their curve-hugging ensembles. Sebastian could have his pick of any of them. It's a depressing thought, even though I already know he's off-limits.

But then I see him scanning the crowd, searching for someone. Our eyes meet and his lips turn up in a smile. I grin back, color flooding my cheeks. I can feel Theo watching me and I know I should play it cooler, but I can't seem to stifle my smile—not even after the game has begun.

Theo suggests we toast Sebastian's winning match at the Old Ticket Hall, a bar and live music venue nearby. Sebastian manages to extricate himself from the admiring Stick Chicks and disappears into the locker room, returning in dark denim jeans and a button-down shirt under a black vest. Watching him, I can't help wishing he weren't so ridiculously good-looking. If only he'd grow a crazy unibrow, or do *something* to take the edge off my attraction.

The three of us jump into a black cab, and after a quick drive through Windsor Great Park and into town, we arrive at the Old Ticket Hall, located on a quaint street, with revelers spilling out the doors. Sebastian leads the way inside, miraculously finding us the one remaining booth. I slide in beside him, with Theo following me.

"What are you drinking?" Sebastian asks.

"Well, considering the drinking age is a lot older in my

part of the world, I don't have much experience with booze," I admit. "How about you pick something out for me?"

"We'll make it a Pilsner, then," Sebastian decides. "That's a good starter beer."

When our drinks arrive, I raise my glass.

"To another win for Oxford," I say, smiling at both of them. "And to old friends."

We clink beer mugs, and I take my first sip. The Pilsner tastes bitterer than I expected, and I can't help making a face.

"Water, please!" I call out to a passing waitress as Sebastian and Theo burst out laughing.

"Don't give up on Pilsner just yet," Theo says with a gentle nudge. "It'll taste better once you get used to it."

"Ugh. Okay, let me try again." I take another swig, which tastes just as gross as the first. But by my fourth sip, it tastes almost . . . sweet.

"It's got a cookie flavor!" I exclaim, slamming my mug down onto the table like I've seen people do in the movies.

"Whoa, someone's already tipsy," Sebastian chuckles. "Good thing I only ordered a half pint."

Half an hour later, my mug is nearly drained and I'm positively giddy. The conversation flows easily, and I keep bursting into fits of laughter over Sebastian and Theo's dry British humor.

When I hear the sound of a jazz band starting their instruments, I sit up excitedly.

"Come on. Let's go to the dance floor!"

Theo wrinkles his nose.

"But it's jazz night."

"Music is *music*," I tell him seriously, as if saying something deeply profound. I grab each of their hands and pull them to their feet. "Let's go, let's go!"

The musicians in the trio give us grateful smiles as we approach the stage. We seem to be their only audience—all the other clubgoers are steadfastly ignoring the music, continuing to talk and laugh loudly among themselves.

"Who wants to dance?" I ask tipsily.

Theo steps back, smiling awkwardly. "I'm not much of a dancer."

"You, then." I grab Sebastian's hand.

"How does one dance to jazz, anyway?" he wonders.

"Like this."

I place his arms around my waist and wrap mine around his neck. His touch only escalates my exhilaration, and it takes all my self-control to not blurt out my feelings then and there, as we dance to the rhythmic lull of a saxophone, piano, and guitar.

"I never knew until now that I actually like jazz," I murmur in Sebastian's ear. He grins down at me.

As the trio amps up their song, getting into a more swinging section of the piece, we kick our amateur moves up a notch. Sebastian twirls me around, even dipping me at one point, and we draw closer together, flushed and laughing.

The song ends, and the saxophonist puts down his instrument, picking up an accordion instead.

"Ooh. Wonder what he's up to with that?" I nudge Sebastian in the ribs.

The guitarist leans into the microphone and begins to sing slowly.

"The falling leaves drift by the window,
The autumn leaves of red and gold.
I see your lips, the summer kisses,
The sunburned hands I used to hold."

The singer's raspy, haunting voice tugs at my chest. Sebastian's arms return to my waist, and I lean against him as we sway to the music. The accordion joins in on the chorus, and it is so beautiful, so heart-wrenching, that everything else in the room seems to fade away until there is only me, Sebastian, and the song.

"Since you went away, the days grow long,
And soon I'll hear old winter's song.
But I miss you most of all, my darling,
When autumn leaves start to fall."

My eyes meet Sebastian's, and I know we're both thinking the same thing. This song could be about *us*, about the summer we said goodbye. He leans in closer, and my heart skips a beat. Is he . . . going to kiss me? But then I see him looking somewhere beyond me, his jaw tensing.

"My brother doesn't look too happy. I wonder if he wishes he were in my place right now."

"Oh—but he's the wrong brother."

I blurt the words out before realizing what I'm saying, and then I clap my hand over my mouth in horror. Did I just admit my feelings? In the middle of a bar? Sebastian stares at me, his green eyes wide. Apparently I did.

The song ends, and I hurry back toward Theo, my cheeks

burning. For the rest of the night Sebastian and I make a valiant effort to pretend I didn't say anything. But the words linger, taking up space between us.

⇛

I return home that night to find Teddy furiously barking outside my bedroom door.

"What is it, Teddy?" I bend down to give him a hug. He jumps up, his paws on my legs, nodding his head toward my room. And then I smell smoke.

Instantly sobered up, I throw open my bedroom door. The wastebasket beside my desk is glowing, with flames climbing its sides, threatening to spill onto the carpet and set the room ablaze. I whirl around in a panic, my eyes searching for a glass of water. But there is nothing, and time is running out fast.

I move closer to the wastebasket. Teddy gnaws at the hem of my dress, trying to pull me back to safety, but I shoo him away. I've never done anything like this before—but if there was ever a time my Elemental skills could come in handy, it's right about now.

I place my palms over the fire, focusing my mind on the image of water. But nothing happens, and Teddy's barking grows increasingly frantic as I wave my hands over the wastebasket like some kind of wannabe wizard. What am I doing differently? Why isn't the gift working? What am I *missing* this time?

My mind flashes back to the Shadow Garden years ago, to the pangs of envy in my stomach as I watched Sebastian and Lucia before growing a flower with my hands. I recall the overpowering grief spilling out of me the night I created the ball of fire, the desperate yearning for my mother a few weeks ago when I grew a rose, my longing for Sebastian when I changed the colors in the Maze. *Heightened emotion.* That must be the trigger to my gift.

I squeeze my eyes shut, forcing my thoughts away from the fire in this room and back to the nightclub in Windsor. Swaying in Sebastian's arms, my head nestled beneath his chin, our faces nearly meeting—

My eyes fly open as the sizzling sensation returns to my hands. I watch in awe as tiny cracks begin to form in my fingertips—and water comes sprouting from them.

Teddy howls in shock as I move my hands over the wastebasket, the water from my fingers extinguishing the fire, until all that remains is a smoky aftermath. Teddy leaps into my arms, licking my face in relief.

"We're okay, buddy. We're okay." I hold his furry little body close, and after setting him down, I stare at my hands in wonder. They've returned to normal, the cracks are gone. What I've just done is completely insane . . . but also a miracle.

I lean over to peer into the wastebasket, which is filled with discarded papers—and a match. I stare at it with a jolt of panic. I certainly didn't put the match in there. Did someone deliberately try to set my room on fire?

I hear a knock at the door and stiffen, expecting Maisie. But to my relief, I find Oscar standing outside, clad in a robe and slippers.

"I'm so sorry to disturb you, Your Grace, but I heard all the barking and I thought—" He breaks off. "Is that *smoke*?"

"Yes, it is." I lead Oscar to the wastebasket, conscious of

my body trembling. "I think someone tried to set a fire in here. I suggest you question Mrs. Mulgrave and Maisie immediately."

❧

But Oscar can find no evidence that the Mulgraves had anything to do with the fire. The next day one of the housemaids, Betsy, comes to find me at afternoon tea, her face splotchy with tears.

"Your Grace, I can't even begin to tell you how sorry I am! I lit the fireplace in your room last night so it would be nice and warm when you got home, and I—I suppose I must have dropped the match without realizing? I had no idea, and I am so awfully sorry. To think what might have happened . . ." Her voice breaks off as she bursts into fresh tears.

"It's okay, Betsy," I assure her. "It wasn't your fault."

I'm definitely not convinced she was the one to drop the match anyway; my money is still on Mrs. Mulgrave or Maisie. One of them could have easily gone in and put the lit match in the wastebasket, knowing it would be blamed on Betsy. But without proof, there's nothing I can do. I'm forced to work alongside Mrs. Mulgrave in preparation for the Rockford Fireworks Concert while my suspicions continue to grow.

I wake up on the morning of the concert nauseous from nerves. My first event as hostess means having to meet countless new people, with all eyes on me, watching and judging whether I'm fit to be the face of Rockford Manor. At the same time, Sebastian and Theo are planning to attend with their parents, and I'm anxious for Sebastian's return to Rockford to go smoothly—and for my beer-laced admission to be forgotten.

The house is a sea of activity from the moment I get out of bed. The caterers have arrived and taken over the kitchen, while the orchestra follows on their heels and files outside to set up their bandstand. On the South Lawn beneath the Fountain Terrace, I find handymen laying a dance floor atop the grass, while footmen line the garden with buffet tables and set up smaller dining tables and chairs. The Fountain Terrace and the Rose Garden are strung with lights, while across the lake, the fireworks operators set up their aerial devices. Oscar and Mrs. Mulgrave are at the helm of the operation, surveying the work and calling out orders.

"Is there anything I can do?" I offer, making my way over to them.

Mrs. Mulgrave just stares at me, her dark gaze giving me the uneasy feeling that she knows I accused her of the fire. I quickly shift my focus to Oscar.

"Thank you, Your Grace, but I believe we have it all under control," Oscar says kindly.

"I guess I'll start getting ready then," I say, feeling a bit useless. "Everything looks amazing."

I take my time doing my hair and makeup, all too aware of the many photos that will be taken tonight. Maisie knocks on my door offering to help, but I tell her I prefer to get ready alone. Ever since the Stanhopes' dinner, I don't exactly trust her.

As I slip on my first couture dress, a red knee-length Alexander McQueen, I feel the sudden, unexpected sense of belonging in this role. Glancing in the mirror, I realize that I look like an actual duchess—and for the first time, I feel like one too.

The first guests arrive at four o'clock, and before long the lawn and gardens are filled with Wickersham locals, the children playing organized games in the Rose Garden, while their parents sip champagne and feast on hors d'oeuvres. I stand under a flower arch Max built for the occasion, greeting each guest, shaking hands and smiling until I think my cheeks might fall off. Though it's definitely tedious, I find I'm happy. Everyone is so sweet and excited to meet me that I feel humbled, and grateful to be here.

As the hour reaches six, I spot a familiar group heading toward me. My stomach flutters as I watch Sebastian's confident stride. He is gorgeous in his suit, and I'm reminded of one of Carole Marino's favorite phrases: "too handsome for his own good."

"You've done a beautiful job," Lady Stanhope says, after we exchange greetings. "Rockford looks magnificent."

"Oh, well, I didn't have much to do with it," I admit. "It's great to see you all."

I glance at Sebastian, and he gives me a grin that makes my heart leap. Maybe my words at the pub haven't ruined things between us after all.

Dinner is served, at seven, and I'm finally able to give my feet a rest. I join the Stanhopes' table, making shy conversation with his parents and joking around with Theo—but

Sebastian is quiet. I imagine he must be seeing visions of Lucia everywhere he looks, remembering past fireworks concerts here with her, and the thought brings an ache to my chest. At one point, Mrs. Mulgrave and Maisie walk together past the lawn, and I watch as they both stop and stare at Sebastian. Are they, too, recalling memories of him and Lucia together?

At last, it's time for the main event. The guests make their way toward the lake for the best view of the fireworks, while the band starts up a rousing rendition of "Rule Britannia." And that's when I feel Sebastian gently take my hand.

I turn around, suddenly short of breath as I look up at him.

"Come with me?" he asks.

I can do nothing but nod. No one seems to notice as we drift away from the crowd, finding a hiding place beneath a tall oak tree on the opposite side of the lake. We're close enough to see the fireworks, but too far away to be heard.

"I'm not sure where to begin," he says, the moonlight casting a glow against his green eyes. "I've been wondering for two days now, and I just had to come out and ask you. . . . Did you mean what you said the other night?"

I swallow hard.

"Um. God, this is embarrassing. . . ."

"Don't be embarrassed." Sebastian takes my hand again, and looks beseechingly into my eyes. "You can probably guess why I'm asking."

I shake my head.

"You already know, don't you?" I manage a nervous smile. "You've known since we were kids. I could never hide my feelings well."

"I guessed how you felt then," he says quietly. "But I'm not as sure now."

"I've loved you since I was a little girl," I whisper. "I never stopped. But I know you can never feel the same, and I understand. Lucia was the one for you and I could never take her place—I know that."

I realize I'm on the verge of tears, and I turn to hide my face from his, slightly in shock over my own confession.

I feel his hand touch my cheek, gently pulling my face toward his.

"I have to tell you something," he says in a low voice. "My relationship with Lucia . . . it wasn't all everyone thought."

"What do you mean?" I ask, my face still burning from my big reveal.

"I—I didn't love her."

I stare at him uncomprehendingly. I must have misheard.

"She changed, or maybe I did too, but . . . it turned out she wasn't the girl I wanted to be with. I held on because of the bond we once had as kids, but it just wasn't the same when we got older. Every time I tried to end it, she reminded me of our history and made me feel like an arse for trying to leave her. My parents, too, were so attached to the idea of us ending up together, and our families uniting. I was trapped in our relationship, unable to get out without hurting people I cared about. Then, when she died and everyone felt so awful for me, I—I couldn't stand myself. I felt like a fraud. Because the truth was, we stopped being a real couple long before she died."

He breathes a deep sigh, as if a weight has been lifted off his chest.

"You didn't . . . love her?" I echo in disbelief.

"I never did." Sebastian inches closer. "But I think I'm falling in love with you."

Stunned, I open my mouth to speak. But before I can say a word, his lips are on mine, our mouths are moving together, and I have never felt anything like this before. He pulls me closer to him as he buries his face in my hair and brushes his lips across my neck. I let out a gasp of pleasure.

As if on cue, the first display of fireworks explodes in the air. The crowd cheers, and Sebastian and I turn to face the sky, our arms still wrapped around each other. My heart soars, my mind replaying his words: "I think I'm falling in love with you." It's everything I dreamed of but never dared to expect.

Our moment of bliss is interrupted by the sounds and sights of a sudden skirmish down by the lake. Two men bulldoze their way through the throng of guests, waving something in the air and parting crowds in their wake. The orchestra abruptly stops playing.

"What's going on?" I ask Sebastian.

He shakes his head.

"I can't tell."

And then we see Theo, gasping as he runs toward us, his eyes wild.

"Sebastian!" he hisses, ignoring me altogether. "You have to get out of here *now*."

"Why? What's going on?" Sebastian asks.

"The police are looking for you," Theo says, his voice wobbling in panic.

"The police? Why would they be looking for *you*?" I stare at Sebastian in confusion.

But we're too late. The two men we saw across the lake

are officers, the object they're waving in the air is an arrest warrant—and they've just found us.

The world moves in slow motion as the officers tackle Sebastian, cuffing his wrists.

"You can't do this!" I hear myself scream. "This is my house—you shouldn't be here! He's done nothing wrong, let him go!"

But the officers pay me no attention, and as I look at Sebastian in terror, it strikes me that *he doesn't look surprised.* What could he have done?

"Sebastian Stanhope, you are under arrest for the murder of Lucia Rockford."

"What?" I scream. *"What?"*

Sebastian stares at me, shaking his head.

"Ginny, I can explain—"

"It was an accident!" I shriek to the officers. "She wasn't murdered."

"I'm afraid we have new information that proves otherwise," the first officer says, before turning back to Sebastian. "Anything you do or say may be given in evidence—"

And suddenly my vision blurs, my legs buckle, as Sebastian cries out my name.

PART III

The dark side of the British peerage was exposed tonight. At half-past eight, Lord Sebastian Stanhope of Great Milton, was arrested for the murder of his girlfriend, the late Marchioness of Wickersham, Lucia Rockford. Stanhope was taken to the Oxford County Jail, and it is unclear whether he will be allowed bail. Said arrest took place amidst the Rockford Fireworks Concert, causing the hostess, Duchess Imogen Rockford, to fall into a shock.

A spokesman for the Stanhope family insists, "This has been a grievous mistake. Sebastian Stanhope is innocent and will most certainly be proven so." Meanwhile, the Rockford spokesperson simply states, "The Duchess of Wickersham and her staff are cooperating with the investigation."

This is a terrible and disturbing business for all involved. One can only wonder how the seventeen-year-old duchess—rumored to have grown close to Stanhope—is coping with the revelation about her cousin's deadly end.

XIII

"Your Grace? I spoke to the police officer. He agreed to return for your statement tomorrow."

Oscar's voice draws me out of my thoughts and back into the present.

"How—how long were you gone?" I ask, my voice dry from lack of use.

"Only twenty minutes, Your Grace."

I shake my head. It seems impossible that he only just left the drawing room, when my mind has relived days, months, and years in the short time he's been away.

I turn to glance out the window. Members of the household staff are outside clearing the gardens, removing all traces of the party that was so suddenly halted by Sebastian's arrest. But two key figures are missing.

"Are you sure I shouldn't call the doctor?" Oscar watches me with concern. "You seem to be in an awful state."

"I don't need a doctor—I need to know why this is happening." I look up at Oscar in dismay. "He didn't kill her. He couldn't have. Why would they pin this on him? Why do they even *think* she was murdered, when everyone knows it was an accident?"

Oscar takes a deep breath, lowering his eyes to the floor.

"If you know something, Oscar, you have to tell me," I plead. "Now. Please."

He slumps onto the seat beside me, his face ashen.

"It all happened so fast. One minute we were enjoying the concert, and the next thing I knew, the two officers were there, banging at the gates. They had a warrant out for Sebastian's arrest, and I had no choice but to let them in. Apparently . . ." He clears his throat. "An anonymous witness came forward—someone who was too frightened to say anything before, who claimed family pressure kept them from speaking up. The witness recalled seeing Lucia walking to the Maze the night she died—but someone was *with* her. Sebastian Stanhope. And they appeared to be fighting.

"The autopsy report determined that Lady Lucia was killed by the force of a blunt object to the head and the assumption before tonight was that she hit her head on the stone pillar where her body was found," Oscar continues grimly. "But in light of the new information that Sebastian was reportedly seen with Lucia that night, the police obtained a warrant to search Stanhope Abbey earlier this afternoon. In the Stanhopes' garden shed, they found a polo stick with traces of Lucia's blood, and Sebastian's own fingerprints."

I begin to shake violently, my knees knocking together. His

words earlier tonight, so welcome at the time, now come back to haunt me. *"I didn't love her. . . . I never did."*

"There has to be another explanation. There's no way he did it. Sebastian is *good.* He could never hurt anyone—"

I break off as I remember the incident with the statuette weeks ago, the way his temper exploded out of nowhere. And his interest in helping me through the Maze . . . Could he have been looking for something himself? Like evidence that pointed to him being Lucia's killer?

Have I misjudged Sebastian completely—and fallen in love with a monster?

Against my will, images from tonight whir together in my mind with scenes from the past, set to the music we danced to at the bar. *"Since you went away, the days grow long . . ."*

I close my eyes, remembering Sebastian kissing my cheek as a child, and kissing me passionately on the lips this evening. Playing together in the gardens as kids, and dancing together in Windsor all these years later. His hand on my waist in the Maze, his gaze full of warmth. *"But I miss you most of all, my darling, when autumn leaves start to fall."*

I rise to my feet, emboldened by my memories. Sebastian is no cold-blooded killer. There's more to this story. I know it. And just like he believed in me all those years ago when I trusted him with my secret . . . it's my turn to believe in him.

"I'm going to my room," I tell Oscar. "I need to be alone."

Without giving him a chance to reply, I turn and hurry out the door. As I reach the Marble Hall, I freeze at the sight of Mrs. Mulgrave descending the grand staircase. Her usually pallid face is splotched with red, her eyes grotesquely swollen. She's been crying.

I slip behind a statue so I can watch Mrs. Mulgrave unseen. Surely there's only one thing that could have caused this formidable woman to break: the news that Lucia might have been murdered. I'm torn as I watch her, part of me sympathizing with her attachment to my cousin, while the other part of me shudders at the sight of this possessed-looking woman, her expression dark enough to kill. And then a thought occurs to me.

I've never once seen Mrs. Mulgrave behave in such a devoted, attached manner to her actual daughter. I rack my brain, trying to remember an instance of warmth between them, a hug or a kind word—but nothing comes to mind. Mrs. Mulgrave seems almost indifferent to her. Is Maisie a disappointment to her mother, for some reason? Did Mrs. Mulgrave love Lucia more? And did Maisie know she was second in her mother's heart?

My stomach lurches as I wonder . . . Is it possible *Maisie* could be the one who had it in for Lucia all along?

I wait for Mrs. Mulgrave to cross the hall into the next room, before thundering up the stairs to my bedroom. I am certain the Mulgraves played some sort of role in what happened to Lucia—and now it's up to me to find out what.

Instead of going to bed that night, I sit at my desk, waiting for all the household sounds to quiet and till I'm sure no one else could still be awake. Finally, at three a.m., I tiptoe out of my bedroom and steal through the halls, crossing over to the west wing when I reach the stairs.

My heart hammers in my chest as I slowly make my way toward Lucia's bedroom; I feel as frightened as if I'm opening the lid to her coffin. I almost expect to find her ghost there, sitting in plain sight on the bed, or gazing into the mirror. But when I finally step into her room and my shaking fingers switch on the light, it's empty. The bedroom looks serene and utterly normal, as if its owner is simply away on vacation and will return any day now.

Her bed stands in the center of the room, perfectly made up, with crisp linens and monogrammed pillowcases. A white nightgown and matching satin robe are folded on her pillow, with a pair of slippers on the floor beside the bed. Every indication points to the person who inhabited this room still being among the living. Fresh flowers spill out of crystal vases on Lucia's bedside table, above the fireplace, and on the corner of her desk. I shudder at the realization that Mrs. Mulgrave must be changing her flowers every day. What a macabre ritual.

Lucia's hairbrush, perfume, and makeup are arranged in orderly fashion on her vanity, and it's then that I recognize the jasmine scent that has been wafting in and out of my bedroom over the past weeks. The scent is *her perfume*.

I look around the beautiful but creepy bedroom, my legs trembling as I wonder where to begin my search. Thanks to Oscar, I know Mrs. Mulgrave keeps Lucia's room exactly as it was before she died, and I'm certain she hasn't thrown anything out. So the question is, where will I find the smoking gun?

I check the desk drawers first, but they are surprisingly low on anything personal, filled instead with all of her Oxford textbooks and binders. I try her walk-in closet next, but all I find are hangers upon hangers of stale-smelling, expensive-looking clothes.

Think, Imogen, I instruct myself. *Where would I choose to hide my most personal possessions?*

And with a flash, I remember. Eleven-year-old Lucia in summer 2006, honoring me with the knowledge of where she kept her diary as she pulled it from its hiding place to read me the bit about the boy who chased her in the schoolyard for a kiss.

I race back to the bed, digging my hand between the mattress and bed frame. There is no longer a diary tucked away, but my fingers close around a small, cold object. Just as I'm about to consider my mission complete, my hand hits a wad of papers. Adrenaline floods my veins as I pull the items out from under the mattress.

The cold object turns out to be a bronze locket. I pry it open, and what I see inside causes me to let out a cry of shock.

I know the couple in the photo. The man is Lucia's father, my uncle Charles. But instead of Aunt Philippa, the woman leaning in to kiss his cheek in the photo is none other than— *Mrs. Mulgrave.* She is a much younger, far better-looking Mrs. Mulgrave, but there's no denying that it's her.

I can't look away from the photo; I'm struck by how different she is. This isn't the ghoulish, sullen Mrs. Mulgrave I'm used to, but an attractive young woman with bright eyes and flushed cheeks.

What changed her so terribly? Could she have been in love

with my uncle Charles? Did his death destroy her? And why would Lucia have kept this incriminating photo of her father's affair tucked in a locket? Unless . . . ? I gasp at the thought but just as quickly dismiss it. There's no way Lucia could have been the product of the affair. When we were little she was the spitting image of Aunt Philippa, and my aunt adored her the way any mother would love their firstborn. So had Lucia held on to the locket as some kind of ammunition against her father? None of it makes any sense.

I set the locket down in confusion and pick up the stack of papers. Looking closer, I see that they're letters, all bearing the same handwriting. I begin reading the letter at the top of the stack, dated one year ago—two days before Lucia died.

October 23, 2013

Dear Lucia,

I'm going bloody mad over what you put me through yesterday. I don't think I can stand it any longer. I can't pretend anymore. I'm going to tell the truth.

You asked me to prove my love for you, and I have, over and over again. I would do anything to be with you. Whatever it takes. Now it's your turn.

Yours,
Theo

"Theo?" I yelp.

That can't be right. I frantically skim the rest of the letters, all of them from the year of her death, and each one more obsessive than the next. They all end with the same signature, marked by a swooping T.

My thoughts race, the pieces coming together in my mind. Lucia and Theo were seeing each other behind Sebastian's back. Theo sent her a series of pleading, lovesick letters. And suddenly, Maisie no longer seems like a prime suspect.

If someone did kill Lucia . . . was it *Theo*? Were these letters some sort of threat? Or could Sebastian have found out that his girlfriend was cheating on him with his own brother, and flown into a deadly rage?

An icy fist closes around my heart as I realize that the odds are pointing to one of them—the boy I love, the friend I cherish. One of them is guilty. And I owe it to my cousin to find out the truth.

❦

I wake up in the morning with a jolt, roused from my sleep by the loud ringing of my cell. Theo's letters to Lucia are strewn across my bed, and I'm still wearing my formal dress from the ill-fated party. I don't even remember having fallen asleep.

"Hello?" I answer, groggily.

"Imogen, darling!" comes Carole's panicked voice. "Thank God you're all right!"

"Why wouldn't I be?"

"It's been all over the news here—your cousin's murderer arrested at your party!" Carole sobs. "I knew I should never have let you go back to Rockford. Keith and I just booked our flight. We'll be there tomorrow to bring you home."

"You *what?*" I sit upright. "Wait—you've got it all wrong. Sebastian didn't kill anyone. At least, we don't know for sure. I need to be here, I don't want to go back."

"Well, the police changed their ruling on Lucia's death to homicide. So if Sebastian didn't do it, then that means there's a murderer at large. Either way, how could you want to stay there?" Carole frets.

"Because—because—" I grasp for the words to explain that I'm tied to all three of the players in this mess, that I'm tied to the manor, and I can't leave until I know what really happened and why. "I can't explain everything now, but I promise you I'm safe. You don't need to worry."

"I'll be the judge of that when I see you tomorrow. Our flight gets in at ten a.m."

"Oh . . . okay."

I close my eyes and lean against the headboard. I do miss Carole and Keith, but now couldn't be a worse time for them to visit. Figuring out how to solve the mystery of Lucia's death is going to be hard enough, but doing so under their watchful eyes will be next to impossible.

"After all you've been through, this was the last thing you needed," Carole continues. "Lauren's mother gave me the name of a new therapist who she's heard wonderful things about, and I'd really like for you to give her a chance—"

"Please, no more therapists," I moan. And then I gasp, remembering the clue I've completely forgotten about.

Lucia had seen a psychiatrist. What was his name? Something about a bird . . . Dr. . . . Dr. Heron! She might have gone to him until the very end. And if so, he could hold the answer.

"I have to go," I tell Carole breathlessly. "I'll see you when you get here."

As soon as I hang up, I race to my computer and Google "Dr. Heron, London psychiatrist." I hold my breath as I dial the number that pops up on the screen.

"Dr. Heron's office," a woman's voice answers briskly.

"Can I speak to him please?" I burst out. "It's urgent. Seriously urgent."

This time when she speaks, her voice takes on a slow and sweet "I'm talking to a mental patient" tone.

"May I ask who's calling?"

"It's Imogen Rockford." Then, realizing I might need to call in the big guns, I add, "The Duchess of Wickersham."

"Is that so?" she asks skeptically.

"I swear. You can call the listed number on the Rockford Manor website and someone on the staff will come get me, if you need proof."

"That won't be necessary . . . Your Grace," she allows. "But I'm afraid Dr. Heron is with a patient now."

I want to scream.

"Please, can't you do something to—to get his attention? I'm telling you, it's urgent. Surely you must have read about my cousin in the papers."

"I did," she says soberly. "I'm very sorry for your loss. But I'm under no circumstances allowed to interrupt the doctor during a session. He should be wrapping up in ten minutes, however, and I'll do my best to see that he calls you back immediately."

I spend the next fifteen minutes pacing back and forth, returning to my old nail-biting habit, until my cell phone rings with an unfamiliar UK number.

"Hello?" I practically yell into the phone.

"Is this Her Grace, Imogen Rockford?" a pleasant man's voice responds.

"Yes! Are you Dr. Heron?"

"I am. How can I help you, Your Grace?"

There's no smooth intro for a conversation like this. I have to just come right out with it.

"I know my cousin Lucia used to be a patient of yours. And now the police are saying she was murdered, which I—I just can't wrap my head around. Please, can you tell me . . . everything you know? Did she have any secrets, any enemies?"

Dr. Heron clears his throat.

"Your cousin is protected by the doctor-patient confidentiality agreement. I'm afraid I can't tell you anything about my sessions with her."

"But—but—someone is being charged with *murder*!" I sputter. "Isn't there a rule that you have to speak out when it comes to life and death?"

"If I knew anything, I assure you I would have called the police long ago," Dr. Heron says. "But the fact is, I haven't seen Lucia in seven years. I don't think any information I have would be of any use at this point."

I freeze.

"You stopped seeing her the year of the fire? Wasn't that when she needed you the most?"

"I would agree with you on that point, Your Grace, but she chose to end her sessions after the fire. And without her parents to insist on her continuing treatment, there was no way to force her."

"But what about my grandfather?" I ask, perplexed. "Wouldn't he have encouraged her to keep seeing you?"

Dr. Heron sighs heavily.

"Your poor grandfather was overwhelmed by his own grief. He chose to ship Lucia off to boarding school in Switzerland."

My jaw drops.

"He just abandoned her? After she lost her *parents*?"

"Not entirely. He sent the housekeeper with her as a chaperone, and the housekeeper's daughter as a companion of some sort." He pauses. "Shouldn't you know all this?"

"I—we lost touch," I murmur, my mind still reeling from his words. Our grandfather sent Lucia to Switzerland with the Mulgraves. . . . Why did no one ever mention this to me?

"Thank you, Dr. Heron," I say shakily. "Please don't hesitate to call if you think of anything."

As soon as I hang up, I send Oscar a text.

> Please instruct Mrs. Mulgrave and Maisie to meet me
> in the library in five minutes.

Five minutes pass and then ten, with no sign of Mrs. Mulgrave or Maisie. But as I stand to leave the library and hunt them down myself, the door opens. Mrs. Mulgrave and a stone-faced Maisie step inside.

"You wanted to see us?" Mrs. Mulgrave says, in a voice devoid of emotion.

"Yes. Please sit." I wait till they're both seated stiffly on the hard-backed sofa. "You heard the news about Sebastian."

"Wretched business," Maisie murmurs, lowering her eyes.

"The thing is, I don't believe it. And if you knew Sebastian like I think you do, then you wouldn't believe it either."

"I saw the way he was cavorting with you last night," Mrs. Mulgrave hisses. "Is that how a grieving boyfriend behaves?"

I'm momentarily stunned into silence.

"Please don't forget that you're working in my home," I say when I find my voice, surprising myself with the sharp edge to my tone. "You have no right to speak about me or my friends in that way."

"And what do you say to the evidence found at Stanhope Abbey?" Mrs. Mulgrave challenges, as if she didn't hear me. "You can defend him after that?"

"Evidence can be faked and planted. Haven't you ever seen *Law and Order*?"

Mrs. Mulgrave stares blankly at me.

"Anyway, I asked you here for two reasons. First, can you think of anyone who might have had it in for Lucia?" I look closely at Maisie. "Anyone she was close to who might have been dangerous?"

Maisie shakes her head.

"Only Sebastian Stanhope," Mrs. Mulgrave says crisply.

I exhale in frustration.

"And what about the trip to Switzerland that you took with Lucia after the fire?"

Their reaction to my question is palpable; it catches me off guard. Mrs. Mulgrave's face twists into an expression I've never seen before, vastly different from her usual haughty, controlled demeanor. She looks almost . . . afraid. And Maisie's hand flies to the plain pendant around her neck, as if checking to make sure it's still there.

"Well?" I persist. "Since when does a student bring a housekeeper and a companion to boarding school with her? You have to admit it's unusual. And why did I never know about it?"

"Is this a trick?" Maisie blurts out, eyes darting to her mother.

"What do you mean, a trick?" I ask, bewildered.

Mrs. Mulgrave gives Maisie a sharp look and then takes a breath.

"There's nothing to it, Your Grace," she says regaining her smooth tone. "We simply accompanied Lady Lucia at her grandfather's request, to help ease her loneliness after the deaths of her parents. And I'm sure you'll recall that you were not a part of your cousin's life after the fire. How could you expect to have been informed?"

"We hadn't been apart that long when you guys left. She wanted me to stay at Rockford, to visit—she would have told me if she was going away," I insist.

"Well, then I daresay you misunderstood her wishes," Mrs. Mulgrave says curtly.

"What did you mean before, Maisie?" I ask, turning my attention to her. "Do you know something that could help me figure out what happened to Lucia?"

Maisie hesitates for the slightest second before shaking her head firmly.

"No, Your Grace."

"Then that will be all."

I watch the Mulgraves leave the room, drained from trying to pull answers out of them. My mind spins with the names of the suspects. Theo. Maisie. Mrs. Mulgrave . . . Sebastian.

I can't keep wondering what Sebastian does or doesn't know, what he did or didn't do. I have to talk to him.

XIV

I keep my eyes trained on the ground, tucking my face into the collar of a trench coat, as I walk the long mile from Rockford Manor's front door to its gates. I cringe every time my shoes crunch against the leaves or gravel, panicking that I'll blow my cover and turn around to find Oscar—or worse, one of the Mulgraves—behind me, reminding me that I'm not allowed to go anywhere, not when the police are coming to collect my statement.

I try to shake the nagging thought that I'm doing something wrong. After all, it's now or never. Once the protective Marinos arrive tomorrow, there's no chance of my being able to slip off alone to the home of a presumed murderer.

Murderer. I shudder at the word. It can't be Sebastian—it can't. My stomach lurches as I try to imagine the confrontation ahead of me. Will he or Theo become violent when I reveal the letters? Will I be the next victim? But as quickly as I envision Sebastian's hands closing around my neck and shutting out my breath, I remember the sigh of his lips against my cheek, the softness of his arms around mine. And I know that whatever he might have done . . . he won't hurt me.

I haven't been able to reach him on his cell, but the *Telegraph* website reported he was out on astronomically high bail and under house arrest until a pending court date. All I can do is hope the reporter is right—and that I'll be able to see Sebastian today.

I give the cabdriver the address for one of the Stanhopes' neighbors, then jog all the way up to the Stanhope Abbey gate. The footman who answers the door looks pale and weary, as if he got about as much sleep as I did last night.

"Your Grace," he says dully. "I'm afraid Lords Sebastian and Theo are not allowed visitors at this time."

"Please," I beg. "Can't you just . . . try? I've come all this way, and it's urgent."

"I'll speak to her ladyship and see what I can do," he says with a sigh.

I wait anxiously in the entrance hall for what feels like ages. The person who finally comes out to meet me is not Sebastian or Theo, but Lady Stanhope. I've never seen her look anything less than polished, and it sends a shiver through me to see her hunched over, eyes red-rimmed.

"Your Grace," she murmurs, unable to make eye contact. "How can I help you?"

"I was hoping to see Sebastian and Theo." I give her an imploring look. "I'm trying to help, honestly."

"That's very kind of you, dear, but our lawyer has instructed all of us not to speak with anyone."

"But—"

"I'm sorry," she says firmly. "Is your driver waiting, or would you like me to call you a car?"

There's no arguing with her, I can see that much. I think quickly.

"No, I—he's coming to get me. I'll just wait outside."

"Thank you," she says quietly. "Goodbye, Lady Imogen."

I head outside, racking my brain over what to do. I can't just turn back and go home now. Slowly, I walk the perimeter in front of the house, staring up at the windows. And then I see his face against the glass, in one of the rooms on the second story. Sebastian is watching me through an opening in the curtains, his expression grim as he raises his hand in greeting.

I notice the tall beech tree hovering above his window—and I get a slightly crazy idea. I've never been the athletic, tree-climbing type, but maybe now with my Elemental power, I can do it?

With a deep breath, I sprint toward the tree and jump onto its lowest-hanging branch. It isn't until I'm struggling to inch my way up the trunk that I realize my gift is likely only tied to the Rockford land. After all, I never had access to my powers in New York.

Sebastian throws open his window and reaches for me. In the most ungraceful maneuver imaginable, I flail toward him from my shaky perch on the tree branch and he grabs my waist, hoisting me through the window. I topple in straight on top of him.

"Ouch," I groan as my forehead hits the wall. I glance down, and realize he is lying underneath me—which would be pretty hot if it weren't for the multitude of fears swirling through my mind. I scramble to my feet. "I'm sorry. I just—I had to talk to you."

"I can see that," he says, trying to smile as he pulls himself up.

I look around. I am in Sebastian's bedroom, which is surprisingly clean for a college guy. The furniture is all masculine dark wood, and his walls are adorned with a combination of modern art and framed polo memorabilia. I feel a wave of sadness. At any other time, I would have been thrilled to find myself in here. But everything is different now.

"Are you here to ask if I'm guilty?" he says quietly.

I glance at the door, wondering how much time we have before one of his parents comes in to check on him.

"I don't even know where to begin. But last night I went looking in Lucia's room for evidence, something that could prove your innocence. I found something, but I'm not sure if you already know about it. And if you don't, I'm afraid you might not want to hear it."

"What did you find, Ginny?" he asks urgently.

I pull the stack of letters out of my cross-body purse.

"Letters to Lucia from Theo. They were seeing each other behind your back. And from the tone of the letters, I—well, anyone could sense a motive."

Sebastian grabs the letters. The color drains from his face as he rifles through them, and then he stops and stares numbly at the top missive.

"Sebastian? Please say something."

"I already knew," he says. "I've known for a long time. But you have to promise me you won't ever say a word to anyone else."

"What?" I yelp. "Your brother went behind your back with your girlfriend and maybe even *killed* her, and you're going to take the fall for him?"

Sebastian stands as still as a statue, silent for what seems like forever.

"Everything I'm about to tell you stays between us," he finally says.

"Okay . . ." I sit down on the bed, and he sits beside me.

"There were rumors, in the months before Lucia died, that she was cheating on me," he begins. "I confronted her about it when I tried to break up with her, I asked her why she even wanted to stay together if she had someone else—but she always denied it, and I never had any proof. But I did know one person who was once infatuated with her. Someone who was hurt when she and I got together."

"Theo?" I guess.

Sebastian nods.

"I didn't take his feelings seriously enough. I figured she was just one of the many girls he was into. I didn't realize until—until after she died, that he'd been in love with her. Or at least, he thought he was."

"So what happened?"

Sebastian sighs heavily.

"The day Lucia died, she sent a text to me and Theo. She wrote that there was something she had to tell us both, and to meet her outside the Maze that night at nine. That's when I knew that my own brother was the guy she was seeing on the side. I figured that night she was planning to make some sort of confession to me, and then tell us who she wanted to be with. By that point, we hadn't been romantic in ages—our relationship was pretty much only for show—and I felt relieved at the thought of being free. To be honest, the only reason I bothered going to the Maze that night was for Theo—to support him, in case she hurt him in any way."

"You mean you weren't mad at him?" I gape at Sebastian. "Even if you were technically over Lucia, he didn't know that, right? He still *betrayed* you."

Sebastian shakes his head.

"You could say the same about me. I went out with the girl my little brother liked. I didn't realize I was hurting him, but I was. And the truth is, Theo's always gotten the short end of the stick in our family. Ever since he was born, he knew it was all about the heir. Me." Sebastian grimaces. "And then the one thing I found that I loved to do, polo, brought even more attention to me, and less to Theo. I think it all just . . . messed him up. And I let it happen."

I take his hand.

"It's not your fault. None of this is."

Sebastian looks away.

"A huge storm broke that night, and it made driving miserable. I was late leaving Oxford, and when I made it to the Maze . . ." He shuts his eyes.

"What?" I urge him on. "What did you see?"

"I saw Lucia lying there, lifeless and covered in blood," he whispers. "Theo was crying hysterically over her body. My polo mallet was next to him on the ground."

I cover my mouth in horror. My heart breaks for Lucia—and for the brothers I always believed were the good guys.

"He—he *planned* to hurt her, then?" I ask, my voice shaking. "Why else would he have brought your polo stick?"

"No!" Sebastian says emphatically. "There's no way Theo would have planned it. This was a retired polo stick that I'd signed and given to Lucia back in the beginning—in better times. Theo must have found it at Rockford Manor, and when he got angry . . . it became a weapon."

"So—so he really killed her, then? What did he say? Why did he do it?"

"He didn't say anything; he didn't have to. It was obvious to me what happened. And I knew Lucia. She wasn't the same kid you remember from before, Ginny. When she came back from boarding school, she had this darker side to her. She could sometimes say the sharpest, cruelest things," Sebastian tells me. "I think Lucia said something to brutally hurt Theo—and he hit her without realizing what he was doing. My brother's not a violent person. He was a complete wreck that night. All I could do was keep telling him it was okay, that it—it looked like an accident, and if anyone should find out it wasn't, I would take the fall." Sebastian's voice lowers, and for a moment it sounds like he's trying to convince himself. "He's not a killer. This was a—a horrible fluke."

"But how could you cover it up? Why didn't you just explain to the police what happened right away? Then you wouldn't be in this mess now." I look at him helplessly.

"Because I love my brother," Sebastian says simply. "I couldn't let him go to jail. Not when it all could have been prevented if I'd only taken better care of him, and if I'd had nothing to do with Lucia in the first place."

His eyes lock with mine. "I know I've made mistakes, Ginny. Do you think you can ever forgive me? For what happened to your cousin?"

"I don't blame you," I tell him. "And I can't stand to see you shoulder all the blame for what Theo's done."

"I know, but you'll have to," Sebastian says. "Promise me you won't tell anyone about Theo."

"I don't think I've ever known anyone so loyal," I say, staring at him. "You're really willing to face jail for Theo's crime?"

"I know it sounds mad, but . . . if you had a younger sibling, you might understand."

My mind flashes to Zoey's smiling face. I would jump in front of a car, I would take a bullet to save her if I had to. Is this any different?

"I get it," I say softly, tears springing to my eyes. "I wish I could talk you out of it, but I understand."

His fingers interlace with mine.

"In case I don't see you for a long time . . ." He swallows hard. "Will you do something for me?"

"Anything," I tell him.

"Kiss me," he whispers.

Tears spill down my cheeks as I wrap my arms around his neck. I kiss his lips softly at first, then hungrily, as he lowers me onto the bed. His mouth brushes across my neck and kisses my tears as I hold him tighter.

"I love you, Ginny," he murmurs into my hair. "I should have known it was always going to be you."

"I love you too." I lean forward, looking him in the eye. "I've never stopped, and I never will."

The sound of footsteps echoes outside the door, and Sebastian hastily pulls me to my feet. He leads me to the window, and we kiss one last time before he helps me out onto the tree. As we say goodbye, I see countless emotions play across his face. I don't know if I'll ever again see anything so beautiful . . . or painful.

⁊⁓

During the cab ride back to Rockford, I find myself silently repeating *Theo killed Lucia* over and over, to make it seem more real. But something is nagging at me; a voice in the back of my mind tells me it doesn't all add up, that there's something I'm missing. Yet I can't put my finger on what it is.

My phone buzzes with a new message. I retrieve it from my purse, and find an email from the Bodleian Library.

> *We are pleased to inform you that the book you requested* [The Unearthly Duchess: A Biography, *by Humphrey Fitzwilliam*] *is now available and reserved under your name in the Special Collections Reading Room.*

"Sir," I call out to the cabdriver. "Change of plans. Can you drop me off at the Bodleian Library instead?"

With a grumble, the driver swerves into the Oxford exit lane. I glance at the time on my phone screen and bite my lip nervously. It's already been a couple of hours since I left Rockford Manor, and I imagine I'll be at least that long at the library, since I'm not allowed to take the book off the premises. I'll have to skim the book as quickly as I can—and hope I make it home before the police arrive to collect my statement.

The cabbie drops me off in front of a massive, fortresslike

building in the middle of Oxford's green quadrangles. I push my way past the groups of tourists oohing, aahing, and taking photos on their phones and iPads and hurry inside, following the signs to the Special Collections Reading Room.

A simply decorated chamber awaits behind the closed door, filled with long wooden tables lined with desk lamps at each seat. Bookshelves reach to the ceiling, and a middle-aged librarian sits at a counter behind the reading tables, supervising the small handful of students perusing textbooks and scribbling furiously.

"Hello," I say as I approach the librarian. "I'm Imogen Rockford. There should be a book waiting for me here, *The Unearthly Duchess*."

The librarian's eyebrows rise as she looks me over.

"Ah. Welcome to the Bodleian, Your Grace." She reaches into a shelf behind her desk, and hands me a thin volume covered in protective binding, along with a magnifying glass. "You'll find the font size much smaller than we're used to in modern times. Now, I must remind you that you are not to leave this room without first returning the book. I also need to see your ID. It's standard procedure for any of our valuable books and artifacts."

After handing over my ID and promising to obey the multitude of rules, I settle into a seat at an empty corner of one of the reading tables. Holding my breath in anticipation, I open the book.

The pages are thin and delicate, the font as small as the librarian promised. I hold the magnifying glass up to the first page and am surprised by the warmth flooding my chest as I begin to read about my ancestor. It feels as if some undiscovered part of me was looking for her all along.

> Imagine that you are just a teenager from America, chosen to be a duchess. The adjustment would be quite an undertaking on its own, but add to that a supernatural gift, and it is no wonder Her Grace Lady Beatrice struggled immeasurably in her time at Wickersham.

My spine stiffens. This is sounding awfully familiar. The biographer might have been writing about . . . me.

I quickly flip to the table of contents, scanning the chapter titles. The book covers the length of Lady Beatrice's short life and includes chapters with such soapy headings as "Scandals and Country Terrors." But the one that interests me the most is Chapter 7: "The Elementals."

> Lady Beatrice insisted that she was no witch, but an Elemental. This is an unfamiliar term to most, but certainly not one invented by the late duchess. References to Elementalism are found as far back as in Greek mythology and Ancient Egyptian writings.
>
> An Elemental is known as a child of nature. Unlike mere humans, they are one with the four elements, able to manipulate the air, earth, water, and fire around them. There are those who find it a frightening concept, but I have interviewed two of the late duchess's acquaintances who profess

that she used her gift for good. A Wickersham tenant farmer who was growing destitute from the lack of thriving crops recalls that Lady Beatrice visited his land, and shortly after her departure, the soil came back to life and grew fertile. I of course asked the man in question why he did not come forward with his testimony when Lady Beatrice stood on the gallows. He insists that he tried, but no one cared for the testimony of a peasant farmer against the word of the furious duke. . . .

I lift my eyes from the page, relief washing over me. My father was right. Lady Beatrice was no villain. And that means . . . neither am I.

The late duchess wore around one finger a diamond icicle band, known as a water-stone in Elemental mythology. There is no definite word on where Lady Beatrice procured the water-stone, but legend has it that the stone appears to those who belong to it—those who are Elemental. My studies of Elementalism suggest that wearing the ring is a form of communicating with nature.

Aristotle noted long ago that "with the water-stone on your skin and your hands on the land, you will have the answer to all you seek." The water-stone is said to work with the hand of an Elemental to use the four elements to his or her advantage. And seeing as the elements are the truth of our world, so the water-stone *reveals* the truth.

The water-stone reveals the truth. . . . What exactly does that mean?

> The only time Lady Beatrice was seen without the water-stone was on the night of her hanging. She professed to have buried it where only her true descendant could find it. If she is to be believed, and there is a "true descendant," then the second coming of Lady Beatrice will be upon us.

I let out a slow exhale as my mind spins. I know what I need to do.

I'll return to Rockford and deal with the police, and the Marinos' visit—but the earliest chance I get, I'm going back to the Maze. It's time to find the water-stone.

XV

I struggle to sleep that night, my mind busy rehashing my visit with Sebastian and my stilted conversation with the police. Did I tell them anything I shouldn't have? Did they believe my statement? The officers were so poker-faced, it was hard to tell *what* they were thinking.

Just as I'm finally beginning to drift off, I wake early in the morning to the sound of familiar voices downstairs in the Marble Hall. I hear what sounds like Oscar making conversation with Carole and Keith—and *Zoey*?

I leap out of bed, throw on a robe, and race down the stairs.

"Zo!" I squeal as soon as I see her beautifully familiar face. "I didn't know you were coming too!"

She throws her arms around me.

"I wouldn't let them leave without me," she says, grinning impishly. "I literally hid their passports until they booked a ticket for me."

"Only you!" I laugh. I turn to Carole and Keith, and the three of us form a tight group hug.

"We missed you," Carole says, touching my cheek. "Thank God you're all right."

"Of course I am." I link one arm in hers and the other in Keith's. "Come on. I want to give you all the tour."

Hours later I'm curled up in an armchair in my room, watching fondly as Zoey naps on my bed. Having my almost-sister here is just what the doctor ordered, and spending the day together, catching up and showing her around my new home, has made me the lightest I've felt in days. But now that she's fast asleep from jet lag, I'm once again alone with my worries. Will Sebastian actually get charged with *murder*? When will I see him again? And why do I still get the feeling the Mulgraves have something to do with all this?

The words from Lady Beatrice's biography flicker through my mind, and I glance at Zoey again to make sure she's still sleeping peacefully. Then I tiptoe out of the room, closing the door shut behind me. I'll be back by the time she wakes up.

Without Sebastian leading the way, the Maze is oppressive and lonely. I creep forward through the green labyrinth, mentally keeping track of my movements so I can find my way back. It strikes me how far I am from the house, how no one will hear me if I scream, and I shudder in the unnaturally fierce wind.

A half hour passes, and then another, until I'm on the verge of frustrated tears. I'm walking in circles, no closer to finding the center of the Maze, with nothing remotely ring-like in sight.

And then the thought hits me, as obvious as the gusts of wind inside the Maze. *If Lady Beatrice left the ring for her descendant . . . she would need proof, a way of knowing for certain who that person is.*

I reach my arms out to my sides and brush my hands against the hedge walls, just as I did two weeks ago with Sebastian. The hedges once again change color, my hands painting them a vivid periwinkle. But this time the dirt path beneath my feet also begins to glow with an ethereal yellow light. I gasp as the light beneath my feet winds forward . . . *leading* me.

I pick up speed, keeping my hands on either side of the hedge walls as I run, following the twists and turns of the glowing path before me. And at last I am in a place I've never been—a curving corner of the Maze highlighted by a bed of hydrangeas, the only flowers I've encountered within. Dad's words from years ago return to me.

". . . remember the hydrangeas. When you see them, that means you're close."

My breath catches. This must be the Maze's center.

I reach out to touch the hydrangeas, and a pressure fills my hand. The flower beds quake, and I watch, heart in my throat, as something pushes out of the dirt. The *water-stone*?

I stare at it in amazement. It is unquestionably the same ring from my dream, the very one Lady Beatrice wore in her long-ago portrait—with the diamond icicle set into an ancient silver band. The water-stone is the most extraordinary object I've ever seen, and I shiver, simultaneously terrified and awe-struck. There's no turning back now. I slip the ring onto my fourth finger.

The ground beneath me shakes violently. I scream, clinging to the purple hedges, then scramble away from them in fear as they rise higher and higher, connecting and forming a *domed ceiling* overhead.

"Help!" I scream, though I know it's futile. I'm trapped, and no one will ever be able to hear me.

Suddenly there is a rustling within the hedges—and then the sound of whispers, incoherent all but for one word.

"Imogen."

I jump.

"Lady Beatrice?" I whisper back.

There is no answer, but the wind blows more fiercely in response.

"Wh-what is this?"

A swarm of hushed whispers echoes around me, and I strain to decipher them. At last, I make out the words.

"You've made it to the Whispering Gallery. You won't see me, for I am on the other side. But you can hear me."

Trembling, I stare up at the domed ceiling above me. It's unbelievable, like something out of a frightening dream, and yet it's real. I am the true descendant of Lady Beatrice; I am an Elemental. And now I possess the water-stone.

"With the water-stone on your skin and your hands on the land, you will have the answer to all you seek." Remembering

these words from my research, I keep my eyes on the dome overhead and nervously whisper my question.

"Why am I here? What really happened to Lucia?"

The whispered voices go quiet, but wearing the stone, I suddenly know what to do. I am drawn like a magnet closer to the evergreen walls, until I am touching the purple-hued hedge with the water-stone.

Flashes of light and shadow dance across the hedges. I stumble backward, stifling a scream, as the shadows form distinct shapes, playing against the walls of the Maze like a macabre puppet show.

Two shadows morph into the image of two girls, walking alongside each other. The girl on the left abruptly stops and leans into the girl on the right—until she overtakes her. Until they have switched sides. Switched places altogether.

I watch with a frown. Is this supposed to be me and Lucia?

A third girl's shadow joins them, looming larger over the other two. Her hand closes around one girl's wrist, covering it entirely. The sound of soft singing wafts through the hedges, familiar and dreadful all at once.

> *"I know dark clouds will gather round me,*
> *I know the road is rough and steep. . . ."*

Suddenly a voice interrupts the singing—the voice of twelve-year-old Lucia, coming from nowhere, yet as clear as if it were playing on speakers. She speaks words I remember from that long-ago day in the Shadow Garden.

"Where did her flower come from? Is this a trick?"

I jump in shock as my *own* voice echoes through the Maze—but my mouth isn't moving. These are words I said yesterday.

"Since when does a student bring a housekeeper and a companion to boarding school with her? You have to admit it's unusual. And why did I never know about it?"

And then a third voice joins the echoes in the Whispering Gallery, replying just as Maisie had responded to me.

"Is this a trick?"

She asks the same question as Lucia. But that isn't the only similarity. When I hear them back to back, something strikes me about the two voices.

"Is this a trick?"

Is it *all* a trick?

And then I lose my breath as everything hits me at once.

I know why Mrs. Mulgrave is obsessed with Lucia and seemingly indifferent to her own daughter, Maisie. I know why the Lucia I've been hearing about from Sebastian seems so removed from the cousin I remember, the cousin who loved me. I know what's been nagging at me, the pieces that failed to fit.

Something unbelievable has happened, and finally, I know the truth.

I sprint back to the house, gasping for breath, reeling from my discovery. I slow down as I walk into the Marble Hall, forcing a smile for the housemaids and doing my best to act normal, like the world as I know it hasn't just taken a 180-degree turn.

I hurry up the stairs, whipping my head left and right as I look for her. And then I freeze. The song I heard in the Maze—Lucia's song—is coming from my bedroom. And now I know I've been hearing it since I returned to Rockford. It wasn't the sound of a ghost, or my imagination after all.

But what is she doing in my room, when Zoey's alone in there napping? I run to my door and fling it open.

Zoey is nowhere in sight. Maisie is calmly making my bed, her back toward me as she hums under her breath.

"Where is she?"

Maisie turns around.

"Good afternoon, Your Grace. Where is who?"

"Zoey." I struggle to keep calm. "She was in here sleeping when I left."

"The room was empty when I came in. She must have gone downstairs to explore. I can ask Mother—"

"I know she's not your mother," I reveal. "You've both been lying to me—to everyone—all along."

The color drains from her face.

"I—I can't possibly know what you mean," she stammers.

I grab "Maisie's" arm, catching her off guard, and unfasten her thick wristwatch.

"Don't!" she cries, struggling to yank herself free and keep her wrist covered. But I'm stronger. I tear the watch off and it falls to the floor. And there, on the inside of her wrist, is Lucia's spade-shaped birthmark.

"Lucia." My voice shakes, the room spins, as my incredible, unthinkable discovery is confirmed. My cousin, *alive,* and looking back at me behind her disguise. "Maisie Mulgrave is the one who died. Not you."

"No," she gasps. "You're mad. I'm Maisie. Lucia is dead. I'm *Maisie!*"

A hysterical laugh bubbles out of her, a laugh that convulses into a sob. And then she crumples to the floor, nearly gagging as she struggles to repeat the name. "Maisie—I'm *Maisie*. Lucia is dead!"

I watch her in horror. Dr. Heron's notes come back to me. *Still struggling with delusions and violent temper. Patient should see me on a more frequent basis.*

Something is terribly wrong with my cousin—something serious enough to result in an identity switch of this magnitude. I crouch beside her, placing a nervous hand on her arm. "Talk to me, Lucia." I try to adopt a soothing tone, but my voice is high-pitched with shock. "Tell me what happened. Why did you do this? How could you do this?"

She lets out another frightening wail, beating the carpeted floor with her fists. I look from her to the door in a panic. Should I get help? I need to find out the truth from her but I don't know what I'm doing, I'm not equipped to handle her nervous breakdown.

"Lucia, it's me," I try again. "Your cousin, Imogen. Once we were the closest of friends. Don't you remember?"

She lifts her head. Her face is red and swollen, but the wild animal in her seems to have calmed. Relief mingles with despair in an expression I've never seen before.

"You're going to hate me," she whispers.

"I won't," I tell her, though I know that's something I can't promise.

Lucia hesitates, her eyes flicking nervously back and forth. "I don't think I can say it. But—" She reaches for the pendant around her neck. I watch, astonished, as she opens the pendant . . . and pulls out a tiny flash drive.

"What is that?"

"I knew that when I died, I wanted to be buried as me," she says haltingly. "The real me. So I wrote my story and kept it in here. That way whoever found my body, whether it be in the near future or later years, would discover this drive and learn what really happened."

I reach out my hand and Lucia drops it into my palm, squeezing her eyes shut as if in pain.

"I—I hope you won't think too much worse of me after," she whispers as I hurriedly plug the drive into my computer.

XVI

LUCIA
AUGUST 2007

I'm huddled on my bedroom floor, studying the framed photograph in my hands. The room is in a complete state of chaos, with clothes and books strewn about and untouched trays of food in a row by the door. Anyone would assume I haven't ventured outside these walls in days. And they would be right.

I'm so fixated on the photo of my parents that I don't notice someone else has entered until I hear the voice.

"Well. You've certainly made a mess of things," says Maisie.

I leap to my feet, holding the photograph protectively against my chest.

"What are *you* doing in here?" I demand, staring daggers at the hateful maid. "Get out at once!"

"I've come with a solution to your predicament," Maisie says smoothly.

"Didn't you hear me?" I draw myself up to my full height, until we are nose to nose. "I said. Get. Out."

"Oh, I don't think you're in a position to give me orders any-more," Maisie says loftily. "Not after what you did."

I freeze.

"What are you going on about?" I ask, a touch too loudly. "I didn't do anything."

"Maybe you need me to refresh your memory."

Maisie pulls a cell phone from her pocket, the same cutting-edge model my father had.

"How do you have one of those?" I ask, my pulse racing in fury at the thought that she might have taken it from my father.

"Dad bought it for my mum," Maisie answers, scrolling through the phone as she looks for something.

"*My* dad. Not yours," I snap.

"It's a little late to be in denial," Maisie retorts. "Look."

Reluctantly, I glance at the phone. The screen is filled with . . . a moving image of the Rockford gardens. A cry escapes my lips as I see myself enter the frame, dressed in pajamas and carrying a lantern as I stand outside the Shadow Garden's gate.

"You were filming me—*spying* on me," I gasp. "How dare you! Why would you do something so twisted?"

"It turned out to be rather bright of me, actually," Maisie boasts. "I had to know if you were going to tell Imogen the news at your little sleepover, so I followed from a distance. Then, when I saw you leave in the middle of the night, I knew you had to be up to no good."

I recoil as my father enters the screen. My undoing, my most terrible act, has been caught on film.

"What are you doing out here so late, darling?" Dad asks, swaying slightly as he holds a martini glass aloft. "Shouldn't you and Imogen be in bed?"

"She is. But I heard you all carrying on out here," I say disdainfully, "and I couldn't sleep. Where are Mum, and Uncle Edmund, and Aunt Laura?"

"They're having a nightcap in the Shadow Garden. I should be there with them, and you, my dear, should be in bed. Let me walk you back—"

"No." The force of my voice catches my father off guard. "If you want to know the real reason I can't sleep, it's because of what that foul little maid of ours told me yesterday."

"What did she say?" Dad seems to sober up instantly. "What did you hear, Lucia?"

"Maisie said you are her father," I spit. "She said you had an affair with Mrs. Mulgrave and that you two are still in love. As if anything could be more ridiculous!"

But Dad doesn't deny it. He simply stares at me, a sad look in his eyes.

"Tell me it's not true!" I shout. "Tell me, and then sack the pair of them. Please!"

Dad takes my hands in his.

"I can't. I hoped you wouldn't find out until you were much older, but I . . . I can't lie to you."

"No," I mutter, shaking my head violently. "It can't be."

"Mrs. Mulgrave nursed me through my injuries after a near-fatal accident during my military training almost twenty years ago," he says. "I suppose I fell for her then. But I was already engaged to your mother at the time, and I loved her too, in a way."

"In a way?" I echo, my voice rising to a hysterical pitch.

"Shh." Dad looks anxiously at the Shadow Garden's gate.

"I've been a good husband and father, despite my faults. Your mother is happy, and you have everything you could ever want. You are the Rockford heiress, not Maisie. Please, darling, try not to let this trouble you. Many British families we know have a secret like this one. We're no better or worse."

"Sack them," I demand. "I can't live in the same house as your disgusting second family. If you love me, you'll get rid of them."

Dad rubs his forehead wearily.

"Darling, I do love you, more than anyone. But I can't send them away. Maisie is my daughter."

And those are the words that send me over the edge.

"I'll never forgive you for this. Never!" I shriek, throwing my lantern onto the grass.

"No!" Dad yells as the lantern hits the trunk of a tree, shattering into pieces. The exposed flame latches onto the grass, and I freeze, watching the flame grow and spread, moving toward the Maze.

"The others!" Dad cries. He grips my shoulders. "Lucia, get out of here now. Go back to Imogen and call for help. I have to get your mother and Edmund and Laura out of there."

"But—" I stare at the flames in a panic.

"Go!"

The screen darkens. I crumple to my knees, sickened with regret.

"You killed your parents. *Our* father," Maisie says bitterly. "Not to mention your aunt and uncle. How can you live with yourself after that?"

"I—I don't want to," I whisper. "I wish I died instead."

Meeting Maisie's eyes, I am filled with renewed rage. "But it's all your fault. If you had only kept your knowledge private, and not tortured me with it—"

Maisie snorts.

"You can hardly blame it on me. How was I to know you were mental?"

I shrink back at the word. *Mental* . . . That's just what I always feared I was, after Mum and Dad started making me see Dr. Heron.

"Besides, I'm the one who called 999 right away," Maisie continues. "If it hadn't been for me, your precious cousin and everyone else in the house might have died too."

"Why are you doing this?" My eyes fill with frightened tears. "I'm suffering enough. There's nothing you can say to make it worse."

"Yes, there is. I could show this tape to the authorities." Maisie leans forward. "You'd be shipped off to juvenile prison or a mental institution, and would forever be known, in the papers and all over the world, as the girl who killed her own parents."

I feel myself gagging, choking on the thought of what will become of me. And what will Grandfather and Imogen do when they learn the truth? They are my only family left, though surely they will despise me and cut me off for good if they discover what I've done.

"Please, don't," I beg. "I'll do anything."

Maisie smiles.

"I thought you might say that. And as it happens, I've got a brilliant idea. I have a feeling you'd rather be anyone but yourself right now. Correct?"

"Yes," I admit through my tears.

"Then switch places with me."

My head snaps up.

"What?"

"Switch places," Maisie says, her voice taking on a silky, alluring tone. "And no one will be the wiser about what you did that night. You can start over again—as me. Put those terrible memories, and all your guilt, behind you."

"But—but—" I sputter. "No one would ever believe it. I know we look alike—I *hate* how much we look alike—but still, we're not identical!"

"Oh, I have a plan for that too," Maisie says calmly. "You are going to beg your—our—grandfather to send me and Mother to Switzerland with you, as your guardian and companion at boarding school. While there, you and I will give each other lessons on how to successfully 'be' each other. We'll make the physical changes too of course, like dyeing our hair. But our best tool will be distance. You'll stay away as long as possible, spending the summer with 'friends' instead of coming back to Rockford after the school term. By the time you return home a year later, everyone will expect you—*both* of us—to have grown up and changed. Being away for so long will make the switch much more seamless and believable when we return. Mother will help too."

"You're serious," I whisper. "You want me to turn over my life to you and become a *maid*?"

Maisie's eyes flash.

"Don't act as if it isn't deserved. I was born six months before you. If the world were just, I would have been our father's heiress, not you. But let me tell you, being a maid in this house is nowhere near as terrible as being stuck in a mental institution or prison. The choice is yours."

273

"Your mother actually approves of this idea? She wants me posing as you?"

"She argued against the switch when I first told her about it," Maisie says with a shrug. "But she quickly became enamored with the idea of her own daughter living as an heiress, next in line to be the Duchess of Wickersham. In her mind too, it's my rightful place."

"And you really think changing our appearance and teaching each other the ways of life belowstairs and above is enough to convince Grandfather, Oscar, and everyone else of the switch?" I ask in disbelief.

"It's simple. You're leaving on the cusp of adolescence, and will return at the end of term as a teenager—you'll be expected to look a little different. And I don't know if you've noticed, but our grandfather isn't exactly *with it* these days. I highly doubt he'll second-guess that I am the real Lucia when I sashay into Rockford just like you." Maisie closes her eyes dreamily for a moment. "And as for you . . . well, take it from me. No one pays much attention to the housekeeper's daughter."

I move to the window. Despite myself, I'm growing tempted by Maisie's offer. The chance to escape my crime, to be someone else, is too much for my tormented mind to resist.

"Okay," I say softly. "I'll do it."

XVII

I reach the last word of Lucia's story and turn away from the computer to look upon her—this person I never really knew. I have so many questions, but all I can think of in this moment is what might have been, if she had just stayed in the boathouse that night.

"My parents," I whisper, tears welling up in my eyes. "You—*you* took them away from me."

"It was an *accident*," Lucia wails. "You can't really think I would ever mean to hurt my own parents, or yours. I loved them—all of them."

"But it was an accident that you caused. If you hadn't decided to start a fight with your dad that night, our parents would still be alive." My chest tightens with pain, but I can't give in to my grief. Not yet.

"I know." Lucia's face crumples. "I can't forgive myself either, and it's the reason for everything I've done."

I shake my head in shock.

"Why didn't you ever come to me and tell me what happened, and that Maisie was blackmailing you?"

"I was too scared," she admits. "I knew it was impossible to expect you to forgive me for the fire—and I had to tell you about that for you to understand everything else."

She's right. I believe her that the fire was an accident . . . but forgiveness will take a long time.

I push my emotions aside. There's much more I need to find out before I can process everything fully.

"How could you stand it, being around them every day, after everything?" I ask.

Lucia shakes her head grimly.

"You'd be surprised what a person can stand when there doesn't appear to be any other option. I thought it was either live as a maid or spend the rest of my years in lockup."

"But then you . . . killed her. Didn't you?" I ask nervously.

I'm calling her bluff, trying to catch her in a confession. But I already know the answer. I knew it as soon as I discovered Lucia was alive.

Lucia buries her head in her hands. When she looks up at me, her cheeks are wet once again.

"When she finished boarding school and began living here year-round while attending Oxford, Maisie became even more unbearable than before. To outsiders, she was a little princess, but to me and anyone else who got too close, she was verbally abusive. And then she became obsessed with Lady Beatrice and Elementals—obsessed with *you*." Lucia pauses. "Did you ever get the letter I sent your parents? Warning you about something?"

"*That* letter? From more than a year ago?"

She nods, and I gape at her in surprise.

"That was from *you*? But neither Harry or Oscar recognized the handwriting."

"Because I used my old penmanship, not my Maisie handwriting," Lucia explains. "I would have typed it up but I couldn't risk getting caught, since we only have shared computers in the staff quarters."

"What were you trying to warn me about?"

"Maisie wanted to—to get rid of you. She was horribly insecure about having to pretend to be me in order to live the life she wanted, and she was terrified of you coming in and getting everything if the prophecy were true. And I knew she was plotting something." Lucia looks at me earnestly. "You were like a little sister to me growing up. You were *my* Zoey. I always cared about you, even later on, when we weren't talking."

I glance down. I'm touched by her words, but I don't want to be. I'm still too angry.

"The night she died, I saw her sneak out in the middle of the storm," Lucia continues. "Her behavior had been maddening in the days before, and I could tell she was up to something. So I followed her. She was swinging one of Sebastian's old polo sticks as she walked toward the Maze. At a certain point I made a noise and she turned around and caught me."

"And?" I whisper.

"She started taunting me, telling me it was no use following her, that I'd never again get to have her life. And then . . ." Lucia's tears fall freely. "She told me she'd uncovered a way to *eliminate* you, just like I had done to my parents. And I

277

snapped. It was like everything I'd been feeling toward her all these years, all the pain and hatred, came to the surface—and I lost control." Lucia takes a shallow gulp of air. "Maisie was going into that Maze with the polo stick, to take something of yours. I don't know what exactly she was planning, but from everything she'd let slip, I knew she considered you the biggest threat to her title. And so . . . whatever she planned to do, I stopped it. I took the polo stick from her hands when she was caught unaware, and I struck her on the side of the head." Lucia looks down. "She died instantly. I didn't mean for it to go so far—I only wanted to stop her."

I cover my mouth with my hand.

"I heard someone coming, so I hid. It was Theo. He lost it when he saw that she was dead. He kept crying aloud that it was all his fault. I never understood what he meant, and I was so nervous someone would catch him at the scene. But then Sebastian came and took him away."

"He thought Theo did it . . . and Theo must have thought *Sebastian* was the one," I realize suddenly. "That's why he kept saying it was all his fault, because he and Lucia—or rather, Maisie—were seeing each other behind Sebastian's back. He probably saw the polo stick and the body and figured Sebastian killed her in some kind of jealous rage."

I feel a rush of relief that neither of the brothers was responsible—and I am moved by the lengths to which they were both willing to go to protect each other in the end.

"You've got to come forward and clear Sebastian's name," I say urgently. "He is completely innocent in all of this. And if you meant what you said about your guilt over the fire, then

278

this is the way to start making up for it. You're the only one who can set him free."

Lucia nods, staring at the floor.

"I know. I've always known it was only a matter of time."

I release the breath I've been holding.

"You'll be doing the right thing."

We sit in silence for a few moments, and then I remember another of my endless questions.

"How did you hide the truth about Maisie's death from Mrs. Mulgrave? I'm guessing she would have lost her mind if she'd known from the beginning that it wasn't an accident."

"The way she fell, with her head up against the pillar, it looked like an accident. So that's what everyone thought for over a year, including Mrs. Mulgrave—even though she's the one who saw Sebastian at Rockford that night. But she was convinced Sebastian was madly in love with Lucia, that no one could possibly want to hurt her *perfect* little daughter. It wasn't until she saw the way Sebastian was with you, that she began to think differently."

"Mrs. Mulgrave was the witness," I realize, flushed with anger. "*She* called the police on Sebastian."

Lucia nods.

"I think she's the one who found the polo stick, too. I watched Sebastian and Theo throw it in the lake that night, but it must have washed ashore—and whoever found it clearly planted it at Stanhope Abbey. It seems obvious who that was. Mrs. Mulgrave."

"Did she set the fire in my room the other night too?"

Lucia shifts uncomfortably.

"I saw her afterward with a matchbox. I didn't know what she was doing with it until I heard about the fire the next day. I'm sorry. . . ."

"And when you were being Maisie, how could you act like you were Lucia's biggest fan? You clearly hated her, and for good reason."

Lucia smiles sadly.

"I spoke about her as if she were me—as if I were the one studying at Oxford and dating Sebastian Stanhope and doing everything I dreamed of but she got to do instead."

I stare at my cousin. When we were little I always knew she was complicated, but I never could have imagined how so. I thought she was glamorous and dramatic, when in reality she was struggling with her embattled mind, a sickness that brought her to this point. And then after the fire, when I assumed she'd forgotten me, she was being held hostage by the Mulgraves all along.

I reach across the space between us, and take Lucia's hand. I might never be able to forgive all that she's done . . . but in this moment, I choose to forgive *her*.

A knock sounds at the door, and Lucia quickly turns away to wipe her eyes while I answer it. Carole stands in the doorway, her expression uneasy. For a moment I'm shocked to see her. I've been so immersed in my discoveries, I nearly forgot she and Keith are here.

"Hi. How are you guys liking your room?" I grin, but she doesn't smile back.

"Sweetie, have you seen Zoey?"

Something in her tone gives me pause.

"No. I came back from my—my walk and she wasn't here. I thought she might have been with you guys."

Carole wrings her hands.

"One of the maids saw her leaving a little while ago with the housekeeper, Mrs. Mulgrave. I'm sure she was just showing Zoey around, but the trouble is, they were supposed to be back by now for dinner."

A cold wave of fear washes over me. But I can't let Carole see.

"Mrs. Mulgrave was probably just—just giving Zoey a tour of the gardens. I'll go find them." I force a smile onto my face. "Don't worry."

I'm growing hysterical with worry as Lucia and I race outside; I curse myself for leaving Zoey alone. What was I *thinking*?

Nightfall makes the Rockford grounds look even vaster and more impenetrable, and I swear loudly in frustration and fear. How am I supposed to know if she's by the lake or the park, in one of the gardens or on the riding trail?

The water-stone. In all my panic, I nearly forgot that I am wearing my greatest ally on my ring finger. Drawing a sharp breath, I bend down, touching the diamond icicle to the earth beneath my feet.

"Where's Zoey?" I whisper to the land around me.

I feel the ground heat up beneath me, and Lucia shrieks as a path lights up in front of us. Just like in the Maze.

"So it's true?" Lucia cries. "You really *are* an Elemental?"

Ignoring Lucia's questions, I grab her arm and break into

a run, following the lit path that leads into the gardens. Lucia and I sprint alongside each other, and for a while the only sound is our panting breaths and our shoes pounding against the dirt and gravel, until the path stops near the Shadow Garden. We turn to stare at each other, and in her eyes I see my own uncertainty reflected.

"I—I can't go in there," she stammers.

"We have to."

I pull her along with me, and suddenly I smell . . . smoke. Lucia looks at me in horror.

Please, I pray silently. *Let me have a chance to fix it this time. I can't lose her.*

The gate is ajar. Lucia and I step inside—and I hear us both scream.

The Shadow Garden, now a wilderness of climbing, writhing weeds, is starting to burn once again. A gasoline can lies carelessly on the ground, while a growing flame licks the fallen leaves and inches toward the two figures huddled at the other end of the garden.

"We can go together," I hear Mrs. Mulgrave say to Zoey, who is wearing a dress I recognize—the very dress from Lucia's State Room portrait. "It will be so easy. We'll be rid of them all, and with our Charles again."

Zoey screams as the flame multiplies in two, and I dart forward. Holding my palms above the flames, I try to concentrate, to make water with my hands even though I'm crying and sweating too hard to think—

The water shoots from my fingers. From the corner of my eye, I can see Zoey's body quake with shock as she watches me. Relief fills my lungs as the fire goes out—but I'm not done yet.

Mrs. Mulgrave lunges toward me, but before she can catch me I pull two gnarled vines from the dirt and aim them in her direction. The first vine ties her arms around her back; the second ties her feet together until she can no longer move. Zoey is free from her clutches. She runs sobbing into my arms, while Mrs. Mulgrave and Lucia both gape at me in astonishment.

"What *are* you?" Mrs. Mulgrave hisses.

I ignore her question and ask my own.

"What were you doing with my sister?"

"That's not—she isn't—that's *Lucia*. Those are her clothes, her necklace—" Mrs. Mulgrave blinks and her face contorts in dismay, as if she is awakening from a dream and seeing Zoey for the first time.

"I went exploring after you left," Zoey says through her tears. "And I found this room with a closet full of beautiful clothes—I didn't realize—"

"It's okay, Zoey," I try to assure her. "Everything's going to be okay."

I squeeze her hand a little tighter, and with a deep breath, I turn back to Mrs. Mulgrave.

"I know the truth. This whole time, you haven't been mourning my cousin at all. It's your own daughter, Maisie, who died. They switched places. And you helped them do it."

Mrs. Mulgrave recoils against the vines that bind her, staring at me in shock. Her mouth opens and closes, but no sound comes out.

"It's over," Lucia calls to Mrs. Mulgrave. "She knows, and soon everyone is going to know."

Mrs. Mulgrave lets out a sound like a howl as she lunges

toward Lucia, but the vines hold her captive. As I watch her, I see a woman whose grief turned her insane, whose distorted reality has finally caught up to her. It is a harrowing sight.

"I'm getting Zoey out of here," I say shakily. "I'll deal with you later."

With that, I shepherd Zoey and Lucia through the gate and out of the garden.

"Are you okay?" I ask Zoey frantically as soon as we're breathing clean air.

"I think so." She clutches my shirt. "You saved my life, Imogen. How did you do that, with the water and the vines? When did you become one of the X-Men?"

And even at a moment like this, Zoey manages to make me laugh.

"I'll tell you later. It's . . . it's quite a story."

⁊⳺

The three of us barrel into the Marble Hall, where Oscar stands looking at us in bewilderment.

"Zoey, there you are. Maisie, we've been looking for your mother. Where has she—"

"Oscar, call the police and get security over to the Shadow Garden now," I interrupt him.

"The Shadow Garden?" he echoes, uncomprehendingly. *"Police?"*

"Mrs. Mulgrave went crazy," I pant. "She took Zoey to the garden and tried to set fire to the place."

Oscar lets out an anguished cry.

"I've got to take care of Zoey. Can you get security to the

Shadow Garden *now*?" I urge him. "And, Lu—Maisie has something she needs to say to the police too. Make sure to keep her with you until they get here." Even though I can tell Lucia is ready to get the burden of truth off her chest, I can't take the chance of her disappearing before she clears Sebastian's name.

Oscar springs into action, pressing the security button on the Marble Hall intercom while simultaneously dialing 999 on his cell. I usher Zoey upstairs to Carole and Keith's suite, the two of us doing our best to downplay the episode and keep her parents from a heart attack. Thankfully they seem more concerned with making sure Zoey is okay than asking questions, but I know the questions will come soon.

In the bathroom, Carole and I help Zoey out of her scorched clothes and I breathe a huge sigh of relief when I see that she escaped the fire unscathed. Once I'm convinced she's safe and in good hands with the Marinos, I race back down the stairs. I find Oscar and Lucia still in the Marble Hall, but they are now surrounded by two police officers. Lucia is sweating bullets, while Oscar's Adam's apple bobs up and down nervously.

"Mrs. Mulgrave isn't there," Oscar blurts out as soon as he sees me.

"What?" I cry.

The shorter of the two policemen steps forward.

"We only found residue from the fire and a can of gasoline, Your Grace, but no bodies."

"She got away," I murmur. "I don't believe it." Did the vines come loose once I left the garden?

Oscar turns to Lucia.

"Maisie, I know this is a difficult position you're in. But

please, is there anything you can tell us about what happened tonight?"

Lucia glances at me, and then at the two police officers. I give her an entreating look. *Do it, Lucia. Tell the truth. Be brave.*

She takes a shaky breath and steps forward.

"Yes. I do have something to say."

EPILOGUE

Two Weeks Later

I lean against Sebastian, relishing the feel of his arm around mine as the nine of us sit around the fire in the State Room. The room's been made friendlier now that Fake-Lucia's portrait has been removed, replaced with an oil painting of Lady Beatrice that Sebastian helped me bring down from the attic.

We've been in hiding ever since the story of the Real Lucia exploded across the media, unable to set foot outside the confines of Rockford grounds without a paparazzi chase or a barrage of questions from tabloid reporters: *"How did you find out Lucia was really alive? How did she and the Mulgraves keep up the charade for so long? What was Sebastian Stanhope's reaction to the news that he was dating the wrong girl? How do you FEEL about all these shocking revelations?"*

My answer to that question would probably surprise everyone, but the truth is, I feel a strange sense of relief. For the first time in seven years, my life is no longer a question;

I finally know the truth. And now that we are free from the lie that permeated these past seven years, we can begin again. Even Lucia has the chance for a new start. After a DNA test proved that she is who she claimed to be and that the dead girl in the Rockford Cemetery is the blackmailing daughter of the housekeeper, the police changed their tack. The murder of Maisie Mulgrave was ruled self-defense, with Lucia charged only for the crime of cover-up. She's been sentenced to ten years' probation, and she is currently serving the first week of a yearlong, court-ordered mental rehab stay. I have faith that she'll return a healthier version of herself; that this is far from the end of her story.

The other reason I'm smiling, despite the fact that my family's dirty laundry is splashed on the cover of every magazine in Britain? It's the people who surround me now, my closest loved ones, all in one place as we weather the media storm together in Rockford Manor—which has never felt quite this cozy. Not knowing when I'll be free to leave the house gave me an added excuse to send Lauren a plane ticket to come visit, and having her here now, with the Marinos and the Stanhopes, makes it feel a lot more like a vacation than a hideout.

Lauren catches my eye now, wiggling her eyebrows suggestively at me and Sebastian. I giggle into the crook of his arm. It came as a definite shock to everyone when they discovered that I have a boyfriend, and the shock was all the greater when they learned that (a) he was the original suspect in the Lucia Rockford case, and (b) he's too handsome to be legal. But it didn't take long for Lauren and the Marinos to see who Sebastian really is: the good guy.

I'm not the only one giddy with relief. Lord and Lady

Stanhope can't stop thanking me over and over for uncovering the truth and proving Sebastian's innocence, while Sebastian keeps smiling at his brother—a smile that touches my heart, because I know how much it means to him to know that Theo is innocent too. Even Carole and Keith—whom Zoey thankfully decided to spare the details of my "X-Men tendencies," instead telling them that my "serious jujitsu skills" saved her from Mrs. Mulgrave—seem pleasantly surprised by how I've adjusted to my new life at Rockford Manor and how well it fits me.

And it's true. Despite everything that's happened here, this is where I belong. I wouldn't hesitate to throw away the title, the fortune, or the notoriety—after seeing what the allure of high society did to the Mulgraves, I don't want *that* anymore. I'm not sure I ever wanted it. But it's the land that I belong to, the very earth that was here long before the manor was built. I feel my connection to it every time I step into the gardens and see them thrive at my touch; I hear it in the wind as it calls my name. Rockford is my home.

The only wrinkle now is that we still haven't found Mrs. Mulgrave. I can't help worrying that she'll show up one day, unannounced and out for blood. But if she does, I'll be ready for her. Sebastian and I are learning more about my gifts as an Elemental, and one thing is for sure: I no longer see myself as a freak, or this gift as a curse.

It's just like Dad once wrote, I think as Sebastian pulls me closer. *There's a big difference between perception and misconception.*

AUTHOR'S NOTE

Suspicion was born out of my love for the gothic suspense novels of Daphne du Maurier and the psychological-thriller films of Alfred Hitchcock. The two collaborated on a few projects, but the one that forever impacted me was *Rebecca,* both Du Maurier's novel and Hitchcock's film adaptation. I remember reading *Rebecca* when I was thirteen (maybe a bit too young!) and being utterly transfixed by everything from the world inside a British manor house to the chilling plot and slow burn of the mystery. Hitchcock's film version brought the story to life in a whole new way, and from the moment I was first introduced to *Rebecca,* I knew I wanted to pay homage someday.

Meanwhile, like millions of other TV viewers around the world, in the past few years I became hooked on *Downton Abbey.* Just like with *Rebecca,* I fell in love with the upstairs-downstairs world of a British estate, and I found myself intrigued by the British peerage, which Julian Fellowes so compellingly portrays in both *Downton* and his film *Gosford Park.* I found myself wondering what the status of all these earls and countesses, dukes and duchesses is today—did the titles even still exist?—so I did a little research and discovered that the British peerage is very much alive and well. In fact, pick up any issue of the popular UK magazine *Tatler* and you'll notice that lords and ladies are treated with the same wide-eyed admiration and scrutiny we bestow upon our movie stars here in the United States. Reading *Tatler* is like entering a new world, with its entertaining cover stories like "How to Bag a Lord" and "So You Want to Be a Duchess?" as well as its expansive coverage of the lifestyles of the British peers, from the schools they attend and the sports they play to their country houses, parties, romances, and scandals. I knew this was something I had to explore: the *modern-day* world of young British peers. This, coupled with my idea for a suspense novel in the style of *Rebecca,* is what led to *Suspicion.*

While studying the Vanderbilt family for my previous novels, *Timeless* and *Timekeeper,* I was fascinated by Consuelo Vanderbilt's experience going from American heiress in New York City to becoming the Duchess of Marlborough at Blenheim Palace in Oxfordshire. So when it came time to write *Suspicion* and create the fictional Rockford Manor, I knew I wanted to base the house on Blenheim. I traveled to England with my mom as travel companion and photographer, and we had the most amazing time exploring Blenheim and its grounds (which include a maze!), as well as the surrounding land of Oxfordshire. If any of you reading this are planning a trip to England, my number-one recommendation is to take a day trip to Oxfordshire and visit Blenheim Palace, which is like something out of a fairy tale. Plus, you'll get to see the basis for Rockford Manor! ☺ If England is too far, I highly recommend the book *Blenheim and the Churchill Family.* Written by Henrietta Spencer-Churchill, the daughter of the 11th

Duke of Marlborough, the book is filled with personal anecdotes about growing up and living in the palace, as well as gorgeous photographs.

For the best coverage on the British peerage during the Victorian and Edwardian eras, I recommend one of my favorite books ever: *To Marry an English Lord* by Gail MacColl and Carol McD. Wallace. This incredibly entertaining and informative book will transport you to another time and place, and you'll have a hard time putting it down! For up-to-the-minute coverage on the current crop of British aristocrats and peers, definitely pick up *Tatler*. It's been invaluable to me in learning about the life of modern-day lords and ladies for *Suspicion,* and I haven't stopped reading it since finishing the book. *Tatler* is pure fun, and gives you entrée to a glamorous world across the pond.

I hope you've enjoyed reading *Suspicion* as much as I've enjoyed writing it! This book has truly been a labor of love, a way for me to combine my passions and interests into one project, and I'm grateful for the opportunity to share it with all of you.

ACKNOWLEDGMENTS

This book has been a joy to write and publish, and I have so many people to thank, starting with the two amazing women who have championed my career: Krista Vitola and Beverly Horowitz. I'm still pinching myself with excitement that I get to work with the two of you, and I'm beyond grateful for your continued belief in me and my work. Beverly, thank you so much for taking me under your wing and guiding me through this industry. It's truly an honor to be one of your authors. Krista, thank you for sharing my vision for this book, and for your invaluable notes and feedback. I couldn't ask for a better editor!

Thank you to Alison Impey, designer extraordinaire, for the best cover I've ever had. You captured *Suspicion* so perfectly—I can't get enough of that gorgeous image!

Many thanks to the brilliant copyediting duo Veronica Ambrose and Colleen Fellingham, for helping me improve upon my book with your amazing attention to detail. Jocelyn Lange, thank you for all your enthusiasm and foreign sales savvy!

Thank you to my fantastic team at the Gersh Agency: Greg Pedicin, Joe Veltre, Lynn Fimberg, and Jessica Amato. I'm thrilled to be working with you all, and I'm grateful for your awesome support on all my projects. And many thanks to Chad and Todd Christopher (my favorite twins!) for bringing me into the agency.

Family is one of the most important themes in *Suspicion*—in no small part due to my overwhelming love for my own family, starting with my hero, my father, Shon Saleh, whom I adore! Thank you for building my wings and giving me the courage to use them. Your unwavering belief in me since I was a child is the reason I'm living this dream, and I couldn't be more grateful. And thank you for reading multiple drafts and making *Suspicion* better with your valuable notes.

Thanks and love to my mother and guiding light, ZaZa Saleh, who accompanied me on an unforgettable mother-daughter research trip to England for this book.

Arian, you are such a huge part of who I am, and I'm so lucky to have you as my brother. Thank you for helping me grow, and for your super-helpful feedback on all my books-in-progress. Sainaz, my sister-in-law, you've been like family for so long and I'm so glad that it's now official!

To my Saleh and Madjidi grandparents and relatives near and far, thank you for all of your love and support!

Chad Christopher, thank you for being a great lawyer and friend. You officially rock!

Many thanks to Heather Holley and Rob Hoffman for your help building my career with the many songs we recorded together.

Dorothy Robertiello, thank you for your love and kindness!

Brooke Kaufman, thank you for ten years (!) and counting of your friendship, support, and belief in me. To my mentors, Maury Yeston and Kirsten (Kiwi!) Smith, thank you for teaching me so much about writing and the biz.

Mia Antonelli, thank you for your wonderful friendship, and for all your enthusiasm and encouragement of my dreams.

Thank you to Chessa L. Donaldson, who read and critiqued two drafts of the *Suspicion* book proposal and then celebrated with me over a *Forsyte Saga* marathon the weekend it sold! ☺

Thanks and love to my great friends, who have all been so wonderfully supportive: Kirsten Guenther, Christina Harmon, Camilla Moshayedi, Roxane Cohanim, Marise Freitas, Ross Donaldson, the Robertiello family, the Bratman family, Dan and Heather Kiger, Dani Cordaro, Ami McCartt, Adriana Ameri, and Jon and Emily Sandler.

And to the special someone I saved for last, Chris Robertiello: for every love story I write, ours is still my favorite. My life with you and our doggies (shout-out to Honey and Daisy!) is a dream. I love you so much.

ABOUT THE AUTHOR

Alexandra Monir is an author and recording artist in her twenties. *Suspicion* is her third novel published by Delacorte Press. It is the follow-up to her popular debut novel, *Timeless,* and its sequel, *Timekeeper.* Alexandra lives in Los Angeles, where she is working on her next novel, while also composing an original musical. Her music is available on iTunes. For more, visit her website at alexandramonir.com and follow @TimelessAlex on Twitter.